SPY IN CHANCERY

To the mild-seeming Ambassador the very word 'espionage' is an anathema, and at first he flatly refuses to believe that there can be a Russian spy among his staff at the Embassy in Rome.

Yet, once convinced, he acts with unexpected vigour and cunning – so much so that Peter Craig, whose unwelcome job it is to root out the traitor, finds he has to curb His Excellency's unorthodox incursions into the espionage business.

A tangled spy thriller of move and counter-move, bluff and double-bluff, with action moving from a macabre cemetery in France to the secret headquarters of the Mafia, this is the third of Kenneth Benton's stories featuring policeman Peter Craig.

Other titles in the Black Dagger Crime series:

SPY IN CHANCERY

Kenneth Benton

·BLACK·
DAGGER
·CRIME·

First published 1972
by
William Collins Sons & Co Ltd
This edition 1987 by Chivers Press
published by arrangement with
the author

ISBN 0 86220 712 6

British Library Cataloguing in Publication Data available

For
Tanya and Selwyn Jepson

The personalities, procedures and lay-out of
Her Majesty's Embassy in Rome and any other
organizations described in this story are wholly fictional

Printed and bound in Great Britain by
Redwood Burn Limited, Trowbridge, Wiltshire

FOREWORD

It is agreeable in any book, more particularly, for some reason, in a thriller, to be able to say, 'Clearly this chap knows what he is talking about. He is allowing us into a private kingdom of which he has the key.' As with Dick Francis in the world of racing or Emma Lathen in the world of Wall Street (the latter 'chap' being two nice American ladies), so with Kenneth Benton in what is now comprehensively called the Foreign Service.

It is a world of Embassies, Legations and Consulates, of Trade Counsellors, Military Attaches and Scientific Advisers. Above all, of that innocuous-sounding appendage to the Embassy formerly known as Passport Control, in fact the local branch office of the British Secret Service.

Kenneth Benton's authority to write about such matters is impressive. Vienna in the late thirties under the heel of the Nazis. Riga in 1940 under the equally oppressive heel of the Russians. A hazardous circuit of the globe to get back to base in London. Madrid, a notorious wartime centre of international espionage. Rome, Peru, Rio de Janeiro. With such a wealth of background material one's only surprise is that Kenneth should have waited so long to cast this valuable metal into the mould of fiction. Was he afraid that, whilst he was in post, the eye of Big Brother was on him? It was not until he was sixty, and retired, that he wrote his first novel.

That does not imply, of course, that this was his first experience in writing. A member of the Foreign Service is constantly writing reports, memoranda and letters. And not only writing them, but doing so under the discipline and correction of superiors who wield a heavy blue pencil, cutting out not only indiscretions, but ambiguities, split infinitives and prepositions at the end of sentences. It is a training which any writer might envy.

All these felicities are present in *Spy in Chancery*, his third book, his second with an Intelligence background. The setting is Rome, one of his best loved cities. The time the unchanging present; the unchanging enemy the Russians.

The incidental delights are all there too – especially the delights of the table. "Caviar in a bowl of crushed ice, with Bernkastleer Doktor, dewy with cold. Roast suckling lamb, with garden peas and asparagus and Château Lafite Rothschild, Premier Crû. And finally, strawberries and Moët Chandon." They did themselves well, the diplomats, in Rome in 1972!

Although the book starts with the normal disclaimer to the effect that the personalities, procedures and lay-out of Her Majesty's Embassy in Rome are wholly fictional, I must confess that I wondered. I knew three of the British Ambassadors in Rome, all of them men of mark, and I could not help feeling that His Excellency, Sir Watkyn Rees (one of the best characters in the book) with his dislike of MI6, his taste in secretaries and his love of orchids, must have been based on one of them. Possibly he was based on all three.

MICHAEL GILBERT

THE BLACK DAGGER CRIME SERIES

The Black Dagger Crime series is a result of a joint effort between Chivers Press and a sub-committee of the Crime Writers' Association, consisting of Marian Babson, Peter Chambers and chaired by John Kennedy Melling. It is designed to select outstanding examples of every type of detective story, drawing on the early works of CWA members, so that enthusiasts will have the opportunity to read once more classics that have been scarce for years, while introducing them to a new generation who have not previously had the chance to enjoy them.

CHAPTER ONE

PARIS; THE KILLING

Howard sat in the café, watching the steps which led down to the Métro. He didn't think he had been followed. When he had entered the station in the Place de la République he had waited until the Number Three train was just about to leave before he pushed open the barrier, ran round a blue-overalled Madame Lafarge as she waved her little flag at him, and jumped into the train. It was the oldest trick in the business, but it seemed to have worked.

As he drank his coffee in the glass enclosure in front of the café in the Place Gambetta he could see the crowd from the following train coming up into the square, and no one looked remotely like a 'tail' who had guessed the right station and was trying to spot him in the milling crowds. There was a fine drizzle falling on the slippery pavements, and the people looked disgruntled, as the French always do at nine o'clock in the morning, hurrying along with heads bent, full of domestic cares.

He glanced at his watch. Six minutes to spare. Exact timing was essential and he had already ascertained how long it would take him to reach the rendezvous. He relaxed and lit a cigarette. He liked to get his thoughts in order before a task as important as this one.

The meeting was to take place—ironically, as it turned out—in a cemetery. Howard had been chosen for the job because he spoke Russian fluently, and what was more had made a special study of defector cases. And there was another reason. The Controller who had briefed him in the old MI6 building in Westminster had put it quite bluntly.

'It could be a plant,' he said, 'and we're not going to risk blowing any officer from our Paris station. We know quite a lot about the Russian who's made the approach—Alexei Kuznetsov—and he isn't the type of KGB operative one would expect to make a run for it. But he's a man with nasty habits and he may have got himself into a jam.' He had fiddled with a paper knife, glancing at the rather stolid young man who sat facing him squarely across the cluttered desk. It would need subtlety to handle a slippery bastard like Kuznetsov, and he wondered whether Howard had it.

'Why risk blowing me?' asked Howard, with a slight smile.

'Because you're known to the Russians already—' he raised a hand against Howard's protest—'of course you are. After that business in Beirut—and I know it wasn't your fault—we *must* regard you as blown. It's tough, at your age, because it limits the number of places you can be posted to, but there are still a lot of ways you can be useful to the Service, and this is one of them. If all the Paris *Rezidentsiya* is trying to do, by making defector noises in the general direction of our station, is to make one of our Paris officers break cover, it won't succeed. Kuznetsov will meet *you*, and you're on their books already. But if he's genuinely asking for political asylum you're the man to handle him. You talk his language in more ways than one, and you know how a defector's mind works and how to bargain before making promises. You've got to get him to produce something solid at this first interview—something we can check on.'

'Even then it can still be a plant,' pointed out Howard. 'Look at Berensky—he gave us a sheaf of genuine KGB reports before we caught him out.'

'Yes, I know. But that's a risk I've got to take. Your job is to minimize that risk by getting Kuznetsov to come across with something really hot. He ought to be able to—he was in the satellite intelligence branch in Moscow before he was posted to Paris. It's all there.' He pointed to a stack of files on his desk. 'Apart from that, your main job, of course, is to get him to stay put, at least for a week or two, so that he can work to a brief.'

'If he does agree to that, can I handle him from this end?'

'Yes, I promise you that. And once we're fairly sure of him you'll have to make personal contact from time to time, both for detailed briefing and to persuade him to remain in his job. Your interview will be recorded, of course, and you may be able to use that as a lever if all goes well. But all this is the second stage. At this meeting you have only three things to do—satisfy yourself that he's genuine, get the pay-dirt, and make clear that the longer he stays put the more golden his future. Right?'

'Yes, sir.'

'Then, if you think he's OK, fix a letter-drop and come home. *No* contact with the Paris station. You'll go out the day before, so that you can reconnoitre the ground and get ideas for the letter-drop.'

'If he insists that he's got to be given asylum at once—?'

'Use your judgment. And don't worry about definitions of political asylum. If we've got his voice on that tape— and you must *make* him say things that are compromising —he'll have political grounds all right. OK, then.' He watched Howard pick up the files and walk to the door. Then he called him back.

'I just want to say this. It's a stiff assignment I've given you. You've got to be tough and persuasive at the same time. So good luck, Michael. If you can make him trust you, so that he will go on working for us under your direction like a second Penkovsky, you'll make a killing.' He waved his hand and reached for his In-tray.

Afterwards, he wondered whether those last words had been inspired by a premonition of what was to happen.

Howard paid for his coffee and stood up. He put on his fawn Burberry and adjusted the camera case that swung from his neck, so that it lay correctly against his chest. Then he went out on to the square and crossed towards the Avenue du Père Lachaise. The rain was stopping, which was just as well if he was to pose credibly as a photographer on his way to the tomb of Sarah Bernhardt, and he walked briskly up the street towards the main entrance of the great cemetery, passing the mournful row of florists' and undertakers' establishments, and so through the iron gates into the empty solitude of Père Lachaise—empty except for the crowded dead and the tall chestnut trees. He went to the ticket office, showed his permit for the camera and bought a ticket.

The routes for both men had been exactly prescribed; Kuznetsov was to enter by another gate on the far side of the cemetery. Howard went along the Avenue de la Nouvelle Entrée to a narrow path which struck off to the left between the heavy grandeur of the tomb of the Marquis de Casariera and a strange dolmen-like entrance to a family vault. The path took him in a straight line between the dwellings of the dead, some severely simple, others covered by tall monuments of a rich mixture of styles, some with tiny chapels like sentry-boxes with rusted iron grilles through which he could see derelict altars and sometimes a few faded flowers.

At the end of the path there was a neo-Roman temple, and beyond he could see the tall trees lining another of the great avenues, but just this side of the temple Howard discovered, on his left hand, the tomb of Sarah Bernhardt, a solid slab of glistening granite opposite a small open space which could not be observed either from the path or the road.

A man was standing there. He wore a grey plastic mac-intosh and a soft brown hat pulled down on his forehead, above the tinted glasses.

Howard ignored him and busied himself with his camera, sighting at the inscription on the Bernhardt tomb and twisting the focus ring on the lens mounting. He shook his head in frustration and backed away, as if to get a better angle. This brought him near the other man and he glanced at him over his shoulder.

'*C'est difficile, vous savez, avec les réflexions.*'

The man replied hurriedly, stumbling over the French

words, '*Vous n'avez pas de photo-flash, monsieur?*'

The passwords had been exchanged. Howard straightened and spoke in Russian. 'I am glad to meet you, Alexei Stefanovich. Take off your glasses, please.'

The man hesitated, then quickly snatched them off. Howard's face showed nothing of the immense satisfaction he felt. It was Kuznetsov all right; he had seen the photograph on the file. And it was a very frightened Kuznetsov. The man's face was pale and sweating. This was no plant; this was the genuine article. So much for the Controller's first point. 'Thank you,' he said calmly. 'Do put them on again, if you wish.'

'You are Mr Dixon?'   *824286*

'Yes,' said Howard.

'Mr Dixon, you must help me. I have to leave quickly.'

'You would be of interest to us only if you stay at your post. Why are you so anxious to leave?'

'I cannot explain it all now, but I'm in trouble with my colleagues. I am sure they are watching me.'

Howard started. 'Could they have followed you here?' he asked coldly, his eyes fixed on the man's pale face.

'No. I was careful. I'm sure they cannot know about this meeting. It isn't that, it's—Oh God, listen!' He turned away and doubled round the end of the little temple. Howard heard two gardeners approaching along the path. He was busy with his camera as they passed, smoking their little clay pipes and talking about football. They did not even glance at him. He called the Russian.

'It's all right. Pull yourself together.'

Kuznetsov re-appeared. 'I have to get away,' he said earnestly, catching hold of the Englishman's sleeve. 'Somewhere I can hide and change my name. I will tell you everything I know. And there is much.'

Howard shook his arm free. 'What branch of the KGB were you in before being posted here?'

'Satellite intelligence,' said the man eagerly. 'I was trained at the scientific school in Kiev. Our spy satellites carry some new and very sophisticated devices for monitor-

ing earth installations. I saw the E.487 demonstrated and
it is extremely efficient. I can tell you its specifications and
I know most of the programmes—at least, what we were
told on the course.' He peered into Howard's face anxiously. 'You must believe me, Mr Dixon,' he muttered, turning
his head from side to side, searching the labyrinth of
vaults and tombs and monuments with his restless eyes. 'I
have a great deal to tell your colleagues . . . A-a-ah!' It
was a muted cry of sheer panic. He gestured towards
something behind Howard's back. The MI6 man turned
round.

A sad figure, wearing a long black overcoat and a black
hat with a turned-up brim, was moving along between the
graves, carrying an enormous wreath of lilies. He was at
least fifty yards away. They saw him find the place he was
seeking, for he posed the wreath carefully against a stone
cross, walked round it and adjusted the black silk banner.
Then he sank down on his knees and was hidden by the
wreath.

'He can still see us! He can look through the flowers.'

'He sees two men talking,' said Howard scornfully.
'Listen, Alexei Stefanovich. I am going to have trouble in
getting you asylum. You are obviously very worried and I
should like to help you, but we have enough Soviet defect-
ors in the West already. Think of the spin-off from the
Olympic Games! And then there was Sudakov and Moisic
and Mamoulian—'

'I am not an Azerbaijanian weight-lifter,' said Kuznetsov, affronted, 'I am a KGB officer.'

'Yes, so you said when you made your approach,' said
Howard calmly, 'but you must prove it. We had never
heard of you before, and what you've told me so far—all
that about the spy satellites— well, any man walking along
the Nevsky Prospekt could have told me that. I've no
doubt, myself, that you are what you say you are, but my
colleagues are suspicious-minded and I have to make a case
for you. Now, what can you tell me that will prove that
you are a KGB officer?'

He was glad he had taken the Russian's mind off the figure crouching by the stone cross. He had no doubt that it was someone sent by the Paris station to keep an eye on the meeting. But he was wrong.

The man in black was carefully sighting a long tube which was hidden in the lilies and foliage of the wreath. A wire ran from the near end to an ear plug which he had screwed into his ear. He was far beyond normal earshot, but as long as he had his tube trained on the two men by the Roman temple he could hear every word, and Howard's Russian was clear and precise.

'That's not good enough,' he was saying. 'What else?'

Kuznetsov groaned. 'There is something else, which is very important for you, but I know only a part of it. It is in the super-secret category.'

'Well?'

'When I was in the satellite section I was shown a report about the Euratom conference which took place in Rome. It was marked "Top Secret" '—he used the English words—'but it didn't tell us anything of importance.'

'What's the good—' began Howard. 'Did you say "Top Secret"—in English?'

'The report was in English, which I can read though I don't talk well. It was a photostat of the original document, which was a letter with an embossed coat of arms at the top and the heading of the British Embassy in Rome. They told me they had a high-level contact who had been in the Embassy for about two years.'

Howard's head jerked up. 'Tell me exactly what the document was like—the subject, the size of the paper, the date, and everything else you can remember.'

The mouth of the man behind the wreath of lilies tightened, and he began to talk quietly through his throat microphone, which connected with a transmitter in his pocket. Then he listened—and drew a deep breath. '*Da*,' he whispered, '*da. Kharasho*!' He quickly pulled out of his over-coat pocket a long-barrelled Mauser, a silencer and a light frame which fixed on to the butt. He had the whole thing assembled in twenty seconds and was squinting along the sights, the frame tucked snugly into his shoulder, the ten-inch barrel with its silencer peering out between the lilies.

Kuznetsov had finished his description and was looking apprehensively over Howard's shoulder. But there was nobody else in sight, only the man hidden by the wreath in the distance. He waited impatiently for the Englishman to speak, but the stolid young man was in no hurry as he went over in his mind the details the Russian had given him.

'When was it that you saw this document?'

'Towards the end of March.'

'And the date on the letter, you're sure it was March 5th?'

'Sure.'

'The copy,' said Howard suddenly. 'You said it was a photostat. Couldn't it have been a carbon copy?'

'No,' said the Russian emphatically, 'it was a photo-copy, and what struck me as so curious was—' The Eng-lishman's body was thrown against him, and for a moment hands clawed at him for support. He sprang back, thinking that Howard was attacking him, and then the other man's body crumpled forward and lay on its face and Kuznetsov saw the hole in the fawn cloth, just below the shoulder-blade, on the left-hand side.

He screamed, and looked up. And there, still forty yards away, came the man in black, waddling forward between the graves like a great vulture. He leaped on to the flat top of a monument which stood in his way, and for a moment was silhouetted against the sky, with the great wreath and the audio tube in one hand and the Mauser in the other.

Then down to ground level again, and on. But always in a straight line for Kuznetsov, who remained frozen with terror like a hypnotized rabbit.

The killer stopped at the Bernhardt tomb and crouched

behind it for a moment, staring balefully at Kuznetsov with the gun propped on the granite slab. Then he evidently decided that there was no danger. He laid down the automatic and pulled out his transceiver. When he had made his report he unclipped the shoulder frame from the gun and folded it together. He left the silencer on the gun, which always lay near his hand, and slowly telescoped the audio tube, which he put in his pocket with the frame. He looked round carefully and then laid the wreath in the centre of the granite slab, over the gold letters which spelt out the name of the woman who lay in the tomb below.

Finally, relaxed, he took off his black hat, brushed it lovingly with his sleeve and put it back squarely on his round, close-cropped head.

A hearse drew up quietly in the avenue beyond the temple and three men came running. One of them had an air of command and a thin, intelligent face. He turned over the fallen body with his foot and peered at the face. 'It's no one from the Paris station but I've seen his face somewhere. Petrov,' he addressed one of the men who had come with him, 'take a good look and check later with the MI6 list. I think it's a man called Howard, a good officer.' He looked at Kuznetsov. 'Too good to die for offal like you.' It was the first words he had spoken to the man who stood shivering with his back to the wall of the temple. 'And next time, Alexei Stefanovich, you make a rendez-vous with the enemy, don't choose a cut-out who has been in our pay for several years.'

The man in black behind the granite slab spoke urgently. 'There's someone coming down the path. He can't see you. Shall I—?' He made a gesture towards the Mauser.

'Don't be a fool, one's quite bad enough. Come over here—slowly—and help. Leave the wreath—that was a good idea. How far away?'

'Fifty metres.'

'That'll do.' He issued orders in a low voice. 'Frisk Kuznetsov and take him away. Get the Englishman in there.' He pointed to one of the sentry-box chapels whose rusty half-grille door stood ajar. They dragged the body inside and propped it against the wall behind the door, the camera case still hanging round its neck. One of the men pulled the camera free from its retaining strap and thrust it into his pocket. Then he felt Howard's clothes. 'No tape recorder.'

The leader was listening to the footsteps approaching along the path. 'Leave him,' he whispered urgently. 'Back to the van, quietly.'

The hearse rolled away slowly, decorously, over the glistening cobbles towards the Avenue de la Nouvelle Entrée. The coffin inside it was no longer empty. Kuznetsov lay in the dark, screaming, but no one heard him through the thick oak lid. When they had gone some distance the man in the black overcoat opened the lid to change the air and then clamped it down again. No one wanted Kuznetsov to die just yet.

Inside the little chapel, as the man on the path drew nearer, Howard's body slumped over sideways against the iron door, which creaked protestingly and closed with a loud clang.

There was no further sound which the man could hear, but he remained completely still, straining his ears, a gun in his hand.

The tiny whirr of the tape recorder was muffled by the false bottom of the camera case in which it was hidden. It still had a few feet of tape to record the grim silences of Père Lachaise.

Apart from that, the Paris *Rezidentsiya* of the KGB had done its work well.

CHAPTER TWO

S.3

'They want us,' explained the Senior Police Adviser, Foreign and Commonwealth Office, sourly, 'to find their bloody spy for them.'

It was early in May, and the window-boxes in Whitehall were full of red geraniums.

'But it's not our job, Bill,' protested Peter Craig. 'We're policemen, not intelligence officers. Surely MI5 and MI6 are supposed to clean up their own vomit. Why pick on us?'

Sir William Dennistoun did not reply at once. He looked thoughtfully at the younger man's dark-tanned, lined face. That broad, intelligent forehead and the broken nose with its odd twist just about summed up Peter, he was thinking. One of the best officers the old Colonial Service had had, and not just behind a desk. If there was a scrap he'd be in it, and then find the most persuasive reasons why he'd had to intervene. He smiled, and looked up to see Craig watching him curiously. He drained his coffee-cup and sat up in his chair.

'Listen, Peter. I know it's not our job, but S.3 want to borrow you.'

'I've never heard of them.'

'Nor had I until yesterday. Nobody has. It's the Special Security Service, and it only exists at all when there's reason to suspect that a member of one of our diplomatic missions abroad is betraying secrets to the enemy. But then it starts to operate, and fast, with a practically unlimited budget and powers to match. It was set up by the Prime Minister as soon as he took office, all his own idea, and he laid down some basic rules. One of them is that the preliminary investigation abroad is not, repeat not, to be left

to the MI5 or MI6 station, if there is one. In fact, only one
person in the whole mission can be put in the picture, and
that must be somebody who can be regarded, for cast-iron
reasons, as above suspicion.'

'But why, for God's sake? If there are trained intelligence men on the spot—'

'The PM has never forgotten that some time ago one
very important spy was tipped off by a member of MI6
and got away to Russia before he could be caught. Hence
his little rule.'

'But why pick on me, of all people? I've never had anything to do with intelligence, you know that.'

'That's what I thought, Peter, but S.3 seem to know
better. They saw—God knows how—a report from Roland
Mortimer in Lisbon, about some damned scrape he got you
into there. What's it all about?° I haven't seen you since
you got back from leave.'

'I had to re-draft my report, Bill, because there have
been some repercussions in this country. But it's on its way
to you.'

'I'm glad to hear that,' said Sir William grimly. 'But
you know damned well you shouldn't have touched an
espionage case.'

'We'd no idea there was an intelligence aspect to it. A
girl had disappeared and the Ambassador asked me to find
her. He threatened to cable you and get me attached to his
staff if I didn't agree. It was very much a rush job.'

'You should have let him signal. I'd have told him—but
never mind, it's over, and he's very pleased with you, for
what it's worth. It was a glowing report, full of praise. You
seem to have got him off a very nasty hook.'

'If Sir Roland ever glows,' said Craig resentfully, 'it's at
the prospect of causing pain. But I assure you, the espionage side was purely accidental. I just played it off the cuff.'

'I'm sure you did,' said Dennistoun mildly, 'and left a
litter of dead bodies in the process. But listen, there's more
to the S.3 argument than I've told you. The investigation
° SOLE AGENT, by the same author.

into this case has got to take place in Rome.'

'Oh hell!' said Craig, as light dawned.

'Exactly. They know you've got to spend two weeks there from next Monday for the Interpol Conference. So you can solve their little problem in your spare time, that's their idea, instead of ogling the girls on the Via Veneto.'

'This *would* happen to me. Still—you said a preliminary enquiry, didn't you? They want me to sniff around the suspect, if I can get to know him, and report back if he's spending three times his salary on high living. Is that it?'

'Not quite. You see, they don't know who it is.'

'They're crazy. Don't they know the form for visiting firemen? Listen, Bill. As the British delegate to the Interpol Conference I shall make a courtesy visit to the Embassy, sign the Ambassador's book, arrange with Head of Chancery to send my reports home by Bag, get invited, with luck, to drinks with the Ambassador and dinner with H of C—and that's it. I can't stroll round the departments, getting to know the Embassy staff and listening to gossip. Unless you want me to blow my assignment wide open.'

'They've thought of that.'

'I'm glad to hear it. So they won't expect much?'

'On the contrary, they want you to go as far as you can in your two weeks. So they've arranged with Security Department that you'll do the routine security check, which is actually due in July. Head of Chancery is being told it's to save expense. So you'll have all the access you need.'

'Jesus Christ! They think of everything, don't they? And when am I supposed to sleep?'

'Don't make such a fuss, Peter. You'll be fully briefed on the procedure for the security check and you can see the Positive Vetting files of all the home-based staff. If there's anything else you want, ask for it. And now you'd better hear the story, such as it is.' He lit a Burmese cigar, and described why there had been a meeting in the cemetery of Père Lachaise, and what had happened.

When he had finished Craig asked, 'What did the chap from the Paris station do when he found the body? Call the gendarmes?'

'No. He took the tape-recorder, which was hidden in the camera-case, and left him.'

'I always thought those MI6 people were a cold-blooded lot of bastards.'

'He was doing his job,' said Dennistoun severely. 'What did you expect him to do? He couldn't risk a public enquiry. It was discovered next day, an unidentified body— he wasn't carrying papers, of course—and an unsolved crime. That's how they wanted it.' He looked at Craig's disgusted face and continued quietly, 'I know how you feel, Peter, but this isn't police work. Espionage is another kind of jungle, with its own kind of nastiness.'

'Hm. So all we've got is this tape?'

'Yes, and it contains one very important statement by the Russian. He said the KGB had had a high-level agent in the British Embassy in Rome for two years.'

'I see. So that's why the MI6 man was killed. The KGB had been listening in and they couldn't let him get away once he'd heard that. And if they'd picked up the tape-recorder we'd never have known. Then why didn't they?'

'I told you, it was concealed in the camera-case—a beautiful job, apparently—and they must have been in a bloody great hurry, because they snatched the camera out of the case, which was slung round Howard's neck, and scrammed.'

'Not Michael Howard?'

'Yes.' He saw Craig's mouth tighten. 'Did you know him?'

'I met him in Beirut. Close-mouthed, but good company. I liked him.' He paused. 'All right, Bill. I'll do what I can.'

'I know you will. You've still got your flat in Smith Street?'

'Yes.'

'Someone from S.3 will call on you this afternoon at four to brief you fully and give you details of their agent in Rome.'

'You mean the one person in the Embassy I can talk to?'

'No. They have an agent there. Recruited by S.3 and kept on ice, for use by S.3 only.'

'Then who is the Embassy contact?'

'The Ambassador.'

'Oh no! That's too much. What sort of help can he give me about what goes on in his departments?'

'They chose him because he was in Saigon when the Rome spy was recruited two years ago, so he's above suspicion. And of course, there's another reason. He's the one person in the Embassy who can send a signal to London without even Head of Chancery knowing what it's about.'

'And who's going to encode my signals, if I do have anything to report?'

'He is. He's already got a special re-cyphering table for them. Rogers, the Head of Security Department, visited him two days ago and arranged for your security check at the same time.'

'I somehow don't think His Excellency is going to like all this. D'you know him, Bill?'

'Yes. He's a delightful and distinguished man, son of a Welsh post-office clerk, scholarship from Cardiff High School to Oxford, a First in Greats, MC in the Welsh Fusiliers as a subaltern at Sidi Barani, and a very good record since. He has a very quiet, dreamy manner but don't—on any account, Peter—underestimate him. Many people have, and been very sorry for themselves afterwards.'

Craig was to remember that advice.

The man who came to Craig's flat at four o'clock was of medium height, with a dark, weather-worn face and mournful-looking dark eyes under heavy brows. He must have been well over fifty, to judge from his grey hair, but his figure was trim and his movements quick and neat. He didn't introduce himself.

'I'm glad to meet you, Craig,' he said in a pleasant, cool voice. 'I've been hearing a lot about you from various people. We're glad you've agreed to help us out.'

'I didn't have much choice, you know. It's hardly my kind of job. May I ask who you are.'

'No. Sorry. The "need-to-know" rule is applied very strictly and all *you* need to know is that S.3 consists of a small number of people, including me, who all have our own jobs and only come together in a case of this kind. In fact—' he smiled slightly—'this is the first case we've had to deal with, so you can imagine how keen the Prime Minister is to see whether his idea works in practice.'

'But Dennistoun said you had recruited agents abroad?'

'Oh, we've done a lot of background work. The man in Rome was easy, because he's an old friend of mine. His name is Luigi Kahn.'

'German?'

'No. Half Italian, half Russian Jew. Don't worry, you couldn't have anyone better. He's an electronics engineer with a very profitable business. He also runs an industrial espionage bureau.'

'Hm. That's something. Does he talk English? My Italian's rusty.'

'Very fluently. He was a refugee in England during the war and joined SOE. The point is this, he has a profound, and for me inexplicable, love and respect for England. We did nothing for him, so far as I know, except drop him into the wrong valley in the Appenines in the middle of winter —but there it is. Incidentally, he doesn't like the Russians. They killed his father, who was a doctor in Leningrad.'

'What for? Trying to kill Stalin? The Doctors' Purge?'

'Yes.'

'You said he runs an industrial espionage service. Isn't he in contact, locally, with MI6?'

'No. He's been kept clean, for special jobs like this.'

'Could he undertake surveillance work if it's necessary?'

'At the drop of a hat, it's his job.'

'That's useful. How do I get in touch?'

'I shall be seeing him tomorrow and you'll get a note of the rendezvous and passwords before you leave.'

'Passwords!' muttered Craig.

Three days later an official car called at Craig's house in Chelsea to take him to the airport. The man who had briefed him was in the back and the glass partition behind the driver's seat was closed.

'I saw Luigi in Rome and he'll expect you at the rendez-vous on Sunday. Contacting instructions in this envelope. We've had the Embassy swept, by the way; it was made to appear the normal electronic check.'

'Did they find any bugs?'

'Not one, which strikes me as odd.'

'Yes. It is odd. I suppose it's useless to point out that both Bracken, the Head of Chancery, and Walton, who appears to be the MI6 man in Rome, are recent arrivals there and automatically beyond suspicion in this case. Without the help of one or other of those two you're asking me to do something that's practically impossible unless I have a big stroke of luck. I really can't expect much help from the Ambassador.'

'Sorry. The PM laid down the rules and until we can prove his idea doesn't work we're stuck with it. One member of the Embassy only, and in this case it's got to be the Ambassador. Unfortunately,' he added with his wry smile, 'and unlike his Soviet colleague, he's had no intelligence experience. I realize how you feel, Craig, but there it is. Walton, who as you say is the MI6 chap, is bright, and if I were only allowed to brief him he might put his hand on the culprit like that—' his long brown hand tapped the arm-rest between them—'but we've got to go the long way round and use an outsider. Sorry. That sounded insulting. It wasn't meant that way.'

'I'm glad you call a spade a spade. A couple of days' briefing isn't going to make me or anyone else into an intelligence officer.'

'You didn't do so badly in Lisbon, did you?'

Craig changed the subject. 'Did you say the Soviet Ambassador was an IO?'

'He was, and probably still is. But he's GRU, the military boys, not KGB, so he won't be directly concerned in your case. Which is just as well. He's a proper bastard. We had him in London until a few months ago. But he's a very able bastard.'

The car began to slow down at the entrance to Hyde Park. 'I'm getting out here. Good luck, Craig. Give my love to Luigi and his Maria.'

'Whose love?' asked Craig, grinning.

'Tell them Il Gobbo. It means hunchback. He'll explain some time.'

CHAPTER THREE

ROME — SUNDAY AFTERNOON

Whatever Peter Craig thought about intelligence tricks—
the pseudonyms, the 'dead letter-boxes' and passwords—
he had to admit that when it was a question of identifying
someone you didn't know from Adam, there was something
to be said for a fixed formula, however ridiculous.

He had arrived at Fiumicino airport by a morning plane
and had lunched very satisfactorily at the Hotel Eden,
where a room had been booked for him. At four o'clock he
was standing by the Temple of Aesculapius in the Borghese
Gardens, idly feeding bread to the ducks in the artificial
lake, when a voice said, 'Excuse me, sir, but brown bread
is bad for them. It expands the stomach.'

Craig protested. 'But it isn't brown, it's white!'

The tall man by his side gave a roar of laughter. 'I
apologize. You must forgive my impertinence, sir. It is my
sun glasses.' He took them off with a flourish and made a
little bow. 'I am delighted to meet you, Mr Craig. Any
friend of Il Gobbo is my friend, too.'

Craig held out his hand. The newcomer was a big man
in his early fifties, well dressed for a warm day in a pale
mohair suit, with a broad fleshy face dominated by a large
arched nose and lively brown eyes. 'Thank you for coming
to meet me, Mr Kahn. Can we talk for a bit here? It seems
as good a spot as any. What about that seat?'

'Sure.' They sat down on a bench by the water. It was a
pleasant place, with the reflections of the willows and the
little temple in the lake, and nobody around except for a
few nurses and their charges.

'Perhaps you could start by telling me what Gobbo told
you about this business. I haven't had any contact with the
Embassy yet.'

'He said you have a KGB spy, with good access, some-where in the Embassy, and it's your job to find him. He also said that for security reasons you would only have the Ambassador to help you.' He glanced sideways at Craig. 'It sounds crazy, but that's what he said. He told me you'd probably want certain facilities from me. You know my trade?' He spoke English very fluently, with only a slight Italian accent.

'I'd be glad if you could tell me about it. He said you had an industrial espionage service in addition to your electronics business.'

The big man stretched out his legs and contemplated his shining shoes complacently. 'I started here in Rome importing and marketing transistor radios and tape-record-ers, mostly Japanese and American, before the Italian industry got fully started. That was twenty years ago. Then I branched out into record players and the whole hi-fi range —it was the craze here, still is, as everywhere in the West —and I got to know a lot of the big firms, Italian and foreign. Well, it became clear that many of them wanted miniature devices for snooping on their rivals. As you may know, it's one of the best selling lines in Italy, particularly in the north, and I found I could get a lead over my competitors by dealing direct with the firms that wanted the things and making up the devices according to require-ments.'

'And I suppose the next step was to install them in posi-tion. And after that, provide the whole service, including surveillance teams. Is that about it?'

Kahn beamed. 'Exactly. I do the whole thing. They haven't either the time or the men to do it properly, so they leave it all to me. And pay for it handsomely. But of course they've got to be able to trust me and my boys absolutely. Which they can,' he finished simply.

'And you've no objection to providing a similar service for me if necessary?'

'Why should I? Gobbo will pay; he asked me to send the bills to him direct. I have an account in England, because

I have my son at school there, and in any case I go to London frequently. So it will suit me very well. But I'm no expert on political espionage, Mr Craig.'

'My name's Peter. I realize that, and also that you may be sticking your neck out more than you'd want to, other things being equal. If the KGB find out—'

'They must not find out,' said Kahn flatly. 'What is it you'll want me to do?'

'I don't know yet. But certain people may have to be followed after office hours. I shan't ask you to do anything inside the Embassy, of course. But the trouble is likely to be that even if I find out, to my own satisfaction, who it is who's doing the spying, I may not have proof. You see, I can't hold anyone on suspicion, as I could in England, so I've got to be able to make an arrest on a firm charge which in a British magistrate's court would give me custody pending trial. You understand what I mean?'

'I do,' said the big man thoughtfully.

'Well, that's where I shall probably need your help— getting proof. And I have a feeling that your special knowledge about listening devices and so on is going to come in useful. But I'll know more when I've seen the Ambassador and we've decided who are the most likely suspects.'

'OK, Peter. And my name's Luigi,' he added.

'Right, Luigi. Now there's another thing, and it's a bit difficult to explain. I'm trying to get the feel of this place before I go to the Embassy tomorrow. I used to know Rome well, when I was up at Cambridge, because I have an aunt who is married to an Italian up in Tuscany and she used to invite me for part of the long vac. We always spent a week or so in Rome so that she could go shopping, but the excuse was broadening my mind.'

'And did it broaden?'

'It did,' said Craig, grinning. 'In several ways! And I learned Italian. It's rusty now but it'll come back.'

'You must look up some of the no doubt delightful living dictionaries who taught you then,' suggested Luigi slyly.

'Good God! They're probably all married with rafts of

children by now. But seriously, Luigi, what I'm getting at is this : the city's changed a lot since I knew it in the fifties. I don't mean to look at—it's as beautiful as ever—but the whole feel and tempo of the place—that's what strikes me. It's so much faster and more chaotic. I wonder how it affects people who come here for a few years, in Embassy jobs. Does it put any sort of special strain on them?'

Kahn thought for a moment. 'It's odd that you should say that—or perhaps I should say perceptive. What you mean is, why should someone wake up one morning— someone who is a plain, more or less sober Civil Servant— and say to himself, "Damn the Queen, damn the Foreign Office, I'm going to be a Russian Spy!" Is that it?'

'You've got it in one.'

'Well, I think it could happen. There *is* something special about the Roman atmosphere. It's a strange city. It has everything, you see, the oldest virtues and the newest vices. The most beautiful buildings in the world and some of the—what's the word?—some of the shoddiest. Churches and sculptures and paintings that take your breath away. But so do the brothels, I assure you. Every devious taste catered for in the greatest luxury. I tell you, in the top-price ones Petronius Arbiter would feel completely at home.' He paused, looking at Craig, smiling. 'And I forgot to mention the spivs. We have the best. And drug-pushers—very sophisticated, they are. We have hippies, too—we call them *capelloni* because of their hair— but of course they can't compete with the King's Road.'

Craig laughed. 'Go on, Luigi, this is what I wanted. So what effect on the innocent foreigner?'

'Oh yes, it affects him all right. Not the Romans—they take it all as a matter of course. Nor the tourists. But some of the ones who come, as you said, for a few years, away from home, learning new sets of values—some of them, in that very expressive English phrase, come unstuck. One way or the other. Perhaps they're searching for one more beautiful thing, or one supreme emotion, or just another sex experience, and they get to a point when they're never satisfied. It can happen, I don't say it has in your Embassy but I know for a fact that it has in others, and then—bang! Like Harpic, clean round the bend! And the poor devil gets sent home in disgrace.'

'Thank you, chum. That's exactly what I wanted to know—that it *can* happen like that. Look, I mustn't keep you too long, but I might be in a position tomorrow to ask you to put tails on two or three members of the staff. Could you get the teams going without delay?'

'Yes, up to three targets, not more. I've got only one surveillance job on at the moment.'

'Good. I'm staying at the Eden, room 232. I'd like to have another talk with you tomorrow in any case, when I've studied the form a bit. Could you dine with me?'

Kahn smiled. 'As you say in England, there is no place like home. Especially in this city where—I'm happy to say —hidden microphones abound. Please dine with us; my wife will be delighted to meet you. Tomorrow evening at eight-thirty, perhaps. Via San Valentino, number 72, top floor. It's in Parioli.'

'I'll look forward to it, thanks.' He held out his hand. 'I'm very glad to have you on my side, Luigi.'

'It is a pleasure. Goodbye, Peter.' He strolled off, unhurried, towards the Valle Giulia gate.

After dining at a trattoria on the Corso Craig made his way through the Piazza Venezia to the foot of the great flight of steps that leads up between the statues to that grandest and most beautiful of the squares of Rome, with Marcus Aurelius on his charger darkly silhouetted against the softly floodlit façade of the Palazzo del Senatore, shimmering in the reflections of the fountains. To the right of the Renaissance palace a road leads sharply downwards, and at the first curve there is a place where you stand above the floodlit Forum. Craig lit a cigar and looked out across the broken columns and arches to the Colosseum. Far beyond, somewhere in the darkness, lay the Villa Wolkonsky, which housed the British Embassy and its spy.

It had been a quiet evening for Craig—the last for many days—and he finished it soberly, walking back through the noisy, swirling traffic in the Piazza Venezia to quieter streets that led him to the hotel. He was thinking over what Luigi had said.

Could there be something special about the lures and tensions of this place, some strange alchemy that could transmute even a plain issue like loyalty—which to Craig was as natural and essential as the air he breathed—into something questionable, something you could argue about? Something seen not in black and white but with outlines blurred by flickering psychedelic visions?

He shook himself. Remember you're a cop, Craig, and keep your big feet firmly on the ground.

CHAPTER FOUR

MONDAY MORNING

Promptly at a quarter past nine, as Craig was standing on the steps of the hotel, a black BMC 1800 drew up and a chauffeur with the Royal Arms on his cap got out. Craig identified himself and the car drove off through the ruthless traffic rush, crossing the heart of the city, past the Colosseum, climbing on cobbles to the vast Piazza di San Giovanni in Laterano to reach, by way of a couple of shabby streets, the wrought iron gates of the Villa Wolkonsky.

He had a peaceful glimpse of palm trees above the curving wall and then they stopped at the lodge. A man in Embassy uniform handed Craig a pass made out in his name and they drove on, through a gap in the massive structure of the aqueduct of Nero, which seemed to pass straight through the Embassy grounds, and stopped at the Chancery building, the central core of the Embassy.

'Mr Bracken is waiting for you, sir.' A messenger took him up a narrow stair, cut in the thickness of the masonry where the building straddled the aqueduct itself, and along a corridor to a door on the left.

John Bracken, Head of Chancery, a man in his late forties with a tired grey face, looked quickly and appraisingly at Craig as he entered. Then he put down his pipe and came round the desk to welcome him.

'Not that chair, if you don't want a broken spring in your bottom. I keep that for selected visitors. The other's sound enough, and the Ministry won't let me have replacements until they both fall to pieces. There. D'you smoke?'

'A pipe.'

Bracken sat on the edge of his desk. 'I don't know much about you people in the Police Adviser's Department, but I gather that besides attending the Interpol meetings you're going to put us through a security check. That's all right with me, of course, and I'll give you any help you need, but isn't it a bit odd? It's Security Department's job.'

'Cheese-paring,' said Craig. 'I certainly didn't want the job, but I suppose they thought it was too good a chance of saving another lot of fares and subsistence. You haven't been done since last July, have you?'

'No, that's true. Anyway, you can have the Minister's room, three doors along the corridor on the left, and use my PA for your reports. She's been security-vetted, of course.'

'That's Miss Warren.'

'You *have* done your homework. Yes. Diana's a competent girl, and she doesn't chatter about her work to the typists' pool.'

'Thanks.'

'H.E. wants to see you, by the way.'

'Sir Watkyn?'

'Yes. Some ideas he's got about building security, I think. I've no idea what the old boy's got in mind, but for God's sake don't commit yourself, will you? Whatever's decided it'll be me to work out the details.'

Craig smiled. 'Let's hope he hasn't thought up anything too exotic.' He tapped his pipe out and followed Bracken into the corridor.

'The first door you come to from the stairs, Diana Warren. On the left here, the Ambassador's PA, Mrs Ransome; then H.E. and beyond that the Minister's room, which you'll have. He's in Milan. The rest I'll explain later, but it's all here on this floor. Registry, First and Second Secretaries, typists, strong-room and cyphers—the whole of Chancery except Admin., which is in a building down the drive. Right, here we go.' He opened the second door, quietly, without knocking, and stood inside. 'Mr Craig, sir. You said you'd like to see him.'

It was a big, plain room, comfortably furnished, with flowers on the tables and photographs in silver frames on the wide-spreading walnut desk. Sir Watkyn Rees, KCMG,

CVO, MC, was tall for a Welshman and still straight as a
Guardsman for all his fifty-nine years, with a smooth gentle
face of great distinction. His hair was quite white, but
thick and curling around his ears and across the broad
forehead. His eyes were dark and hooded by heavy lids.

He rose to his feet and held out a long slender hand. He
waited until the door closed behind Bracken and said, 'I
won't keep you long, Craig. I realize you've got no less
than three jobs to occupy you while you're in Rome. I'll
see that Bracken gives you all the help you want with your
security check, and I'll do what I can to aid you in the—er
—under-cover task.'

'Thank you, sir. I'm afraid there's a lot I'll have to ask
you.'

'Of course. But what I want you to know is this, just so
that we understand each other.' The quiet voice held muted
Welsh overtones. 'The idea of having a spy on my staff
makes me feel physically sick. At first I refused to believe it,
and was in fact rather rude to poor Rogers. But he convinced me. I have always detested security regulations and
all the paraphernalia of espionage. I can never feel the
enthusiasm which Derek Walton, the MI6 representative,
expects me to show when he's pulled off some important
coup. I've had to dissemble my feelings during thirty-five
years of Government service but remember—they're still
there. That's what I want you to realize.'

'I feel exactly the same, at least about espionage. I'm a
policeman, not a counter-espionage officer.'

'Good. So long as you will understand that I shall get no
satisfaction out of your investigations, however successful
they may be. But on the other hand I'll give you all the
help you need, if you will call the tune. It's my duty.
Right! Now I gather I'm the only person in this office
with whom you can discuss your assignment?'

'Yes, sir.'

'Well, then, it seems to me that we'll have to meet quite
often to discuss the staff and procedure. That's what you
want, no doubt? But won't all this take a lot of time?'

'That's just what I've been worrying about, sir. We can't have frequent discussions in your room without throwing your programme out and causing a lot of speculation among the Chancery staff.'

'Exactly. I've prepared the way by telling Bracken that I have some ideas about building security to discuss with you. But that is of course a fiction. As I've just explained I'm the very last person to have ideas of any kind on the subject. It just served as an excuse for this first meeting. You have my permission to tell Bracken that you listened patiently to my suggestions and dissuaded me from going further. You may add that my ideas were poppycock—or whatever coarse word you care to choose. If I know John his sense of loyalty will inhibit him from asking you for further details. He'd be putting himself in your camp, so to speak.'

'That's neat, sir, if I may say so. I will think of a suitable term.'

'Do that,' said Sir Watkyn, unsmiling. 'Now, the other point. Where can we meet frequently without being overheard or attracting attention?'

'Golf, perhaps? I could borrow some clubs.'

'I do not play the game,' said His Excellency, in a tone of some severity. 'But I am an amateur of orchids. Do you know anything about the *orchis* family?'

'I think I could just get by. My last Governor in Bangasa was a passionate orchid grower and he frequently entertained me on the subject. At great length,' he added, only half under his breath.

'Good. Let us have our next meeting this afternoon at half-past three. I should explain that I am almost always engaged for luncheon, but whenever I can get back in time I have a short siesta until three-thirty and then spend an hour in the orchid house. It restores the perspective. The place is in the private garden, beyond the swimming-pool. If anyone sees you there say I have invited you. In fact I will tell Mrs Ransome to let Bracken know.' He paused, and added suddenly, with a gleam in his eyes,

'Wasn't Gerald Swanson your Governor in Bangasa before Independence?'

'Yes, sir. It was Sir Gerald who took my orchid education in hand.'

'My dear fellow,' said Sir Watkyn, chuckling merrily, 'you must have been no only bored to extinction but hopelessly misinformed. He knows nothing about orchids.' He frowned. 'But I'm afraid we shall have little time for enlightening your ignorance. There will be less pleasant things to talk about. You have the description which that wretched man gave of the document he said he had seen in the Kremlin, or wherever it was?'

'Yes, sir.'

'Good. I shall have some pointers for you on that. I think I have identified the document. We meet then at three-thirty. Among my orchids.'

CHAPTER FIVE

MONDAY AFTERNOON

The Questore of Rome had done his polished best to make the luncheon for the Interpol delegates a success, but nothing could stop the speakers from droning on, and Craig was very glad when he could get away into the quiet streets. Under the hot sun the city seemed to have gone to sleep.

But for some people it was not a time for rest.

In spite of its high ceiling the room in the ultra respectable old house was heating up as the sun battered the blistered *persiani*, and the sheets on the iron bedstead were damp with sweat. The man lay on his back, looking up at the shadowy ceiling unhappily. 'It's all wrong, you know,' he muttered.

She turned quickly and propped herself on her elbows, peering down at his face. 'If you're referring to morals,' she pointed out—and there was the hint of an edge to her low voice, 'remember, I didn't start it.'

He pulled her head down so that he could kiss her, and whispered anxiously, 'Of course you didn't, darling. I know that. It's just—'

'And if you mean it's wrong to meet like this, at least it's safe. And anyway, it's just what we lower orders have to put up with in our clandestine amours. We don't have your umpteen thousand a year for living allowance, you know.'

'Don't rub it in. It's not right for *you*, that's what I mean. It's too sordid for someone so—' He stopped, confused.

'Sophisticated,' she said with a lazy laugh. 'Is that the word you're searching for?' The arm round his neck tightened. 'You're always talking such nonsense, aren't you?' She kissed him slowly, deliberately. 'And wasting such precious time.'

And then of course he was lost, and it was much later that he looked at his watch and struggled to get up. 'I've got to go, and so have you, or we'll be bloody late.'

'You were telling me you didn't care a hoot for the Establishment. I'm glad to see you're such a loyal servant after all.'

'Oh, don't talk rot; it's nothing to do with loyalty. If I don't do my job I shall lose it. It's as simple as that.' He was pulling his shirt over his head, and did not see the calculating look in her eyes. 'And I need the money, you know that.'

On the way to the bathroom she turned back. 'There are more ways than one of earning it, you know.' The door closed behind her slim back. He stared at it for a moment, then shrugged his shoulders, finished dressing, and ran out of the flat.

And later that afternoon, in the inner security sanctum of the Soviet Embassy in Via Gaeta, another kind of activity. The KGB section-leader, sweating in his shirt sleeves in the windowless room, turned up the clanking air-conditioner and let a chilling draught play against his crew-cut head. 'Tell Comrade Zakharov I want to see him,' he said gruffly into the intercom. He stood there thinking, until the cold air made him shiver and he moved back to his desk and picked up some papers.

'You wanted to see me, Sergei Pavlich?' The man at the door was tall and well built, with grey eyes and thick fair hair. The face was naturally pale, with broad cheek-bones. He was a young man, in his first post abroad, and he feared and hated his boss. And with some reason, because Rostov's weakness, as a career KGB officer, was that he was bad with juniors. He had done very well for his Service as a lone wolf attached to the Illegal *Rezidentsiya* in England, but now he was office-bound, and he suspected his subordinates of trying to steal credit that should have been his. But he enjoyed playing cat-and-mouse with them, and his expression now was falsely genial.

'Come in, Sasha,' he said. 'I want to have a talk with you about BX.328, the agent you succeeded in recruiting all by yourself. I've come to the conclusion that this agent needs stimulating.' He raised a hand. 'I know what you're going to say. The transmitter has been installed as planned—a very successful operation. But after all, what risk did 328 run? None at all, simply a question of substitution—it was child's play. All the risk lay in planting the transmitter, and that was done by other operatives.' The young man was silent, and Rostov went on, 'Now, as you know—because they must at least have made a point of this on your training course—these technical operations are tricky. They produce a mass of information we don't want, and a great deal of office time is spent sifting out the few grains of gold. In this case, fresh from your recent training course, you argued that we should use a new device which would be extremely selective. It would only transmit matter likely to be of real value. Is that correct?'

'Yes, Sergei Pavlich.'

'And what, precisely, has this device transmitted to us?'

'Nothing so far, Comrade, but it was only installed on Saturday and yesterday was Sunday, of course, so—'

'But it has been silent all today, too. I took the trouble to check. I'm afraid your invention may prove so selective, Comrade, that it will scorn to produce anything at all.' His voice rose to bullying pitch. 'So what are we left with? A well-placed agent who hasn't succeeded in recruiting a single sub-source in—let me see—nearly three years.'

'But that is being done, Comrade Rostov. I told you we were working on the sub-source, even before I went on the training course. But then of course the agent had no contact with us while I was away, and I did not wish to delegate the task to anyone else. But I assure you, 328 is working on the recruitment very hard, under my supervision. It is not an easy task.'

'So he isn't on the hook yet?'

'No, Comrade.'

'Have you shown the whip?'

'But no, Sergei Pavlich,' cried Alexei Zakharov desperately. 'It is still far too early. It might ruin everything.'

'You have obtained the material to make a whip?'

'Yes, of course, it's all ready. But I assure you, Sergei Pavlich, it is too early—' He saw the look on Rostov's face. 'I assure you—'

'You have been assuring me for weeks, Comrade Zakharov, and there is still no action. We want that man on the hook. You are to show the whip. That is an order.'

Zakharov's face went white, then slowly flushed, but he remained silent, and the other went on, 'I would not be so insistent if 328 were producing a flow of useful reports—'

'But, Comrade, we are getting the reports regularly, and they are factual—not padded at all.'

'I agree,' said Rostov with a sneer, 'but I was talking about *useful* reports. I can't believe that there isn't something more worth while to be extracted from the British Embassy by a source who has such inside access.' He added, harshly, 'I have the feeling, Comrade, that as with your precious transmitter, *selection* is being made, and not in our interests.'

'*No!*' cried the younger man.

'That is my view, Sasha,' said Rostov gently, 'and it is for you to persuade me otherwise. I leave it to you, but be sure you take *some* action. This sort of thing which you sent in half an hour ago—' he flicked his fingers contemptuously at a paper on the desk—'isn't worth a fraction of the money we're paying. Reduce the pay or threaten reprisals—do anything you like within reason, but I want that sub-source on the hook and I want better, inside material in the reports. I would not wish,' he added softly, 'to have to send another mediocre production report to Moscow. That's all.'

Zakharov turned on his heel without a word, and went out, fists clenched and the sweat beading his smooth face.

Sergei Pavlich Rostov smiled. He picked up the report.

'BX/328/451. 5th June 70. Arrival of police officer at the British Embassy.

'Peter Verney Craig, 35, British, Overseas Police Adviser's section, FCO, arrived here yesterday by BEA flight—.

'He is to attend the Interpol Conference. He will also carry out a security inspection at the Embassy. No apparent connection with intelligence or with BX 328's activities.

'Ambassador informed Counseller John Bracken, Head of Chancery, in casual conversation that Craig was an expert on orchids and had His Excellency's permission to visit his orchid house whenever he wished to do so. (Field Note : The Ambassador's main recreation is the culture of orchids.)'

'Orchids !' shouted the section leader with a contemptuous laugh. He crumpled up the report and threw it into the open maw of the destructor which stood in the corner of his room. The electronic eye switched on the machine, which digested the paper in one raucous cough and was silent.

The louvres in the glass roof of the orchid house were open, and the reed matting had been rolled down to give some protection from the blazing sun, although it was still stiflingly hot. But the Ambassador didn't seem to notice it. He was still wearing the black jacket and striped trousers he had worn for an official luncheon, and when Craig came in he was lovingly operating with a razor blade on a gorgeous plant that cascaded over the sides of a bark basket swinging above his head. The air was thick with the sweet, corrupt scents of tropical vegetation.

'Ah, there you are,' said His Excellency, putting down the blade and going over to a dripping tank to rinse his fingers. 'We'll sit down over at the table. As you see, I've brought a catalogue so that if anyone should come we can pretend to be studying it.' There were two cane chairs by a well-scrubbed deal table, on which the catalogue was lying.

'May I take my coat off, sir?'

'Of course, and I'll do the same.' He continued to look elegant in shirt sleeves, and Craig saw that the stiff white collar had not even begun to wilt. 'Now, let me have a look at the description of the document which went astray last March.'

'This is the transcription of the tape recording of the interview which took place in Paris, translated from the Russian, of course. I suggest you begin where I've marked the text.'

The Ambassador read it through slowly.

HOWARD : What's the good— Did you say 'Top secret'--in English?

KUZNETSOV : The report was in English, which I can read though I don't talk well. It was a photostat of the original document, which was a letter with an embossed coat of arms at the top and the heading of the British Embassy in Rome. They told me they had a high-level contact who had been in the Embassy for about two years.

H. Tell me exactly what the document was like—the subject, the size of the paper, the date, and everything else you can remember.

K. About twenty centimetres by thirty. And the date was March 5th.

H. Foolscap. (Translator's note : This word in English.) What was it about?

K. The gas-centrifuge process for extracting uranium. The Italians wished to introduce a discussion of the method at the Euratom Conference. Something like that.

H. Was the report one page only?

K. Yes, it was a letter to the Foreign Office, not an official report.

H. Was it signed?

K. Yes, I saw that. I remember I could not read the signature, but underneath was typed 'HM Ambassador'. (Translator's note : Pause of 26 seconds.)

H. When was it you saw this document?

K. Towards the end of March.

H. And the date on the letter, you're sure it was March 5th?

K. Sure.

H. The copy. You said it was a photostat. Couldn't it have been a carbon copy?

K. No, it was a photo-copy, and what struck me as so curious was— (Translator's note : Speech broken off here. There is a noise like a cough or a gasp. Then silence for 45 seconds, except for unidentifiable sounds, very faint. Two other voices then speak in Russian. See 096/743, copy to Paris.)

The Ambassador raised his head. 'Was that when—?'

'Yes, sir. The British officer was shot dead. The Russian, as was clear from the rest of the tape, which was of interest to Paris only, was arrested and taken away.'

Sir Watkyn sat looking at the table in front of him. Then he shivered and shook himself.

'That's what I feel about intelligence, Craig. It is utterly evil. In that cemetery at Père Lachaise—I know it well; it already has sad memories for me—a brave man went to his death. And for what? For a piece of paper which the Russians themselves probably didn't want. And here we are, you and I, plotting to deceive loyal members of my staff and spy on them in the forlorn hope of discovering which of them is the traitor. It's a terrible thing. Evil never brings good, you know, only more evil. Spies breed spies.' The lilting, beautiful voice stopped, but Craig made no reply. There was none to make. He waited.

'After Rogers gave me the gist of the thing I turned up the file—' He caught Craig's glance and added impatiently, 'Yes, of course I thought up a good excuse. Well, I identified the document. As that Russian said, it was a letter about this rather sensitive question of our gas-centrifuge research. We knew the Italians wanted the whole subject ventilated at the Conference, and although of course we're not members of Euratom we succeeded in persuading them not to. My Scientific Officer drafted the letter and I signed it. It was sent to the Head of Scientific Department in London and the float copy marked to H of C, Minister Commercial and Defence Attaché "after action". The action copies were for my own file, which I keep in my safe, and the Scientific Officer.'

'So the Commercial and Defence people would only see the letter afterwards, in copy?'

'Yes. In the Top Secret float.'

'And of course only the original, which you signed, would have the Royal Arms at the top of the sheet. The carbon copies wouldn't have the embossed seal, only the typed heading?'

'That is right.'

'So the only *officer* to see the signed letter, besides yourself, would be the Scientific Officer. That's Neil Adams, isn't it?'

'Yes,' said Sir Watkyn shortly.

'I examined Adams's file in London. The S.3 people thought I should pay special attention to it.'

'Rogers said the same thing to me. I told him he was barking up the wrong tree.'

'Why, sir?'

'Because—surely you must see—if Adams were the spy he wouldn't have had to send my letter to his confounded spy-masters; he could have given his own account of the whole thing. And incidentally added a lot more about the gas-centrifuge process than appears in my letter, which was only dealing with a question of principle.'

'With respect, sir, I don't agree.'

'Indeed?'

'I'm trying to put myself in a spy's place. What he is always anxious to do, as I understand it, is to provide information which his enemy contact *knows* is true. Anything he wrote off his own bat would not necessarily carry conviction. But a photograph of a letter signed by you would.'

'Oh dear! Oh dear me, I believe you're right. Jumping

to conclusions, wasn't I?' He turned to Craig with a disarming smile. 'I will own up. I was over-anxious not to adopt a *parti pris* towards Adams because, in fact, that would be my natural reaction.'

Craig stifled a groan. 'Could you explain, sir?'

'Certainly. Neither I nor my wife can find anything whatever in common with Adams or his bouncing little wife. I can't talk to him without both of us having to stop just short of losing our tempers. He is wildly left-wing in his political views, contemptuous of his elders and betters, wears the wrong clothes—I think quite deliberately—on formal occasions, and had to be stopped from wearing sandals in Chancery. But I must admit that he is careful in his work and uses his brains, is liked by the Italians and his chaotic household is always open to any lame duck of a love-lorn typist or a visiting fireman. He's a useful member of my staff, and really not a bad boy at all. And as for what you're thinking, if he spied for anybody it would be more likely to be Mao Tse Tung than the—what d'you call 'em—the KGB. But he's no spy, I'm sure of that.'

'You said his political views were far left. So he talks about them?'

'He states them, blandly, on all occasions, and won't argue about them. That's the trouble. You know what some of the young men in the Office are like these days, in their political opinions, but they're taught to leave their feelings at home. But of course Adams isn't a member of the Service, he was brought in as an expert. He refuses to see that when he airs his views about Vietnam the foreigners think it's Her Majesty's Government putting out a subtle feeler, *perfide Albion* at its old game. It's such a pity, because he's got a lively mind.'

'You're giving me just the sort of thumbnail sketch I'd like to have about the others.'

'Which others?'

'Anyone who could have been alone with the top copy of your letter after signature.'

'Well, it's a limited field. There's me, to start with.'

'We can eliminate you, sir,' said Craig.

The Ambassador stared at him. 'That's handsome of you, Craig. May I ask why?'

'You weren't posted here until early last year. The alleged spy had already been working for them for at least six months when you arrived.'

'Well, that's pleasant to know. I suppose if I weren't in the clear they'd never have told me about this business at all?' Craig was silent.

The Ambassador thought for a moment. 'But that lets out the Commercial Minister and—let me see—Bracken and the Second Secretary in Chancery, not Adams—he's on his second tour—not Mrs Ransome or Miss Warren—' He stopped, and turned to Craig with a rather worried look on his face. 'I'm talking nonsense,' he went on quietly. 'The point is that any letter I've signed shouldn't be seen by anybody afterwards except the originator, in this case Adams, and Mrs Ransome.'

'Your PA.'

'Yes. She takes the signature folder from my desk and separates the copies which are to accompany the letter itself from those which remain for filing, and encloses them in the envelope. Then she keeps any copy I need for my own files and sends the others, with the sealed envelope, to Head of Registry for dispatch and filing.'

'She wouldn't leave the letter on her desk if, perhaps, you called her in for dictation?'

'No. If she's with me she locks her outside door if there are any secret papers on her desk. Then if anybody wants to see me urgently they come along the passage to the door which leads directly into my room.'

'You said the originator of the letter might also have seen it afterwards?'

'Yes. I can't remember, but Adams *might* have brought the letter in for signature, and he might then have taken it out to Mrs Ransome.'

'But the only person who *must* have had it in their hands would be Mrs Ransome. I think we ought to start by taking a careful look at her. I've seen her PV record, of course, but it'd help me a lot if you could tell me about her in your own words.'

'Well, as you know, she's the daughter of a baronet who had a lot of money in his lifetime, but didn't leave very much to his widow. Lady Balcombe is half-Italian, and she just had enough to live in Italy and bring up her daughter. She sent her to school in England and Janet got a scholarship to Somerville, where she did quite well. Then she met and married an older man, who was CO of the Green Howards. They had a son, now a boy of seven who started at his prep. school this year. But his father was killed in an aircraft accident soon after he was born.'

'Poor girl!'

'Yes, it was a tragic thing. It left Janet with a miserable widow's pension, so she came out to Italy and lived with her mother for a time and then applied for a job at the Embassy. This was about five years ago. She'd put herself through a secretarial course and was taken on as a typist, "locally employed", and translator. Then she tried to get into the Diplomatic through the Civil Service exam—she came down from Oxford with a good degree—but they turned her down. Still, she got herself established in the Service last year and was allowed to stay on here for her first official posting and became PA to my predecessor, who thought very highly of her. As I do. But I suppose all this is on the file?'

'Well, yes, sir. But what about her as a person?'

The Ambassador hesitated. 'She's not a warm person, or at least doesn't show her feelings much. Not an outgoing personality at all. But she's very pleasant to work with. Her mother owns a house on the other side of the Borghese Gardens and they live together.'

'Security-conscious?'

'Exceptionally so. She's rather a bore sometimes in the way she chases after me, taking papers out of my hand so that I don't leave them about.'

'I see.'

'But don't think for a moment that *she*'s the spy. She's as traditionally upper-class as they come.'

'It doesn't necessarily hold, sir,' said Craig drily.

'No, of course not, that was stupid of me. But I can't imagine her for a moment being disloyal.' He paused. 'There was something about that particular letter I can't remember—' He suddenly struck his head with his hand. 'Great heavens, man!' he cried, and the Welsh overtones were very strong. 'How daft of me! I had forgotten altogether. I told you Adams drafted the letter. Now it comes back. He brought it to me for signature. I signed it. But when he'd gone I realized that there was only a passing reference to the part he had played in the negotiations, which in fact he'd handled very well and with—for him—remarkable tact. So I asked for it back and scribbled something pleasant at the end, something like "I am indebted to Mr Adams, my Scientific Officer, for the neat and skilful way etc., etc.," and I told him to get my PA to re-type it to include my remark. Which she did.'

'Mrs Ransome did?'

'Yes, I suppose. But the point is, Craig, *I signed both letters*. From that conversation we saw just now we can't possibly tell which letter the Russians got hold of.'

'I see. You just wrote in your piece about Adams in the margin or underneath. You didn't strike the first letter through?'

'No,' said the Ambassador slowly, 'I don't think I'd ever do that, when I'd scribbled on the top copy. It wouldn't be necessary. The typist would cancel it when she'd re-typed the letter.' He paused. 'But—'

'But more probably,' finished Craig with a sigh of frustration, 'she'd simply throw the first letter into the confidential waste bin as soon as you'd signed the second one. I'm afraid, sir, we're back at Square One.'

Bracken was saying, 'Well, I'm at your disposal for the next half-hour if I can help. Where d'you want to start?'

'The main thing we're interested in on this trip is your

confidential waste disposal. Could you give me an idea about that?'

'Confidential waste? That's odd. Rogers didn't mention that, as far as I know. He said you were just going to make a general inspection.'

'So I am, but the thing he laid stress on to me was the problem of waste. There are some new devices, you know.' He hoped there were.

'Oh well, that's interesting. We still burn everything in the special incinerator—everything "Restricted", that is. The lower grade stuff is disposed of by the departments in their own time.'

'What's the procedure for the higher grades?'

'It's all kept in combination safes and collected once a week by a Chancery messenger, home-based, with one of the diplomatic staff in attendance. They then parade through the garden to the incinerator, which is fired by gas, with a forced draught, and leaves nothing but fine ash. But the diplomatic officer has to inspect the thing afterwards and satisfy himself that it's worked efficiently.'

'That's a bit of a call on an officer's time, isn't it?'

'It is. It's a colossal bind. But everybody below Counsellor is on the roster, so it only happens every few months for each chap.'

'And what happens, exactly, while the stuff is waiting for the weekly cremation ceremony?'

'I'll show you. Come next door.' He led the way through the communicating door into Diana Warren's room and introduced Craig.

She was a tall girl with fair hair, and long, attractive legs under the brief summer dress. She opened a safe and pulled out a large paper bag sealed with Sellotape, with her signature scrawled across the tape. He turned it upside-down, and saw with approval that the bottom end of the bag had been secured in the same way.

'And the shredding?'

'Oh yes, I forgot. Every paper marked "Secret" or "Top Secret" has to be shredded before it goes into the paper bag.

Look here.' He pulled out the bag in current use, and Craig saw that it was half-full of what looked like paper straw. 'At the end of each day the girls put all the high-grade waste—drafts, carbons, and so on—through the shredders and put the straw into the bags, and *they* go into the safes, as you see.'

'Well,' said Craig, 'that looks pretty efficient. Thank you for showing me.'

So if, as he had been thinking, what Kuznetsov had seen was a copy of the first Adams letter, why hadn't it been shredded?

Craig was introduced by Bracken to Head of Registry and the heads of other departments housed in the Chancery building and left to get to know them and discuss their security problems. It was after seven when he returned to Bracken's room. They talked for a few minutes, and then Diana Warren came in to pack up Bracken's files.

'Sorry,' said Craig. 'I'm keeping you.'

'No, you're not; I've got to go on for a bit anyway. Diana, don't wait, I'll lock up here. You might show Mr Craig out and see if there's a car to give him a lift into town. Oh Peter, Althea said would you care to dine with us tomorrow? We'll get some of the staff to meet you.'

'That's very nice of you, John.'

'Good. Eight o'clock then, in what you're wearing.'

'Thanks very much. I'll be in tomorrow afternoon. I've got Interpol all morning.'

CHAPTER SIX

MONDAY EVENING

Craig and the girl went down the stairs together. She was an attractive piece, he thought; those lovely long legs and a calm, composed face that was something more than pretty. 'How d'you like it here?' he asked tentatively.

'It's all right. And I like the Italians, even if they're compulsive pass-makers.'

'Well, you do put them under a strain, don't you?'

'Oh dear! Is Rome going to your head already, Mr Craig?'

'Just making conversation, that's all.'

She turned and looked at him, smiling. 'Do go on. I'm becoming fascinated, rapidly.'

'This is where I shut up. I'm too shy to get past the first bit.'

'Are you indeed? Then my judgment's all wrong again.' She laughed, twitching her fair hair across her shoulder in a gesture which, he thought, was just enough contrived to be flirtatious. 'What a lot of Italian girls are going to be disappointed during your stay in Rome. How long are you here for?'

'Two weeks. Not much, is it?'

'No. There's a lot to see.'

'The trouble is I need a guide—someone who really knows the place. You've been here for some years, haven't you?'

'No longer so shy, are you?' She was laughing at him, but when she looked away, towards the doorway of the hall, her expression changed. 'There's Neil Adams.'

Standing at the top of the steps was a slender man in his early thirties, with a thin, intelligent face. He seemed short beside the tall Diana, but he had long arms, which stuck far out of his sleeves, and his legs seemed to be only loosely jointed to his body. He went down the steps with them, ignoring Craig, with his hand on Diana's arm.

'I'll give you a lift home.' He spoke with a faint York-shire accent.

'No, thanks, Neil,' she said lightly—but Craig could detect a hint of annoyance in her voice. 'I'm being picked up at the gate.'

'Are you indeed?' he said jocosely. 'The gallant major, I presume.'

'Neil, this is Mr Craig from the Police Adviser's section. Now, he *does* need a lift into town.'

'OK, OK, he can come with me. Glad to meet you,' he added to Craig. 'I gather from H of C's circular that you're putting us through yet another security check. But you won't find anything wrong here, chum, under John Brack-en's energetic and popular rule. We're a tightly-knit, orderly and well-behaved bunch, aren't we, Diana? And moral, too.'

'Shut up, Neil.' She walked off down the drive.

'You seem to have said something,' said Craig.

'I didn't mean it. Bloody hell! I never mean it. I can't stop putting my foot in my mouth with some people. I'm sorry, Craig—what's your name? We call each other by our Christian names here, ever so friendly.'

'Peter.'

'Good. Where d'you want to go?' He paused. 'I know. Why not come to my place? Maggie'll be delighted to give you some *pasta*.'

'I'd like to take a drink off you, if I may, but I've got a dinner date, thanks.'

A Volkswagen Mini-bus was parked on the covered car-park in front of the Chancery entrance. 'Get in,' said Adams. 'Do you know these things?'

'Yes. There're thousands in the streets in Rio, all made locally.'

'Rio? Good lord! Were you posted there?'

'No. Just on a visit, a few months ago.'

'I did a stint there for the British Council, some years back.' He was driving down the drive as he spoke. 'That was really fun. So much to do, so many interesting chaps —I mean scientists, of course—and welcoming, the lot of them. God knows why I transferred to this crowd, although of course it's only a contract job. Dress them in woad and shark's teeth,' he added, swinging wildly to avoid a heavy lorry lurching out of the end of the Via Merulana, 'and they're still stuffed shirts. The odd thing is that they're mostly quite good at their jobs.'

'Oh nonsense!' Craig was irritated. 'I came to the Foreign Office as fresh as you did, straight from darkest Africa. The old Colonial Service was as different from the Diplomatic as chalk from cheese, and that's what I was brought up to—first my father and then me—that and a hell of a lot of policemen, black and white. And I find these people easy; I could count the stuffed shirts on one hand.'

'But that's because you talk in that oh-so-decent way—' he was exaggerating his Yorkshire accent more heavily than ever—'and probably went to Oxbridge. Did you?'

'Cambridge.'

'There you are, born with a golden spoon in your mouth. Just like sweet Diana—Roedean, I ask you! You can't get near the girl.'

'D'you want to get so near to her?'

'Oh come on now, I don't want to make a pass at the girl. It's just that she and all those others—my God, you haven't met our Major Partridge, Royal Marines, have you?—he has to be listened to to be believed. I want to know what makes them tick. My interest,' he added, turning to Craig with a wide, infectious grin on his face, 'is purely experimental. Or something.'

He stopped the car in a street of nineteenth-century apartment houses in Via di Porta Pinciana, which faced the Pincio gardens. A shaky lift took them up to the fifth floor and a dark landing with two doors.

'It's old-fashioned,' said Adams with a trace of pride in his voice, 'but large, and we like it. And we've got a lot of children, as you'll see.'

He opened the door and brought Craig into a square hall, gloomy and furnished with hideous imitations of Cinquecento pieces. There were loud cries of 'Papa' and an inner door burst open and a small boy in a dressing-gown came rushing out and wound himself round his father's legs. A plump little girl in a nightdress followed, trailing a Teddy-bear by one arm. Adams took out his handkerchief as he talked to Craig and, hoisting the girl on one arm, cleaned her face. 'This is Claudia, born here, of course, and the boy is Jimmy. They only talk Italian, so far. Their brother Fred is probably helping with the twins.'

'*Five*?' cried Craig, shaken to the core. He wasn't much of a family man.

'The twins were a mistake,' said Adams calmly, 'but there's plenty of room for them all here. Five bedrooms, and I've made bunks in one so that we've converted another as a sort of—'

'Day-nursery?' suggested Craig, smiling.

'Playroom,' said Adams firmly. 'Come and meet Maggie.'

She was sitting on a low stool changing a nappy. There were several smells in the room, all of which Craig vaguely connected with babies. A boy of ten was sitting between two large loudspeakers with the other twin, who appeared to be sound asleep in spite of the roar of pop music that came from the hi-fi. 'Hullo, Dad,' he said, with his father's wide grin. Then he turned his attention back to the radio.

Margaret adjusted the nappy and stood up. 'Hullo,' she said to Craig. 'Would you mind holding this while I kiss my husband?' She was a pretty woman, well-covered, with a cheerful face and wide, intelligent eyes. She pushed the baby into his awkward arms and rushed at Adams, who put one arm round her and kissed her fondly, with Claudia somewhere jammed in between. She clung to him until he disengaged himself gently. There was a look on his face that Craig could not analyse.

Then she turned to Craig. 'How do you do?' she said in a ladylike manner, wiping her hand on her check trousers before offering it. 'Where did you spring from?'

'He's a cop, love.'

'Christ! One of those student-sluggers? What's he doing darkening our threshold?'

'I've got to go,' muttered Craig.

'Not with my baby you don't. Get him some gin, Neil. What's his name?'

'Peter Craig.'

'I really ought—'

'No you don't.' She took the baby back. 'We've got a sort of nanny, but it's her evening off. I'll get them all to bed. They've all had their baths, though you wouldn't think it. Come on, Fred.' The eldest boy switched off the radio and carried his burden out of the room and Margaret shepherded the others in front of her.

It had suddenly become quiet and the room was oddly welcoming. It was very large and led towards a broad covered balcony. The sounds of traffic came in through the open windows softened by the Pincio trees and the overhang of the balcony. At that end of the room there was a bar, laden with bottles, and a number of ugly, comfortable chairs and sofas. Adams settled Craig down with a gin and tonic.

'Sorry,' he said, 'no whisky left. We had the Instituto Chimico here last night and they cleared the lot. But it was a good party—only the odd disc broken.' He sat down. 'That's one good thing about this flat. Ugly it may be—' He looked around. 'Jesus! I could say that again. But although the Office would have given me a bigger rent allowance I prefer it to one of these modern places where they sting you for every splash of wine. And it's near the centre and nobody in the building objects to pop concerts.' He sipped his drink. 'A lot of these research scientists don't have much home life—they come from all over Italy—and we see a good deal of them.'

'Part of your job, isn't it?'

'I do wish somebody would define my job—I haven't a clue what it is. I must ask H.E. some time. That'd shake the old codger.' He imitated rather neatly Sir Watkyn's precise voice with the faint musical lilt, 'My dear boy, I can't be expected to understand the policy of Scientific Department. They didn't exist until a few years ago.'

'I liked him,' said Craig shortly. 'He was showing me his orchids this afternoon.'

Adams raised his eyes to the ceiling. 'He probably knew your father or something. I've never even seen his blasted orchids. The swimming pool is the nearest we get, by gracious permission.'

Craig changed the subject. 'What's your brand of science?'

Adams laughed bitterly. 'It *was* low temperature physics. I was going on to Cambridge, but I dropped out of the rat-race when I got married. I tried the Council, as I told you, and finished up here—an all-purpose scientific expert.'

Margaret came in. She had made up her face and changed into a long peacock-blue skirt and a white lace blouse. Craig didn't flatter himself that it was for his benefit.

She went up to her husband and stood close while he mixed her drink, leaning her head on his shoulder. He turned and sniffed at her hair. 'Scent!' he said with a lecherous grin. 'I like that one.'

She set her drink down and put her arms round his neck. 'I hate it when you have these official lunches,' she said dreamily, and kissed him full on the mouth.

He said nothing for a moment, but held her tight. 'Demonstrative bird, isn't she?' he said to Craig, but his smile was forced.

She came over to sit on the sofa by Craig and began to make conversation. 'Do you know Rome at all?'

'I used to come here quite a bit when I was an undergraduate. I can talk some Italian and I want to get round and see the place properly, if there's time.'

'You know what the Italians say, "*Roma, non basta una vita.*"'

'I'll have to see what I can in a fortnight, then.'

'We'll show you places, won't we, Neil?' she said suddenly.

'Of course, whenever you like, Peter.'

'That's awfully kind. Can I take a rain check on that? As soon as I know how I stand with these Interpol meetings I can figure it out.'

'Have you really got to go out to dinner, or were you just being polite?' He looked at his wife. 'You've got enough *pasta* for him, darling, haven't you?'

She hesitated, and Craig broke in, 'Thanks a lot, but I do have a date, at eight-thirty in Parioli, and look at the time.'

'I'll run you there,' said Adams quickly, but as he spoke there was a sound of crying and Jimmy came drifting in, complaining incomprehensibly in a mixture of Italian and English. Adams scooped him up and comforted him in fluent Italian, promising to tell him a story. They could hear his voice as he carried the boy out of the door, in the classic beginning of all Italian fairy-tales, '*C'era una volta* . . .' Once upon a time. Craig got to his feet and as he turned saw the look of relief on Margaret's face.

'Won't you wait for Neil to take you?' she asked politely, moving firmly towards the door.

Craig smiled. 'No, I'll get a taxi, thanks. I don't want to upset that story.'

'Do come another evening—I'll tell Neil to fix it. To tell you the truth, I wouldn't have had enough cheese for the *pasta*, anyway.'

'And you want to talk to him, don't you?'

She flushed. 'I'm not much of a liar, am I? Nor is Neil, that's the trouble.' She added bitterly, 'I suppose if he *were* a good liar I wouldn't be so worried.'

He stopped. 'Look, Margaret, if I can help—'

'No, Peter. But thanks, all the same. It's my problem.'

But as Craig waited under the tall pines for a taxi he wondered whether it wasn't his problem too.

The entrance to the house in the Via San Valentino was in

an archway which led through to a courtyard at the rear, where Craig could see a row of double garages. The commissionaire at his desk in the marble foyer refused to let him go farther until he had rung Luigi's flat on the house telephone. Then he ushered him ceremoniously into a walnut-panelled lift, pressed the top button, and left him. When the lift stopped the door opened on to the hall of a flat, lit discreetly by lights concealed in cornices and behind vases of flowers. A manservant led him into a living-room at least forty feet long, furnished with chairs and sofas upholstered in white leather, glass and marble tables and an impressive bar glittering in the distance.

Luigi and his wife Maria were standing in the middle of the room, side by side. She must have been beautiful, he thought, before she had put on weight, and her creamy skin and dark, expressive eyes were still very pleasant to look at.

She put out her hand and Craig, realizing that this first meeting was a formal occasion, raised it to his lips. '*Signora*,' he said, '*E un gran piacere.*'

'*Piacere mio, Signor Craig.*' The dark eyes rested on him for a moment, apparently with approval. She had an entrancing smile. Then she asked what he would drink, and the manservant brought him a glass of Chivas Regal and water. Luigi put his big arm round his guest's shoulder.

'As our Spanish friends say, Peter, this is your house. Now come and sit down. Dinner will be served at nine, so we've time for a talk first. Maria—' She gave Craig an impish grin and said, 'I leave you to your secrets,' and went out of the door with a swish of silk.

Luigi took a pull at his whisky. 'You tell me how far you have got, perhaps, and I tell you what I can do to help, right?'

'Right. The evidence on which we base the assumption that there is a spy in the Embassy— Did Gobbo tell you what it was?'

'No. He said there was a spy, that's all.'

'I'll tell you then. I think you've got to know so that you

can understand the conclusions I've come to so far.' He told him about the document seen by Kuznetsov and his remark about something curious in its appearance, then explained why, in his view, the letter might have been copied by either Janet Ransome or Neil Adams or somebody with access to the paper bags of confidential waste.

'The trouble is, of course, that I can't ask questions. But I assume that Mrs Ransome would take the draft, or rather the first letter with the Ambassador's pencil additions, back to her room for typing. There is a photostat machine just inside the registry, which is near her office. So she could have photographed either the original letter or the final one quite easily, without anyone paying the slightest attention. So could Adams, if he found an excuse for asking to have another look at it. But there is another possibility.' He described the procedure for destroying the confidential waste. 'It's a very sound system, except for one thing.'

Luigi chuckled. 'Are the paper bags given separate numbering for each office?'

'You're quick. That's it, of course. I checked, and they're not. Each girl has a stack of the bags in her desk. When the current one in the safe is full she seals it with Sellotape, writes her name across the seal with a Biro and then takes out a new bag and starts to fill that.'

'The idea of the seal is good, Peter. You can't strip the Sellotape off without lifting the surface of the bag, and you can't dissolve it off without smudging the ink. But still, you could take one of those un-numbered bags, fill it with scrap paper, seal it up and substitute it for one containing secret papers. But you'd still have to forge the girl's signature.'

'And run the risk of finding, if she's been conscientious, that all the secret papers have been shredded. The only person who could get away with it and run no risk at all is the typist herself. Instead of shredding the paper she wants to steal she crumples it up and pushes it well down in the bag. Then, at her leisure, when there's nobody about, she opens the bag, takes the paper she wants and puts all the rest into a fresh bag, which she seals and signs in the normal

way. Then she takes away the paper and the old bag in her
handbag.'

'Make it easier for her. She puts the old bag through the
shredder.' He thought for a moment. 'But, of course, if it's
Mrs Ransome, she doesn't have to go through all that, she
just puts the original letter into her handbag and walks off
with it.'

'Exactly. Either way, it looks black for Janet Ransome.
And you'll note that *either* the pencil additions on the
original *or* the crumpling of the paper would account for
what Kuznetsov thought was "curious".'

'Not the crumpling. If a KGB officer isn't used to looking at the contents of waste paper baskets, who is?' Luigi
finished his whisky and looked at Craig. 'Well, Peter, who
do I start with, Ransome and Adams?'

Craig sighed. 'Yes, please. Neither looks like a spy to me,
but I suppose no spy ever should.' He took out his wallet.
'Here are their photographs and this is a spare list of
Embassy staff, which you'd better keep. It has addresses
and telephone numbers. Lunch hours one o'clock to four-
thirty, summer schedule. They normally start at nine and
leave in the evening at seven or later. But of course they
could make contacts on their way to and from the office,
or find an excuse—especially Adams, who's his own master
to a large extent—any time during the day.'

Luigi looked at the photographs with which Craig had
been supplied in London, and whistled. 'Now that's the
kind of blonde for me,' he said—in Italian, for the benefit
of his wife, who had just entered the room. 'Tall and
slender, with dark bedroom eyes—Ouch!'

She gave his back hair another vicious tug. '*Rospo mal-
igno*!' she said sweetly. 'That's what you are, a malign
toad. Let me see the boy. Hm. *Tipo nervoso, poveraccio,
ma simpatico, non è vero?*'

'That's him,' said Craig. 'I can't help liking him. Five
children, Signora, and playing around with another woman
if I'm not mistaken.'

'Is he indeed?' said Luigi. 'That's interesting.'

'Men!' she said, with a wealth of feeling, as she thrust her arm through Craig's and led him towards the dining-room. 'I don't trust any of you.'

The dining-room was lit by a chandelier of Venetian glass, which shone down on the smooth stretch of *antico verde* marble which formed the table. There was caviar in a bowl of crushed ice, with Bernkastleer Doktor in the Baccarat crystal glasses, dewy with cold. Then roast suckling lamb, with garden peas and asparagus, and Château Lafite Rothschild, Premier Cru. And finally strawberries and Möet Chandon. A meal to remember.

Back in the drawing-room Maria served coffee and Luigi offered brandy or grappa.

'Grappa, please.' Craig sniffed the white grape spirit appreciatively. 'I discovered this stuff when I was twenty, and I always go back to it. But this is something special, Luigi.'

'Maria's father has vineyards near Carrara and this is his speciality. Il Gobbo and I hid in a barn on his land for a week, and found the stock he'd hidden from the Germans. He was furious; we'd drunk a lot.'

'If I hadn't hidden his cartridges,' said Maria reflectively, 'there'd have been one fat Russian Jew the less.'

'Is that when you and Maria met, then?'

'Oh no. That's a long story.'

'I like long stories before bedtime,' said Craig, comfortably sipping his grappa. 'If you can put up with me for a bit longer.'

'You stay, Peter. I'd rather he told this story while I'm here.' She shook a warning finger at Luigi, with a ferocious scowl.

'It was when I'd joined SOE in England, to pay off some family scores with Hitler, and they dropped me north of the Gothic Line. I was supposed to be joining a band of Christian-Democrat partisans, but a group of Commies heard the plane coming over and signalled to it.'

'But there must have been some recognition signal.'

'There was. But the pilot was a young boy and very tired and I suppose he'd got his navigation wrong. He'd searched for a long time and when he saw the torch flashes down below he didn't bother about the code but just let me drop. I can't blame him, he probably thought the boys down below had forgotten what they had to do. It wasn't the first time.'

'Luigi always finds excuses for the English,' muttered Maria darkly.

'It's a trait that appeals to me. I may be glad of it before I'm through.'

'You wouldn't have done that—what the pilot did. You look a careful man. *Santo Iddio*! Luigino would have died but for God's help.'

'Go on,' said Craig. 'What happened?'

'No doubt it was God, but he took a most attractive form.' He lifted his wife's hand to his lips. 'It was Maria who got me away.'

'Maria?' He tried not to look at the well-rounded form in the gilt arm-chair.

'You should have seen her then—all legs and scrambling over the rocks like a chamois, with one of my Sten guns strapped to her back and a sort of original mini-skirt, all rags.'

'Don't listen to him, Peter. It's true I had run away from home and joined the partisans—I didn't know they were Communists, just anti-Fascists, I thought—but no girl who wasn't a *puttana* would have showed her legs in that camp. I made myself a skirt from parachute cloth, quite *decente*.'

'But where did you get the Sten?'

'They had dropped a case of them at the same time, and another of ammunition. That's what the Commies wanted, of course.'

'But they wanted the radio more,' cried Maria. 'That's why they tortured him. And he wouldn't talk.'

'But where was the transmitter?' asked Craig, fascinated.

'Il Gobbo had it. They'd dropped him earlier and he

was hiding until I came with the codes and the Stens, in a village twenty kilometres away. The Communist partisans, who had a feud with the other freedom-fighters, gave me a bad time, as Maria said, and she disapproved. So one night she made love to the guard—'

'He was a pig. I did not.'

'She got close enough to him, somehow, to slip a knife between his ribs and cut me loose and took his Sten gun. I couldn't walk easily, but she got me away. That must have been when she got rid of that long skirt,' he added, grinning.

'We had to climb over a mountain,' she explained to Craig, 'and it was very rocky.' She hadn't minded what Luigi said about her killing the guard, but showing her legs was a different matter.

'And how did you get him to where Il Gobbo was?'

'I didn't. When he couldn't walk any more I put him in a stone hut they use for injured sheep—only this was an injured goat,' she interpolated, giggling, 'and I left the Sten with him and went and found Gobbo. He stole a mule and came and picked up Luigino.'

'Then we had to hide in a cold village high up in the mountains, where you could see the approach roads for miles around.'

'That's where,' added Maria, 'we found a priest whom I'd known all my life—he was hiding, too—and he married us.'

'About time, too,' remarked Luigi, under his breath. Maria blushed scarlet and slapped his face. But not very hard.

The big man roared with laughter. 'Her mother was a *Sarda*,' he explained. 'The Sardinians are all like that.'

'Why d'you call him Gobbo?'

'We could always make a generator for the radio, if we could borrow a magneto from a garage and a bicycle to work it, but the transmitter was as big as a family Bible, and as heavy. So Maria made a hump on a wicker frame and we fitted the set inside and strapped it on Gobbo's

back. What a man! There was a time when he wore it for
a week without a chance of taking it off. We were in a
village gaol with a lot of other suspects—they were pulling
in everybody those days—and they stripped Maria and me
but didn't touch Gobbo.'

'He'd stopped washing,' explained Maria, 'as soon as
the *rastrellamento* started, and what with that and the
smell of the untanned sheepskin he wore you couldn't get
near him. And of course we all respect hunchbacks and it's
lucky to touch the hump, so the Italian police never held
him long. When I saw him after the war in London, with
his *chapeau melon* and one of those thin umbrellas, I
nearly died laughing.'

'I'm glad you've told me all this,' said Craig thoughtfully. 'You see, I scarcely know him.'

'He is a good man, Peter,' she said solemnly, 'and the
bravest I've met—except for my old bear.' She placed a
plump, proprietary arm around Luigi's neck.

CHAPTER SEVEN

TUESDAY AFTERNOON

When Craig came into the orchid house at four o'clock, as arranged, he found the Ambassador looking mildly perturbed.

'We've got to take some rapid action, my boy, and I'm not sure what. The American Ambassador—his name's Marchant—came to see me this morning, just before luncheon, and gave me this.' He made Craig sit down at the deal table and took from his pocket a photostat of a message typed in English on a piece of quarto paper. It was, in fact, the report which Rostov had thrown into his destructor the previous evening.

Craig read it through and was silent, thinking. His Excellency became impatient. 'Come on, man, what's it mean?'

'Well, it looks like a routine report from our spy to his control, and it tells us two things. He doesn't know—I say "he" but it could be a woman—what I'm here for, as yet. Which is good. Secondly, it's someone who saw the circular which Head of Chancery put out yesterday morning about my assignment to check security. But as it went to all departments that doesn't help us much. He's given us a sample of his typing, but I'm afraid it's very unlikely that the typewriter is in the Embassy. It'd be flouting every rule in the book if it was. It looks like a portable, so it's probably privately owned.' He looked up. 'But of course what I want to know, sir, is how Mr Marchant got hold of it. And why did he give it to you? Surely that's odd? There must be a line between his CIA people and Derek Walton.'

'There is, but that's something I must explain to you. Marchant isn't a career diplomat, he's a political appointee. He is a distinguished expert on West European affairs and was one of the President's advisers before the election, when Marchant was still a professor at Yale. He got the Rome Embassy partly, I think, as a "thank-you" gesture and partly because his special knowledge makes this a very suitable appointment anyway. He's a close friend of mine —we see one another frequently—and at least from my point of view it's a very useful contact. I think, too, that my willingness to advise him on diplomatic procedures and so on is of some help.' He paused. 'He's got his own Minister (Political), of course, who's a career man and first class, but—not always very tactful.'

'I see. But how on earth did he get this paper?'

'His head CIA man obtained it yesterday.'

'*Yesterday*? Good God! Our spy must have got his report in quickly.'

'Yesterday evening, I believe. But I should explain that apparently the Americans got it before the Russians did. As it seemed harmless they let it go through.'

Craig stared. 'So the Russians don't know? I mean, don't know that CIA had intercepted it?'

'Apparently not. But I don't know any details. Only that Ashbee, the head of the CIA mission, showed it to Marchant this morning, saying he proposed to take appropriate action.' The Ambassador added calmly, 'Marchant forbade him to do so, and retained the paper.'

'But he can't do that,' cried Craig, dumbfounded.

'He's an opinionated man, and like me doesn't like espionage much. He said to Ashbee that it was his duty to consult me first, before any action was taken. He told me he owed it to me as a friend.'

'So it's possible,' said Craig slowly, 'that CIA haven't informed your MI6 representative so far?'

'That's what Marchant told me.'

'Well, sir, it seems we have a choice. We need to know exactly how that paper was obtained; that's the main thing, because it may lead us to an identification of our spy. So either we get permission from S.3 in London to bring Walton into our confidence—in which case I can

E

leave all future action to him. Or I shall have to see the head of CIA and we still keep Walton out of it. Of the two, I should naturally prefer Walton to be indoctrinated and take over the whole case. He's a professional; I'm not —in this game, anyway.'

'I'd quite like you to go on with it, Craig. Walton is a good officer, but once we allow SIS to get involved in loyalty cases—which isn't their job—it's the thin end of the wedge. This is essentially a Security Department matter, through this—what did you call it?'

'S.3.'

'Yes. We'd better get off a signal. I agree to offer the alternatives, as you said, but I hope they'll agree with my view.'

'How did you leave it with Ambassador Marchant, sir?'

'I thanked him, of course, effusively. Then I told him this was a matter I knew about already. That of course delighted him, since it seemed to show that he had taken the right action. He slapped his knee and—er—said he'd always known I was a wily old fox.' He caught Craig's eye and smiled. 'Then I said it was very secret indeed and I would have to obtain instructions. That was when he promised to stop all action until he heard from me.'

'That's splendid. The CIA man will of course think it's some super-secret double-agent case. He'll be madly curious but he'll probably do as he's told and keep mum.'

'Good gracious! I should think so,' said the Ambassador primly. 'Marchant is quite capable of having him removed if he falls out of step. There's no doubt he's got the President's ear.' He thought for a moment. 'Make the message short, Craig, if you please. I shall have to encode it myself. As you know, my arithmetic is not what it was. I can't have you closeted with me in the office without attracting attention.'

Craig tore a leaf from his notebook and began to write rapidly. Then he handed the paper to Sir Watkyn.

REES TO S.3. ONE. PARA ONE. CIA HAVE OB-TAINED COPY OF MESSAGE APPARENTLY

PASSED BY SUBJECT YOUR INQUIRY TO KGB CASE-OFFICER. MESSAGE IS INNOCUOUS, MERELY REPORTING CRAIG'S ARRIVAL AND HIS OVERT MISSIONS. PARA TWO. US AMBAS-SADOR WHO IS CLOSE FRIEND INSISTED GIVING ME MESSAGE PERSONALLY AND STOPPED ALL REPEAT ALL ACTION BY CIA PENDING CONSUL-TATION WITH US. PARA THREE. IMPERATIVE WE KNOW HOW CIA OBTAINED MESSAGE. SUG-GEST EITHER WALTON REPEAT WALTON BE INDOCTRINATED AND BRIEFED DIRECTLY BY YOU OR CRAIG BE INSTRUCTED TO CONTACT CIA REPRESENTATIVE ASHBEE IF US AMBAS-SADOR APPROVES. IMMEDIATE INSTRUCTIONS PLEASE. MESSAGE ENDS.

The Ambassador looked at it gloomily. 'That's about it, I agree; you couldn't have made it much shorter. Would you add two paragraphs, please? Let me see. PARA FOUR. I PREFER SECOND ALTERNATIVE. PARA FIVE. FOR AMBASSADOR MARCHANT SEE MY LAST HEADS OF MISSIONS REPORT.'

Craig finished printing out the signal and handed the paper back. His chances of getting right out of the case were looking slim, he thought. The Ambassador's wishes, stated so unequivocally, would have their effect in London.

His Excellency said, 'It'll take me at least half an hour, and then there's the reply, and heaven knows to what lengths—wait a minute. I'll put the request for instructions at the end and insert BRIEF REPEAT BRIEF before INSTRUCTIONS. That may remind Rogers that I am the cypher officer at this end.' He stood up. 'One thing I don't understand. Why wouldn't Marchant tell me how his man had got the report? He went very cautious when I asked him.'

'It was pretty high-handed of him to take charge of the information, but to have told you—even if he knew, which I doubt, how it had been obtained would be very much out of line. It's a CIA secret, after all.'

'Yes, of course. What are you going to do now? There may be an answer to this tonight.'

'Talk with Bracken, sir. He told me you'd kindly offered to give a reception for some of the Interpol delegates before the Conference closes. I think I'd better help him to work out a list.'

'Good. The radio man will call for an emergency signal contact while I get this ready. I'll have to tell Bracken that it's something very secret I got from the American. At least that's true, and he knows Marchant called on me this morning. But it does distress me to have to deceive him like this. However, with luck the reply will have come in before the office closes. Come round to the Residence for a drink at seven-thirty. We'll be alone.'

As Craig thanked him the Ambassador took a tiny pair of shining secateurs from his pocket and cut a bloom from a plant which sprawled out of a pot standing in a bed of peat and loam. 'For my wife,' he said to Craig, as he carried it carefully out of the scented glass-house into the comparative cool of the garden. 'It's one of her favourites and it must have come out last night. I must ask Mrs Ransome to put it in water until I go back to the Residence.'

After spending some time with Bracken, discussing who should be included in H.E.'s reception for the Interpol delegates—and what was more difficult, who should be left out—Craig went on with his tour of Embassy departments. People were cautious at first, because no inspector is welcome as such, but he had a knack of getting on with strangers and when he had explained that he was solely interested, for the moment, in the disposal of confidential waste, they showed him round their offices very willingly and introduced him to the staff who handled secret papers. He found a few lapses and made some suggestions, so he felt his time had not been wasted. On his return to Chancery he borrowed Diana Warren and dictated some notes. Then he went back to the room which had been lent him and began to draft in longhand his first report on the Interpol meetings. By the time he had finished only one of the Second Secretaries was still working in the Chancery offices and it was time for him to go to the Ambassador.

He skirted the main building and turned into the tarmac forecourt of the Residence. It was an impressively large house. A footman in blue livery showed him where to sign his name in the visitors' book and then led him across the entrance hall and knocked on the door of the Ambassador's study. Sir Watkyn was sitting on a leather sofa, reading the airmail edition of *The Times*. He stood up.

'There you are, my dear fellow. Tell Giovanni what you want to drink. He knows my choice.' The manservant brought a glass of pale sherry and a whisky and water on a silver tray, served them and went out.

His Excellency put down the newspaper with a sigh and pulled a paper out of his pocket. It was a typed telegram. S.3 TO REES. ONE. YOUR TELEGRAM ONE. CRAIG SHOULD PROCEED WITH CASE. OUR BASIC RULE EXCLUDES USE OF WALTON. ASHBEE IS BEING FULLY BRIEFED BY WASHINGTON AND CRAIG MAY CO-OPERATE WITH HIM DIRECT. IF FIRM EVIDENCE AGAINST SUBJECT OUR INQUIRY IS AVAILABLE REFER BACK FOR INSTRUCTIONS. DO NOT REPEAT NOT CALL IN ITALIANS AT THIS STAGE. ENDS.

All Craig's hopes of being let off the hook had gone for a Burton. He handed back the paper. 'You said Ashbee was the top man in CIA?'

'Yes, but I gather from Marchant that he's also the only officer they allow to liaise with other intelligence services, so he also acts for the FBI, who have a mission here. He's a counsellor in the legal section, or at least, that's his—er— cover role. Strange fellow; never seems to have much conversation, so Marchant says. I expect he tried to get Ashbee to tell him all his secrets, and the chap won't play. Quite right, too, according to his lights. I've met him once or twice—and his wife, too, who's a delightful person.' He added cheerfully, 'Well, Craig, I've fixed it all up.'

Craig groaned inwardly. 'Er—what have you fixed, sir?'

'I telephoned Marchant.'

'On the open line, sir?'

'Oh, I was very crafty, don't worry. I told him that in connection with the *legal* problem he'd spoken to me about this morning—I told you what Ashbee's cover is—I had discovered by good luck that our Interpol delegate was something of an expert on the question and would be glad to give his advice to Marchant's legal section.' He looked at Craig triumphantly. 'There was a long pause at the other end,' he added, chuckling, 'and then old Marchant got it. He said that would be very kind of you and they'd be very glad to see you, any time. He repeated the last words. You'll find Ashbee's home telephone number over there, on the telephone table. In the *Corps Diplomatique* list.'

Craig drew a deep breath. 'That was very smooth, sir. It seems to me you're sliding painlessly into the role of an intelligence officer.'

'Not on your life, my boy. I'm only anxious to get the whole thing over as quickly as possible. And as for painlessly, you should have seen me sweating over those telegrams.'

'The typing, sir?'

'Yes, yes, Craig. D'you think I don't know the rules? The carbon, and the one copy I kept of the message, are both in my safe. So is the telegram we sent and the encoded text.'

'And the key to your safe?'

'In my pocket. And if you're thinking of the Cicero case, let me add that I don't leave my keys where my valet can make an impression of them. You mustn't forget that we've been given so many warnings during the last twenty-five years that some security ideas *do* stick, although it's against the grain.' He glanced at Craig's expression and smiled. 'Still not satisfied? Let me see. Oh yes, there *is* another key, kept in a heavily sealed envelope in Bracken's own safe. And so is the combination, which I always work myself before I leave the office. *Now* are you happy?'

'Perfectly, sir.'

'Help yourself to another whisky before you go. Wait. There's one thing I don't understand. What is all this about the Italians? We don't want them in on the act, for heaven's sake.'

'It will be difficult to keep them out, if it comes to an arrest.'

'An arrest! Oh dear, I suppose it might come to that. I'm afraid I can't get used to the idea that there really is a spy, here in this compound. But you're right, of course. You could only arrest him on Embassy premises, I suppose?'

'Yes, sir. And only then if I've got a cast-iron case.'

'So the Italians would have to do it, and that's what S.3 don't want, apparently. Well, it's up to you, my boy. And good luck.'

'I'll get in touch with Ashbee tonight, and if he has evidence to identify the spy will let you know at once. If not, could I report to you tomorrow afternoon, at four? I've got the afternoons free for the time being, since I've managed to avoid being put on any of the sub-committees, but next week we have a full programme.'

'The more reason to get this business settled in the next few days. At four tomorrow, then.'

'There's just one thing, sir.'

'Yes?'

'The last bit of that intercepted report about my arrival. You remember it said that you had informed John Bracken in casual conversation that I was an orchid expert and that you had given me permission to visit the private garden?'

'Yes. I told you I was going to tell Mrs Ransome about it, but Bracken came in and I told him direct. Why do you ask?'

'The spy knew about that conversation. I wonder how.'

'Oh dear, you're right. But no, I'm afraid it's not so simple, when I come to think of it. Bracken would have sent a note to the Administration officer and probably the

head of the security guard, so that there would be no question if you were seen wandering around in my garden,
which is out of bounds—except for the swimming pool—to
the staff.'

'Even so, it limits the field a bit.'

His Excellency smiled. 'On the rare occasions, Craig,
when I have mentioned my delightful hobby to a member
of my staff I have noticed a wary look in his eyes. It may
be that I express myself at some length, when I get started.
So—' he gave a disarming smile—'the story that I had
lured into my—er—net someone new whom I could bore
with my esoteric opinions would go round the Embassy like
a bush fire. With frivolous embellishments, no doubt.'

Craig grinned. It would be difficult, he thought, not to
like this man. 'I think you have the answer, sir. It could
have been anybody on the grapevine. I'm trying to narrow
the possibilities down, but I haven't got very far yet, and
would rather not speculate. Ashbee's evidence may solve
the whole thing, of course.'

'Let's hope so. But from what you said earlier I realize
that even when you're quite sure you'll still have a lot to do
to obtain powers of arrest.'

Craig walked down the long curving drive from the Residence, which met the main drive near the gate. As he came
out a car drove up and stopped. Bracken was waving to
him.

'Some Immediates have just come in and I've got to have
a look at them. Why not come back to my office? I shan't
be long and we can go home together.' Craig had almost
forgotten his dinner-date.

'Thanks. But I was going to go back to the hotel and
change.'

'Good lord, man, you're all right like that. Jump in.'

Back in his office Bracken sat down at his desk, making
notes of action on the decodes as he read them through.
Craig picked up a copy of the Diplomatic List and made a
note of Ashbee's telephone number and address. He

watched the Head of Chancery running through the pencil-written messages with the speed acquired by long practice in stripping down official statements to their essentials. He kept back four telegrams which required action before morning and gave them to the duty-officer. The rest he put into his safe.

'I had a scare this afternoon,' he remarked, as he spun the dial. 'I lost your notes on the confidential waste procedure.'

Craig stiffened. '*Lost* them?'

'Oh it's all right, they turned up. They were only marked secret, of course, but I was really worried for a bit. It seemed so silly.'

'What happened, John?'

Bracken looked up, surprised at his tone of voice. 'It was nothing, Peter. Diana typed your notes, and I only asked for them when I was packing up, so that I could have a glance before meeting you tonight. And she couldn't find them. She said she'd put them on the table in her room where I pick up papers, but they weren't there. Apparently, though, half a dozen people had been in and out of her room and evidently someone had parked some papers on the table and then picked them up with your notes stuck underneath, because they turned up in the Registry, near the big safe where the other sections put their paper at night for locking up.'

Craig hesitated; then he said, 'I wonder if I could have another look at those notes. Could you dig them out?' He went to the other side of the room while Bracken worked his combination, and then took the paper Bracken produced from the safe and put it carefully into his wallet.

As they went downstairs they heard the heavy clang of the Chancery steel door as the duty officer closed it.

CHAPTER EIGHT

TUESDAY EVENING

The Brackens lived on the *piano nobile* of a sixteenth-century palace behind the Piazza Navona. The great doors, twenty feet high and studded with iron bosses, were open, and the car drove through the archway beneath the building into the cobbled courtyard beyond. Craig got out. Water was gushing through the mouths of stone dolphins and trickled down through the mosses of a fountain on the far wall. Beside it, the black twisted stem of an ancient vine meandered up the wall to break out into a thick canopy of green leaves.

From under the archway the great staircase with its broad, shallow steps sloped gentle as a ramp between walls where the busts of departed members of the D'Aste family peered from their niches through the shadows cast by the massive bronze wall-sconces.

Inside the flat on the first floor the atmosphere of gently decaying grandeur was maintained. Beneath the painted beams of the high ceiling brocaded chairs and boiseries were reflected in the inlaid marble floor. The gloomy oil paintings in their heavy gold frames, the chests and cabinets and trinket tables all shared the sad look of family possessions that had been used for untold years by strangers.

But Althea Bracken was proud of her historic apartment, and showed Craig round with a flood of references to members of the princely families of Rome. Then more guests arrived, and drinks were served.

Bracken had invited the Waltons, the Defence Attaché (a naval captain) and several other members of the senior staff. They all seemed to get on well together, and with second drinks in their hands the room became pleasantly noisy.

At dinner Craig sat on Mrs Bracken's right. She showed
no interest in his mission in Rome and he was duly grateful and steered her on to the usual lines of diplomatic small-
talk—previous posts, common acquaintances, the cost of
living in Rome, difficulties with servants and, of course, her
children. She must have been a very pretty girl, he thought,
but various posts in hot climates had left their mark and
although she was a good hostess her face wore the slightly
strained look that Craig had come to expect of a senior
diplomatic wife.

It was partly, to do her justice, that she was finding it
difficult to fit her guest of honour into a known category.
She had expected, vaguely, that he would look like a
policeman, but decided that colonial policemen were more
like soldiers, and she knew how to cope with those. You
got them to talk about The Regiment. She tried talking
about The Force, but got nowhere. He seemed more
interested in *her*, which was unusual, but pleasant. She
liked his slow smile, which made his rather craggy features
suddenly very attractive, and decided he was nice. Then
she learned that he was a bachelor, and leaned forward
confidentially.

'Have you talked to Janet yet?' she whispered. 'On your
right, of course. She really is the most charming girl, don't
you think? But she doesn't seem to go out much—or at
least we seldom run across her. Did you know about her
husband's death?'

'I know he died in a plane crash some years ago.'

Her eyes widened. This was simply not enough. 'But it
was the most *awful* thing. There she was on the airstrip at
Kuala Lumpur, waiting for him to land, and she had Miles
with her—only a baby he was then—and the plane over-
shot the runway and crashed into the trees and everybody
was burnt alive and she *saw* it.'

'What a dreadful experience!' What else could you say,
he thought, and it was true; it must have left a mark.

'Yes, and I sometimes think she's never got over it. Lady
Rees and I invite her whenever we can, but you know how

difficult it is, especially when you feel you ought to ask her Mum as well—there she is, next to John—and of course she's a darling, but—well, it's not the same thing for Janet,' she added, vaguely. 'They haven't much money left, I think; she's worn that dress for I don't know how long.'

'She looks very well in it,' said Craig, without turning his head.

'She'd look right in anything, she's so naturally elegant. What I'd give for that figure! Look, you talk to her.' She turned her attention to Captain Travis, on her left.

When Craig turned round he found Janet Ransome looking at him with a slight smile on her serene face. 'Have you been told to talk to me?' she asked quietly.

'I haven't had much chance until now, have I?'

'She's a dear, but I do wish she wouldn't always try to pair me off.'

'I won't speak.'

'Oh, but you must. We can't let her down.'

'Couldn't I neglect my food and just stare at you with glowing eyes? It wouldn't be difficult.'

'That's a good start. Have you shot any elephants lately?'

'No. I like elephants, at least, African ones. Why d'you ask?'

'Oh, I knew from the List that's where you'd served mostly. And you do look a little bit like a Great White Hunter.'

'Wrong again. I like elephants and I don't like Great White Hunters.'

'That makes two of us.'

'I see. So your first impression was of instant dislike?'

It was an attractive laugh. 'Point to you. Where do we go from here. What about orchids?'

'I'm interested. And I do like your Ambassador.'

Her face lost its quizzical look. 'Yes. He's a very nice man. Since he came my job has been really quite enjoyable.'

'You don't sound very enthusiastic, though.'

'How can you be with a stooge job? I tried for the

Diplomatic, you know, but didn't get in.'

'But they can't take many girls, whatever they say. They'd obviously filled their quota for the year.'

'That's nice of you, but I expect it was something those PV people turned up. Or thought up. They were altogether too smooth and inquisitive. Was there something? You'd know, wouldn't you?'

'I've never seen your Positive Vetting files.' Craig lied easily. 'It's not my job, as you well know.' He laughed at her. 'What did you expect me to say? Something like, "Well, my dear, as a matter of fact, there was that bit about your visiting the Russian Embassy after dark"?'

She looked at him unsmiling. 'It was a silly question.' An ice pudding was being served, and she busied herself with that. 'Is this your first visit to Rome?'

'Oh no, I used to come here for long vacations.'

'But so did I. How extraordinary, we might have met.'

'You'd have been at school still,' he said diplomatically.

'No, Mr Craig. I told you I looked you up, and you're the same age as me, more or less. My mother was living here at the time, so I spent all my vacs here.'

'If we had met,' said Craig, smiling, 'I wouldn't have forgotten.'

'Are you sure you're in the right career? All very smooth for a policeman. But I was very thin and gawky. And earnest, terribly earnest. But I did get to know Rome well.'

'I got around, but I seem to have forgotten most things except picnics in the Castelli and bathing parties at Fregene. You must help me to make up what I missed.'

She turned her head slightly away from him, giving him the smooth ivory line of her cheek and the delicate Italian nose. Her mouth, he thought, was perfect. But her face was cold; there was no light within. 'There must be other people on the staff who'd love to show you round,' she said demurely.

'It's true,' he said, 'that Mrs Adams did offer—'

She swung round. 'Our Maggie? She's a—'

'She's a doll,' he said firmly.

She shook with silent laughter. 'You can't imagine how funny it is to hear you saying that. You don't *look* interested in dolls. Anyway, she's not my idea of a doll. I find them both so brash and they talk so loud, and seem to go out of their way to be awkward with H.E. and Lady R.' She paused. 'They'll show you all the wrong things.'

'Then you'll show me the right ones?'

'I might.' She turned and looked him full in the face. 'I might, you know, if you go on asking me so nicely.' She caught Althea's eye. 'We women have to go. Don't be too long.' He pulled her chair back and she walked away to join the other women, assured, with the slight swing of her hips that made the old dress—if it really was old—look like a million dollars. Craig watched her go, thoughtfully. It was hard to think that she was his Suspect Number One.

The men sat for a time over coffee and brandy, until Bracken made a move and they drifted into the drawing-room with their glasses. Craig had chatted for a time with Walton, a short, square man with an incipient paunch, who spoke with knowledge about some of the police and Carabinieri officers whom Craig had met that morning. By contrast with his lazy body the man's face was alive with intelligence, and Craig felt the anomaly of his position more than ever. This was a man he would have been glad to work with.

Lady Balcombe was sitting by herself on a sofa by the open window, waving a painted fan to catch the evening breeze. He reminded himself that she was half-Italian, and saw it in the strong white hair, so cunningly dressed, and the arched delicate nose she had passed on to her daughter. She caught his eye and patted the seat beside her. He sat down.

'I'm interested in you,' she said. 'I saw you talking to Janet at dinner—going hammer and tongs, it seemed to me. It's unlike Janet, the first time she meets someone.'

'You have a very charming daughter, Lady Balcombe.'

'Yes, isn't she? They were such a happy couple, although

Miles was so much older than Janet. But then, you mightn't think it, but there's a streak of ambition in her, and besides being devoted to him she loved being the Colonel's wife. And I believe she did it very well until—but I suppose you know?'

'Mrs Bracken told me. It must have been bad for you too.'

'Well, yes, it was, because I was very fond of him. But of course it was a joy to me, after living alone so long, to have her and the baby come to live with me here. I still feel a bit guilty about it.' She sighed deeply. 'Oh dear, it won't last much longer. You see, now that she's established they'll post her somewhere else. And since Miles has gone to school she can't plead that any more, as an excuse for staying in Rome. Poor little fellow, he had a bad time at first.'

'How was that?' prompted Craig.

'We packed him off to England in January, for the first time, and within a month the school doctor wrote to say he was being operated on for peritonitis, and Janet got into the first plane.'

Craig was getting restive. For the sake of something to say he asked idly, 'I hope he got over it quickly.'

'Oh no, she had to stay in England until after Easter. There were complications, you see, and poor little Miles was very miserable. She even got her leave extended so that she could stay near him in Dorset.'

He held his breath. 'What bad luck!' he said. 'So she stayed in England the whole term, almost?'

'From the middle of February until after Easter, as I said. She won't get any leave until next year now. And all her holiday last year was spent doing up the house.'

Craig wondered when he could ever get away from this charming but garrulous old lady. He caught Janet's mocking gaze across the room. 'What house is that?' But he was thinking, for God's sake when *was* Easter last year?

'Oh, you see I had a house left me by an aunt, a Contessa Santa Rosa. It's near the British School of Rome in the

Valle Giulia, and that's where we live. But as we're so short
of money we decided to split it and let the ground floor as
a separate flat. And Janet worked so hard on it and did a
lot of the painting and so on herself—it's quite extraordinary what women will do these days, when every little job
costs so much—and now for the past year we've let it to a
businessman from Milan, who's never there, and it's a great
help. We let it first, very cheaply, to that dear girl Diana
Warren, because she helped with the decorating, but afterwards we raised the rent and the Milanese got it. I've never
seen him, but he's no trouble at all. He just uses the flat
when he comes to Rome on business, and then he's very
quiet. No rowdy parties.'

She glanced at her watch and spoke quite sharply, 'You're
keeping me talking and it's half past ten. I always go to bed
early, and so does Janet. She doesn't get a siesta in the
afternoon, because she teaches English to boring people
before she goes to the office. It is so distressing, being poor.'
She reached out a hand and Craig pulled her gently to her
feet.

He made his voice as casual as he could. 'What did poor
Sir Watkyn do while your daughter was away for so long?'

'Oh, Diana stood in for her and never grumbled. *What* a
nice girl!' She collected her handbag and turned to Craig
with a charming smile. 'My dear boy, you've been very
patient with a gabby old woman. You must come and have
a drink with us one evening. And now be kind and tell
Janet I'm waiting, will you please?'

Craig asked Althea if he could use the telephone and she
showed him into the study. The first thing he did was to
search feverishly in his diary for last year's calendar. As
he had thought, Easter had been in April. His Number One
Suspect was no longer Janet Ransome, but Diana.

He rang Ashbee's number, and a voice answered in a
slow Texan drawl.

'This is Craig, Ashbee. Your Ambassador said you'd like
to have a talk sometime about some forensic problem

you've got on your mind. I rang earlier and was told you'd be back about now, so forgive my ringing you so late.'

'That's OK, man. I'd certainly like to meet you. Are you free now?'

'Well, yes.'

'Come right round. You've got my address?'

'Same as in the List?'

'Sure.'

'I'll get a taxi right away.'

'Hold on a minute. What d'you drink?'

'Bourbon and branch water, by preference.'

'I wouldn't recommend the Tiber, but the bourbon's OK. See you, man.'

The man who opened the door was in his mid-forties, very broad and carrying a lot of weight, but when he led the way into his comfortable living-room he moved lightly, padding across the deep-pile carpet like a big cat. 'Take your coat off, friend,' he said in that slow drawl, 'we've some serious drinking to do. And perhaps a little chat about the weather.'

'Stormy,' said Craig, 'from where I see it. And I'm sorry you've been drawn in on the act so late at night, Ashbee. But I'm hoping you've got a solution to a problem which is giving me one big headache.'

'I'm not so sure about that, Peter. My name's Jo, to my friends. Short for Jonas. I may say that I've been kept very busy since my Ambassador, whom God preserve, snatched a piece of paper out of my hand this morning and exit, running.'

'It was news to me that there was still life in the "special relationship".'

'You'd be surprised. But it isn't that, you know. It's just that they're buddies, your Old Man and mine. Here's your bourbon. I managed to find some water.' He paused. 'No ice?'

'No, thanks, just as it is.' He sipped. 'I needed that, chum.' They sat down on a settee near the open window.

Ashbee looked across at him with a thoughtful smile on his lined face. 'We'd better know where we stand, Peter. According to my briefing you have come out to Rome, quote, without any intelligence experience, unquote, to deal with an espionage case that's so durned secret that Derek Walton mustn't know anything about it. Which is fine, just fine.' He took a large swallow of his bourbon and looked Craig in the eyes. 'But I don't get it.'

'You can take the quotes out, Jo. I *am* just a policeman; it's quite true.' He felt the American's cynical stare as he sipped his drink.

'Oh sure. That's what the dossier said.'

'What dossier?' asked Craig sharply.

'It came over the air this afternoon, hot from the computer at Langley. However, if we're going to be friends, as I hope we are, I've got to believe your story. It's certainly a good one,' he ruminated, avoiding Craig's eye. 'Twelve years in the African police, rapid promotion, finishing up as Commissioner of Police in Bangasa, then transfer to the Police Adviser's Section at the Foreign and Commonwealth Office, and at once operational. This year Brazil, Chile and some hanky-panky in Portugal—no details available but it was noted that two GRU operatives died while you were there. Yes *sir*, I'll say that's a good story.'

'I told you—' began Craig, in an ominously quiet voice.

Ashbee raised a large flat hand. 'I meant what a good cover story it *might* have been for an IO. But I accept you're not an intelligence officer, just engaged in some routine security enquiries about a spy in your Embassy while you cover the Interpol Conference. Suits me, but I would like to know how you learned about this spy originally. The Agency wouldn't say. Perhaps you can't, either.'

'My brief is to co-ordinate action with you, and nothing said about what I can and can't tell you. So I'll begin in Paris, where it started.' He told the story as he had heard it in London, without omissions.

Ashbee listened with concentrated attention. Then he got up, took Craig's glass and his own and went over to the drinks table to replenish them. He said nothing until he had sat down again. 'And this S.3 thing? The idea is that when someone in your Diplomatic Service is suspected of spying no one in your MI6 or MI5 is even informed, let alone told to find out the truth. This S.3 agency takes over —is that right?—and selects someone with special qualifications for the job.'

'That's about it.'

'And in this Rome case they selected you, because of your Interpol cover. Anyone else?'

'The Ambassador. No one else at all inside the Embassy.'

'Ah yes, Sir Watkyn. I suppose,' he continued, dead pan, 'that he makes up for your lack of intelligence experience?'

'Oh for Christ's sake, Jo, stop pulling my leg. I can't help it; I was drafted for the job. I'm damned if I wanted any part of it. And incidentally, I have one outside helper here. He's got no connection with the MI6 station here but S.3 think highly of him. I won't tell you his name, if you don't mind. If you do I'll have to get authority from London.'

'OK, feller. I understand. I wonder who the MI6 member is—but never mind. You can't tell me that either.'

'I don't even know his name—only his pseudonym, Il Gobbo.'

Ashbee jumped. 'Jesus, that brings back memories. You don't say that crafty old coon is still around?'

'You knew him?'

'Did I know him? He taught me my first faltering steps —and boy, did they falter.'

'What d'you mean?'

'We were together in Italy at the end of the war. I was in the OSS and he'd switched over to MI6 from the blood-and-glory boys. In OSS we were all fresh from the egg, and he taught me a lot.'

'But who is he?'

'This is where I get my own back, boy. No names, no pack drill.' He grinned. 'But I'll tell you something, Peter. If he's at the back of all this he's not going to stay in London and let us put our big feet into it. You'll open a door some time, and he'll be on the other side.'

'Well, why the hell doesn't he come and do it?'

'Perhaps he's satisfied with you. But what about Sir Watkyn? God's teeth, if that old English gentleman is an undercover agent I will go up the steps of Aracoeli like the good Catholic I am, on my knees.'

'He's learning,' said Craig, grinning. 'I'd better tell you what we've done so far.' When he described the telephone conversation between the two Ambassadors Ashbee gave a roar of laughter. And then sobered suddenly.

'We'll have to watch them, Peter. If they start taking action on their own, God help us.' (That was a remark that Craig was to remember later.) Ashbee continued, 'You do realize, of course, that you're up against some of the best trained operators in the world?'

'Then how did you pick the pocket of one of them, photograph the contents and put it back without him knowing?'

'Good question. It shall be answered. Tell me, Peter. As a flatfoot, on your own ground, if you wanted to trail someone twenty-four hours a day, how many men would you want? *Without* letting him know?'

'Shifts of six surveillance men for shadowing on the ground and three cars, with two men each and intercommunication by radio, replacements for the cars, a control HQ—and a hell of a lot of luck. If the chap is skilled and takes evasive action, even without knowing specifically he's being trailed, he can almost always get away. It's all hit or miss, and you just go on hoping he'll get slack.'

'Exactly. And in a place like Rome, with the traffic like it is, it is one hell of a job. But we decided it was worth trying. So we assembled a full team, twenty-six men all told, Italians trained specially for the job, and six cars in shifts of three, and we concentrated for a month, every day and all day and night, on one known member of the KGB *rezidentsiya*.'

Craig stared at him. 'It must have cost the earth!'

'It did. But it paid off. We caught him in the act yesterday, and I'm darn sure he doesn't know.'

'That's pretty smart organization, Jo. Which KGB man?'

'Alexei—Sasha for short—Ivanovich Zakharov, who we know works in the Foreign Embassies section, headed by a man we know well by repute. Sergei Pavlich Rostov, his name is, and not a pleasant character. But he has a sense of humour, the bastard. He sent me a Christmas card last year, signed *"Attentivamente, Sergei."* '

Craig chuckled. Then he said, 'He couldn't afford to do that sort of thing unless he was pretty sure of himself.'

'You can say that again, boy. He's one of the post-Beriya brand, clever, University-trained, ruthless—and allowed a whole lot of latitude. We've had real trouble with him, more than once.'

'But it was one of his assistants you followed?'

'Yes, a young man, very earnest and doesn't appear very self-confident, especially when he turns up at a diplomatic reception under Rostov's wing. It's fairly obvious that he hates Rostov's guts and we think his boss may be pushing him. And that's always worth knowing. So we thought he was the best choice, and the easiest, since he spends a lot of working time outside the Embassy, making like he's contacting agents. Which he certainly is, but he's bright and well-trained and we didn't catch him at it until yesterday, three weeks after we started the operation. He was just a trifle careless. They had followed him to the Colosseum, where it was easy to keep him under observation, with three men on the job. Then he went across the street, guide-book in hand, and began to explore the Domus Aurea, the Golden House of Nero.'

'Good place for it,' remarked Craig. 'Full of dark passages and stairs underground.'

'Exactly. And that's where he was careless. He stopped in one of the dark rooms with a crowd of tourists. A guide was showing them some of Fabullus's frescoes, using a torch. Then they moved on and Zakharov waited behind, lighting a cigarette. It was almost completely dark, without the guide's torch, but the light of his match showed he had something white in his hand and the third man in the trailing team saw it. Just for a fraction of a second. Next moment it wasn't there. Then the Russian came walking back towards him and when he came out of the dark room he stood for a moment hesitating. He glanced at his watch and looked worried. Then he went off, with the other two members trailing him. The third man groped around in the darkness and found the loose stone. And the envelope. His instructions were not to open it, but he could feel the wad of notes inside and guessed what had happened.'

'Money?' said Craig, puzzled. 'What did he do?'

'Left it there. His job was to identify the contact. Another bunch of tourists was coming into the room, so he went out, found a quiet place where he could use his transceiver and made his report. He said he thought Zakharov's contact was late on the job. Whatever the Russian had expected to find wasn't there. They told him to get back fast and watch. They knew the KGB never leave caches filled for longer than they can help. But when he got back to it he was too late.'

'Oh bloody hell! The contact had been with the second crowd of tourists?'

'I suppose so. There was an envelope there, but not the same one. And no sign who'd done it. I'm sorry, Peter, but that's how the cookie crumbled. Anyway, he took it out, went back to his transmitting post, and handed it in.'

Craig said, 'You got the report, that's the main thing. But how the hell did you copy it without Zakharov knowing? He could have been strolling around, killing time until he could have had another look.'

'That's where the team-leader, sitting in the control car by the Colosseum, showed that little bit of genius that buys him my big bonus. When the receiver bleeped the second time, and he heard what had happened, he told the third man to come straight back to the car, where he'd got some sophisticated tools for opening letters and spotting the security traps in them, and a camera all set up. It's a van, labelled for a national building society and shaped like a country villa. The chimney is a periscope. Nice job, though I say it.'

'But how did he delay the Russians?'

'Again, that bit of genius. He simply told the other two watchers that they were to hold him up for half an hour, even if they had to let him see he was being followed. Otherwise, he said, he'd have their skins for lampshades.'

'What did they do, pick a quarrel?'

'Too chancy. No, they let themselves be seen, but only when he was well clear of the Golden House. As you know, it's one hell of a job to shake trained followers if they don't mind you knowing they're on your trail. Try running across the street just as the lights change, and they're doing the same daring act. Get into your car and they're hugging your rear lights. But Zakharov did it in the end—as I said, he's bright. They lost him completely. But by that time the other boys had had ample time to do their stuff and get the report back into the envelope and the envelope into its cache. I don't think Zakharov connected what he thought was a very clumsy trailing operation with his job at the cache.'

Craig frowned. 'He ought to have done. You mean he went back to it?'

'Yes, he did, an hour later, without returning to the Embassy. I see your point, of course, and it's puzzled me, too. But the explanation may be that he couldn't face going back to his section and reporting that he'd been followed while on an operation. So he *had* to go back and reassure himself that the cache was still unblown. And there was the envelope. I suspect he's kept mum.'

'How d'you know he didn't go back to the Embassy?'

'I've got a standing watch on all the entrances.'

'It was a swell job, Jo. I congratulate you. You'll catch the contact next time, with luck.'

'Don't count on it, Peter. They won't use that drop again for certain. They've probably got a dozen they use in rotation, and at least he'll have the sense to cut that one from the list. But we'll keep up the watch on him and take off the two trailers he can identify.'

Craig thought for a moment. 'What time was the report put into the cache?'

Ashbee smiled. 'I wondered when you'd come round to that. Two-forty-five, give or take a couple of minutes.'

'Embassy lunch break.'

'Yes. Have you narrowed the field at all?' He padded across to the bar with the two glasses, now empty. 'Same again?'

'Please. It's wonderful bourbon.'

'I think so. Well, Peter?'

Craig told him how far he had got. He finished, 'The valuable part of your operation, Jo, is not the report itself, since almost anyone could have written it, as I've explained. What *is* important is, one, that we know that the spy is active *now*; two, he loses no time in reporting to the case officer—that report was written within an hour or two of being lodged in the letter-drop—and three, that the case officer is Zakharov, a young man who may be pushed into doing things he oughtn't to do. I still think he oughtn't to have risked going back to see if the drop was blown.'

'You're probably right. Then there's four, one period used for contacting is the lunch hour.'

'Yes, I'm going to see that there's a special watch put on Diana Warren and Adams between one and four-thirty.'

'I think I know Miss Warren. Tall blonde with a top-drawer look about her. And very good legs.'

'That's the one. She's pretty good-looking altogether.'

'Yes. I've seen her at parties given by our junior staff. I'd better tell you this, Peter; she gets around a lot and has got herself a bit of a reputation.'

Craig sat up. 'Spell it out, Jo. It may be important. Don't spare our national feelings. What is the girl—just easy come, easy go?'

'*Very* easy come and go. She gave Jensen a fling—he's one of my young men, though I shouldn't be telling you, but it may be significant. She ditched him overnight for a Frenchman. If she's your spy I want to know. I don't like girls who make a play for my boys, unless it's straight.'

'She's the obvious chief suspect, at present. Access and opportunity for all three cases.'

'Three? I know about the original scientific letter, and this one. What's the third?'

'This.' Craig drew out his wallet and carefully extracted the sheet of notes. 'Unless I'm mistaken, a photo-copy of this will be the next thing in your letter-drop—or rather one of the dozen others, as you pointed out so depressingly.'

Ashbee picked it up by the edges, read it and frowned. 'What the heck are these notes? Made by you?'

'Yes. Dictated to Diana Warren this afternoon after I'd done a tour of departments looking for security lapses as part of my cover job.'

'Oh boy, you surely are exposing some human weaknesses, aren't you? And you think it's been copied. Why?'

'It disappeared, unaccountably, after she'd typed it. Then it turned up half an hour afterwards.'

'Doesn't sound like the Warren girl, does it?'

'You're right, it doesn't. She could have photostated it or simply taken a carbon copy for herself. But it's all the same the sort of thing the spy—whoever it is—*might* have thought worth another wad of lire. Whether the KGB would agree I would doubt.'

'Why—oh yes, I see what you mean. You've got a point there. What d'you want me to do with it? Test for fingerprints?'

'Yes. But something else. I want to know *if* it was photographed and if so, precisely *how*. Listen, Jo. The photostat machine, in the Registry not far from Diana's room, isn't a Xerox or anything very modern. It uses reflex photography with light for the first operation and then heat for printing out. No liquids, just heat.'

'I know. But the original wouldn't show any sign it's been copied.'

'Wouldn't it? It gets pressed tight against the photographic paper. Wouldn't there be some microscopic trace of chemicals left in the original?'

'Is the Registry air-conditioned?'

'No. I agree that in this Rome atmosphere, with high humidity, the emulsion might be a tiny bit unstable. Could you do anything?'

'I think it's worth trying. Can you leave it with me?'

'Yes, but I'll have to put something in its place. Have you got a typewriter I could copy it with?'

'Sure. There's one over there on my desk. But remember that if the Warren girl sees it she'll spot the difference at once.' He went across to the desk and opened the machine. 'Help yourself. There's some paper of the same size.'

Craig finished typing and gave the original to the American. 'You've made me a much less despondent man, Jo. Thanks a lot, especially for the bourbon. Could we meet tomorrow so that I know the result?'

'Sure. I've been thinking about that. We've got to be able to talk without attracting attention from Rostov and his thugs, so this flat, your hotel and the third row, stalls, in the Colosseum are all out. I also can't ask you to come to the Embassy, except for emergencies. Sorry, but there it is.'

'Open places?'

'Again too risky. No. What I've done, I signalled the Agency this afternoon and asked permission to blow, to you only, one of my safe houses, at my discretion. They agreed. You'll keep the address under your hat, huh?'

'I will. And thanks. I know it's a sacrifice.'

'Sure is, but never mind.' He looked at Craig with a trace of a smile. 'Via Ludovisi number 39, sixth floor, flat A. Got it?'

'Next door to my hotel, you old devil, and you know it. Or just up the street, anyway.'

'Seven-thirty do? P.m.'

'Fine. Can I bring a bottle?'

'Drinks are courtesy of the Agency.'

'Will you eat with me afterwards, Jo? Some quiet place where we can talk—?'

'It'll be a pleasure.' And he sounded as if he meant it.

Sergei Pavlich Rostov was working late, too. Zakharov came in, excited, and waited impatiently until his chief paid him attention.

'All right, Sasha. What progress have you made?'

'The receiving device was visited an hour ago and the reel changed. It had been triggered off sometime this afternoon and fed the recorder for forty-three seconds. The tape is being processed by the night staff in Technical Section.'

'Then where are the results?'

'There are some snags, Comrade. After all, this is the first time, and they are not confident yet of the computer settings.' He saw the look on his chief's face and went on, 'But we shall have the report in the morning.'

'I should hope so. Anything else?'

'Yes, Sergei Pavlich. I also arranged to see BX.328 to-night and gave orders, in a stern voice, in the sense of your instructions. The agent then handed me this, saying it was worth a bonus. I read the report and agreed.' He handed over a sheet of paper.

Rostov read it through carefully, then looked up. His broad flat face was clean-shaven and had no eyebrows, and the very nakedness of the face made the expression in his cold grey eyes more menacing. 'You are not telling me,' he said slowly, 'that you actually paid money for this—*crap*.'

The young officer hesitated for a moment, then he burst out indignantly, 'It is an inside report. This is surely the sort of thing we want to know—the weak points in the British security defences. It's the best thing 328 has given us. I paid the prescribed bonus as encouragement.'

Rostov nodded. 'As encouragement. I see. And whose notes are these?'

'Look at the source information.' Zakharov was feeling more confident. 'Craig. The police adviser. The subject of the report we had yesterday. The report fits with what we were told about his task in the Embassy.'

'Ah, yes. Craig, the security expert. And what would you say, Sasha, was his purpose in compiling these notes?'

'Oh God!' It was little more than a whisper, 'Oh God!'

'Go on, Comrade Zakharov, tell me what his purpose was. You said it was part of his task to write these notes. *Why?*' The last words, '*patamu cho*', were spat at the quivering Zakharov with uncontrolled fury.

The young man, his face dead white, stood to attention. 'He will draw these failings in the security procedure to the attention of the head of the Chancery,' he said in a dull, official voice, 'and recommend changes in the regulations. Where existing regulations have been contravened he will prescribe punishment for those at fault.'

'And what use, precisely,' shouted Rostov—he liked the feeling of the terror he could instil into his staff on occasions like this—'what use will your precious information be then? Get out! No—wait. The bonus will be deducted from your salary. I will keep the report, with a note of your reaction to it, and send it to Moscow for the training staff, as a classic example of false assessment.' He paused for a moment, partly to let the man sweat and because he was thinking that if he drove him too far he would go to the Ambassador, and that wouldn't do at all. 'Unless,' he added, 'your work shows a remarkable improvement. *And quickly!*'

Zakharov was at the door when Rostov called him back. 'I ordered you yesterday to show the whip to 328's potential recruit. Has this been done?'

'Not yet, Comrade. It is not easy—'

'I do not favour easy, comfortable ways of running agents. I favour firm control, from the start. The man has been in touch long enough. Let it be done tomorrow, without fail. Is that understood?'

'Yes, Comrade.'

CHAPTER NINE

WEDNESDAY MORNING

At nine-thirty the following morning Craig went into Diana's room. She was typing fast, her long fair hair over one eye and her shorthand notebook on the desk beside her. He waited until she looked up.

'John Bracken said you might be kind enough to type my notes again.'

'What's wrong with them? I don't make typing mistakes,' she said coldly, holding out her hand for the paper he had in his hand. He held on to it.

'It was beautifully typed, but I've got to re-draft it for use at the Heads of Department meeting.'

'OK. I am ready.' He dictated the notes in the form of a minute to Head of Chancery, adding recommendations for action. Then he said, 'There's one thing I forgot to check. When you have something Secret or Top Secret to be destroyed you shred it, don't you? Is it this thing over here?'

'Yes. It's simple; it's always connected. Switch on and put the paper into the hopper. Give it to me and I'll show you.'

'Don't bother.' He switched on the machine and pushed the page of notes he had copied on Ashbee's typewriter into the hopper. There was a chattering noise, and then it resumed its quiet hum. He removed the paper sack underneath and opened it. The contents were a pile of fine straw and nothing else.

'Splendid. I gather you nearly lost it last night, didn't you?'

She gave him a frigid stare. 'As I told John Bracken, I put it on that table, face down. That's a pretty broad hint that it's not to be looked at, isn't it? Well, some clot must have put some papers on top of it by mistake and carried it into Registry.'

'Oh well,' said Craig, placatingly, 'it doesn't matter as long as it was found. It could happen very easily; you might have done it yourself.'

'I did not,' she said furiously. 'It must have been Reg Newman from Registry or Douglas or Janet or any one of the dozen people who came in and sat down on that chair and talked to me while I was trying to work. They all use my office as if it was a staff common-room.'

'You're such a popular girl, obviously.'

'Yes, Mr Craig. But at this moment a very busy one, and you've got your meeting at ten, so would you be very kind—' she smiled at him with exaggerated sweetness— 'and get the hell out of here?'

Craig wondered, as he went down the stairs, whether she had a special reason for not wanting visitors in her room.

CHAPTER TEN

WEDNESDAY AFTERNOON

Dino Pasquale took a pride in his work. He could go into a public lavatory or an *albergo diurno* (that typically Italian establishment, where you can get a bath, shave, shoe-shine and haircut at any hour of the day) looking like a well-dressed, respectable businessman and come out five minutes later a long-haired student with a beard straggling over his dirty collar. Two minutes behind a bush in the Pincio Gardens, to turn his clothes inside-out and put on another wig, were enough to change a young man in a blue suit into an old man in a brown suit. And his modest Fiat 1200 could keep up eighty-five miles an hour without the slightest strain. Which wasn't surprising when you looked under the bonnet.

Keeping up with the erratic driver of the Volkswagen minibus was no problem at all. He was turning off the Viale delle Belle Arti towards the imposing Lutyens façade of the British School of Rome, and then round and into the quiet Via Mangili, where he stopped. Pasquale drove past for a hundred yards and then got out of his car with an envelope in his hand and began looking helplessly at the numbers on the nearest gates. They were all very respectable houses, standing in their own gardens behind trees and high railings. He looked round. The man was walking towards him. Then he disappeared.

Still with the envelope in his hand Pasquale walked slowly past the gate which Adams had entered. He could see him standing in front of the door of the house, which he opened. The surveillance man went back to his Fiat and called his control. Then he sat back in the driving seat and to all appearances went to sleep.

Half an hour passed before his radio bleeped and a voice

told him that another car had taken over the watch on the Volkswagen. But he was to stay at his post until the target had left.

Another quarter of an hour went by, and Dino saw a second man walking slowly past his car, going towards the gate. Fifty yards beyond it he turned and walked slowly back. Very slowly, this time. Dino was puzzled. It wasn't one of his own team, and he took out his notebook and jotted down a description as he had been taught: height, build, apparent age, clothing, facial characteristics, etc. The man had passed the gate when he stopped suddenly, and bent down to fiddle with his shoe.

The Englishman had come out of the house and opened the gate. As he went towards the Volkswagen the other man began to overtake him. A black Lancia had drawn up just behind the mini-bus. As the man caught up with Adams the Lancia drew out, passed the mini-bus and came slowly towards the two men. Dino began to be very worried. It looked like a snatch attempt. But no; the man was alongside Adams and showing him something white, an envelope. Then he pushed it into his hands and was immediately picked up by the black car, which accelerated past Dino's Fiat and made off fast.

The Englishman stood staring after the Lancia for a moment before he looked down at the white thing in his hands. By this time Dino had his binoculars to his eyes. It was an envelope and Adams was drawing out a thick piece of paper. Dino could see the expressions changing on the man's face—from idle curiosity to disgust and then, suddenly, to the utmost loathing and horror. He held the paper nearer to his face, and seemed to be shouting something. Then he tore it into pieces and threw them down on to the pavement.

He began to walk fast towards his car, but stopped, and turned around and ran back. At the place where he had stood he stooped and began to pick up the pieces of paper. He looked round to see that he had missed nothing and ran back to the mini-bus, which he drove with clashing gears past Dino, who had resumed his notional sleep, and on towards the Zoological Gardens. Dino let him go, and his team-mate's car which came past as well, and went on a search of his own. One solitary piece of paper had been blown between the railings, and he retrieved it. And inspected it, grinning broadly.

The Ambassador listened attentively, sitting in the orchid house with the 'cover' catalogue on his lap, to Craig's report.

'Let me get this straight, Craig. We agreed that the report Marchant brought me yesterday only goes to show that the spy is active. And as far as that document is concerned it could be anyone. As for the first document, the scientific letter, the main suspicion lies on Adams and Miss Warren—it was most remiss of me to forget that she was working for me at the time in question—or possibly Adams's PA or someone in Registry, or anyone who could have got at the confidential waste sacks. Finally, the sheet of notes that was lost yesterday, if it *was* copied—and you don't know for certain yet—could have been—er—borrowed by any one of a dozen people. We haven't got very far, have we?'

'No, sir. But Adams and Miss Warren are very much at the top of the list.'

'I can't imagine either of them as a spy,' said His Excellency, testily. 'It's really unthinkable.'

'We're going to have a surprise whoever it is,' said Craig. 'But I feel strongly that we have enough evidence—purely circumstantial, I admit—to put a watch on those two.' He omitted to say he had made arrangements already.

'You mean—*follow them around*?'

'Yes, sir, I'm afraid so.'

He had expected an outburst, but the Ambassador said nothing, looking at the ground. Then he raised his head. 'I suppose you're right. It's a most distasteful thing to do, but I realize that you've got to get firm evidence. I give you my full approval.' He got to his feet. 'You'll let me know the

G

results,' he said coldly, and walked towards the door of the greenhouse, and the fresh air outside.

Craig rang Luigi from the call-box on the ground floor of the Chancery building.

'There's something interesting, Peter. Are you free now?'

'Yes. Could we meet half-way at Doney's? I'll be there in twenty minutes.'

'OK.'

When the Chancery car dropped him outside the café on the Via Veneto he could see Luigi already sitting at a table on the pavement, under the awning. He ordered an Espresso and sat down.

'I've got the reports in my pocket, but I don't want to wave them about, so I'll give you the gist. First, the Warren girl, and there the team had bad luck. She left the Embassy before lunch in the staff bus and was dropped in the Piazza Venezia. She went down the Corso and turned sharply up a one-way street—traffic against her. By the time the foot-trailer had been dropped she had disappeared. You know what those small streets in the old town are like in the middle of the day. I'm sorry, but there it is.'

'Can't be helped, but did she know she was being followed?'

'No, Peter,' said Luigi in a pained voice. 'My boys really are good, I assure you. Either she dived into a shop before the man could spot her, or she was taking evasive action as a matter of routine.'

'You mean, on instructions?'

'Yes, I suppose so. We'll try again when the offices close this evening, and again tomorrow at lunch-time. Now to the main thing, Adams.'

Craig's heart thumped. 'Didn't he go home?'

'Yes, he did. But at half-past two he came out again and drove to Via Mangili, number thirty-seven. But he parked some way short of the house, as if he didn't want his car to be seen in front of it.'

'Via Mangili? But that's where Mrs Ransome lives. It's odd; I wouldn't have thought they were in the least friendly, to judge from the way she spoke to me last night about Adams and his wife. When did he come out?'

'Four o'clock. Just time to get to the Embassy. Now listen.' He went on to describe what Dino Pasquale had observed. Then he reached into his pocket and produced an envelope.

Craig took out the scrap of glossy photograph. His lip curled. 'It's their standard filthy technique. That's a bit of his leg. They got him into bed with a woman and took photographs, and now they're putting on the heat.'

'Not yet. This is what they call "showing the whip". They'll follow up with a threat to distribute copies if he doesn't co-operate. But why? If he *is* the spy, Peter, already working for them, what's happened? Has he refused to continue? And what was he doing in that house?'

Craig said nothing, watching the strollers passing between the two rows of tables on the pavement—tourists of all types, girls showing themselves off before the cynical eyes of the old roués who sat with their backs to the roadway for a better view, lovers, families from the provinces, rich businessmen from the North. He slapped the table with his hand.

'I've just remembered. Lady Balcombe told me that the ground floor of her house is let to a businessman from Milan.'

'Who's Lady Balcombe? Mrs Ransome's mother?'

'Yes. And she said the tenant was scarcely ever there. I wonder whether he's in that flat now.'

'That I can check. But there's something very odd about the whole incident, Peter.'

'Odd? It was a professional job, of course, not done by a back-street blackmailer. The time and the getaway car show that. I'd say it was the KGB, but how did they know he'd come out of the house when he did? It either shows he's been there often and has been watched, or they've got a contact with the person he goes to see. And—yes, now, that *is* funny. Tearing up the photograph, that's what you mean?'

'Tearing it up and throwing away the bits is something I can't see any trained spy doing.'

'That's it, there was no instinctive reaction against leaving evidence lying about. It was only when he remembered that he went back. And then—I think you said—he searched hastily, slap-dash, or he'd have seen what your man found. So what's the explanation?'

Luigi said, 'There was some other reason for picking up the bits, nothing to do with security. But this is all speculation, Peter. I'm just left with a strong impression that he isn't a spy—not yet.'

'There I agree, but they're going to put the screws on him, the bloody fool, and I've got to find some way of getting him to tell me. What baffles me is the sheer coincidence, if it is coincidence, that he should go to Janet Ransome's house and that this should happen in front of it.'

'It could have been a social call.'

'Not on your nelly. Not at two-thirty on a hot afternoon. If she is mixed up in this business it's incomprehensible. She could not have been responsible for the first leak—we know that for sure—and if she's the cause of the second we've got two bloody spies on our hands.'

'What second leak?'

'Oh lord, I forgot to tell you. The spy is active *now*.' He told him about the discovery of the report of his arrival, but without mentioning Ashbee by name, and the matter of the lost sheet of notes. Luigi sat looking down at the remains of his coffee, thinking.

'You remember telling me what Sir Watkyn said to you about espionage—that spies bred spies. He is right, you know, that old man.'

'I simply don't see Janet and Neil Adams in any sort of ploy together.'

'There's one obvious sort of play,' said Luigi, misunderstanding.

'Oh God, no! She's attractive, all right, but inside she's

as cold as Trajan's Column.'

'I told you before, Peter—funny things happen in Rome.'

It was nearly six o'clock when Craig got back to the Embassy. He went into Janet Ransome's room. She stopped typing and looked up at him, smiling. It was an attractive smile, and he wondered whether he'd been right about Trajan's Column, after all.

'Hallo, Peter, what can I do for you?'

'Can I stick my head in and see if H.E. can spare me a moment?'

'No go, I'm afraid. He's gone to the Palazzo Chigi to see the Minister. Won't be back before the office closes. Anything I can do?'

'No thanks. It's just some gossip I heard today from one of the Interpol people. It'll wait.' He perched himself on a corner of the table. 'I enjoyed meeting your mother last night.'

'You made rather a hit with her. She hopes you'll come and have a drink one evening.'

'I'd like to. Couldn't we combine something? I come to you for a drink and you come out and dine with me and show me Rome after dark. Er—your mother, too, if she'd like to.'

She smiled at him demurely. 'Mummy doesn't like walking very much. But I'd love to do that.'

'Splendid. I've got a date tonight, but what about tomorrow?'

'Sorry. I can't then, but Saturday? At seven o'clock?'

'Fine. I'm interested in seeing your house, after what your mother told me about your heroic efforts to split it up so successfully. That must have saved you a packet, with labour what it costs in Rome these days.'

'Yes, but my God it was a sweat. Why? Are you a do-it-yourself man?'

Come to think of it, thought Craig, that wasn't a bad description. 'In a way. I like seeing what people can do with old houses. And I gather you've let it already?'

'Oh yes, six months ago, after Diana left. Which reminds me, I must get her key back.' She scribbled a note on her shorthand book. 'When you come I'll show you, if you like, provided the tenant's still away. We're lucky; he only uses the flat as a *pied à terre*.'

'Good, that's settled. But I'll see you before then.'

'I hope so. There's lots more we can say about elephants.' She was still leaning back in her chair, looking at him, when he went out.

Now that, thought Craig, had been a surprisingly useful conversation. It was a pity he would have to wait until Saturday to see the inside of Lady Balcombe's house, but still, Saturday would be something.

And that was the understatement of his life.

Adams's offices were in a block of wooden buildings on the other side of the drive. Craig went into the outer room. There was no one there, but he could hear Adams's voice coming from behind the inner door. It was high-pitched and strained. There was still no sign of the PA, so he went forward quietly and listened.

'. . . no intention of meeting you, you filthy swine.' He was talking in English. There was a pause, and then the same voice, strident, so that Craig could hear every word. 'No. *No*, you bastard. You'd get nothing out of her anyway . . . All right, I'll see you there if you promise—if you swear you'll keep your filthy fingers off her. Do you understand?' Adams spoke again, more quietly, but with a passionate rage in his voice that held a real menace. 'I'll accept your promise, and you'll keep it. Because if you don't I will kill you, d'you understand me? . . . All right then, seven-thirty tomorrow evening.' He rang off.

Craig went out into the corridor and entered the outer room again, calling Adams by name. He got no answer and pushed open the door of the inner room. Adams was sitting at his desk with his hand still on the receiver, staring in front of him. At the sound of Craig's voice he gave a start and looked up at him angrily.

'Hullo, Peter, what d'you want? I'm terribly busy, I'm afraid. My PA's been sick for two days and I never seem to be able to get help from the typists' pool.'

Craig settled down comfortably in the visitor's arm-chair and stretched out his legs. 'Sorry, shan't keep you a moment. That's better,' he said, crossing one knee over the other. 'I've been walking my legs off.'

'What is it you want?' Adams had lost any veneer of diplomatic courtesy he might have acquired.

'It's just the routine question we have to ask all members of the staff who have access to Top Secret material.' The man's face did not change its expression; he continued to look at Craig with his mind on something else. 'Just so that we can keep the records straight. Since that last security inspection has anyone outside the Embassy made a pass at you, in the security sense?'

'What on earth d'you mean?' Still that vacant stare.

'There are a lot of people in Rome, Neil—the Russians for a start—who'd like to know some of the things you've got locked up in your head.'

'Are you out of your mind?' Adams was roused at last. 'Nobody would think of trying to pump *me*. I'm small beer, chum. You know that.'

'You'd be surprised what they do want, though, and they do try it on, all the time. And sometimes it's a very gentle approach—they get to know you socially, ask you out and so on.'

'You've been talking to John Bracken,' said Adams contemptuously.

Craig looked at him sharply. 'Why him?'

'Oh, it was last year. One of the Russians asked me to lunch, and it turned out to be a *tête-à-tête*, with this chap— Serov, his name is, on the scientific side—getting very serious all of a sudden. I told John Bracken, of course. There's a standing instruction. But Serov's approach, if it was one, was pretty vague, a lot of obvious stuff about scientists all over the world having to stand together.'

'And then?'

'And then the bloody fool began to talk about Vietnam. Now I'm prepared to talk until the cows come home about what I think of American policy in the Far East, but for crying out loud, *not* with a mucking Soviet imperialist. I told him what I thought about the invasion of Czechoslovakia, and then we lost our tempers.' He laughed. 'I was sorry afterwards, because he's a decent chap, really, but we both became very red-faced and there was a scene about each paying his share of the bill. Then we stalked off in opposite directions.'

'And afterwards, did you see him again?'

'Good lord, yes. Often, at these scientific functions, and yes—that was a bit odd—he came up to me and apologized. Practically clicked his heels. So I apologized, too, for having shouted at him, and I told him he wasn't responsible for what his bloody Government did, and we're on good terms now.'

'But he hasn't asked you to lunch again?'

'No, he hasn't,' said Adams impatiently. 'Look, Peter, I told you—'

'I'm sorry, Neil, but I haven't quite finished. The point is that if Serov's approach was an intelligence one, that may be the beginning of an attempt to recruit you.'

'Oh, that's cock, Peter. Serov is a shy little fellow, he isn't an OGPU man in disguise.'

'He doesn't have to be. They often use a straight man for the first approach—you ought to know this, it's all in the security briefs—and then follow up from a different angle altogether. Has there been *any* other approach?'

'From the Russkies? Good God, no.'

'Nor from *anyone* at all? No kind of contact that you can't explain?'

Adams started as if he'd sat on a drawing-pin. He stared at Craig, his face slowly flushing. Then he made an obvious effort to control himself, and faced Craig boldly. 'No. Nothing at all.'

'Oh come on, Neil! Why are you looking so embarrassed all of a sudden? Nothing at all?'

'Nothing. You're not doubting my word, are you?' he added in a threatening voice. He looked like a Sealyham growling at a bull-terrier.

Craig returned his belligerent stare calmly. Then he got up slowly and walked out of the room. There was no point in pressing him too hard at this stage; let him keep his appointment tomorrow and then tackle him again.

Maggie Adams had been right. Neil was a hopelessly bad liar. But not a spy. Not yet.

CHAPTER ELEVEN

WEDNESDAY EVENING

Just before half past seven Craig got off a bus in the Via Veneto and walked along Via Ludovisi towards his hotel. But he stopped at number thirty-nine and went in. It was a tall apartment block, with four flats on each floor. In the lift he pressed the button marked 6° and on the sixth floor found Flat A. Ashbee opened the door.

It was a small, two-bedroom flat with a fair-sized living-room and a dining-room. The furniture was old, well-worn and miscellaneous, fairly shrieking of 'furnished let', but there was a useful-looking drinks cupboard, a desk with two telephones on it and a couple of deep leather arm-chairs which were comfortable enough. The two men settled down with tumblers of Ashbee's bourbon in their hands. The American was smoking a Canaries cigar and offered one to Craig, but he shook his head and pulled out his pipe.

'There's a lot to tell you, Jo. But first, what about those notes?'

Ashbee drew out of his pocket a sheaf of fingerprint photographs and Craig's paper of notes, which Diana had typed. Craig looked at it curiously. At each of the corners there was a faint brown smudge, and connecting them, like a St Andrew's cross, were two long marks, very faint and too broad to be called lines, that intersected in the middle of the paper in another smudge shaped like a four-leaved clover.

'What on earth do those marks mean?'

'You may well ask; they baffled me. But the head of my photographic section, who's getting on in years and has seen everything, was delighted. Rubbing his hands with glee and jeering at me because I didn't know what it was. Then he told me, and I remembered.' He took a long pull at his whisky. 'During your career in the African bush, Peter, did you do any document photography in the field?'

'Up country, you mean? It was a bit primitive. The station sergeant had a black envelope locked away from his detective-constables. It was document paper, sensitive to artificial light only, and usually covered with dead ants who'd tried to eat it. He also had a sheet of glass. You put the thing to be copied face upwards on a flat surface, then the sheet of document paper face *down*—you tested for the sticky side with a wet finger—and finally the sheet of glass, so that it pressed the two sheets of paper together. Only then did you switch on the desk lamp, if you had one, or wave a torch over the glass, counting seconds and hoping to God you'd got the exposure right. Switch off, develop the doc. paper, fix it, and there was your negative. To make the positive you used the same process all over again, and the result was usually bloody awful.'

'Exactly. The reflex process. But if someone had busted your glass?'

'No go. The glass was essential to hold the sheets tight together.'

'No, Peter, it isn't. You can get some sort of a result this way.' He took a sheet of writing-paper from a desk and laid it on top of the sheet of notes. Then he put his forefingers and thumbs together in the centre of the top paper and spread them outwards until they occupied the corners of the sheet, pressing it evenly down on to the paper underneath.

'My God!' said Craig. 'You've got it. But wait—what do you switch on the light with? Your big toe?'

'Good question. Either you have an assistant or you do it like this. Give me that Guida Telefonica.' He opened the stiff cover of the directory, placed the two papers together on top of the first page and closed the cover. 'Right. Now I switch the light on, so.' He made a gesture with his right hand. 'Now I whip back the cover, smooth down the top paper with my fingers as before and wait, say, ten seconds.

Remember, this paper is slow. Then close the cover down
again with one hand and switch off with the other. Of
course the result will be blurred and there'll be marks
where my fingers were at the corners, *but you can read it.*
And remember, Peter, all your spy has got to do is send the
negative to his contact. The KGB does the rest.' There was
a long silence.

'I know what you're thinking,' said Craig slowly. 'It was
the marks at the corners that Kuznetsov noticed.'

'You're jumping to conclusions, feller. We know only
that this method is used by your spy. Not the photostat
machine so conveniently available. As I said, it only has to
be legible.' He pointed an accusing finger at Craig's glass
and when it was empty took the two tumblers to the bar
and poured out more bourbon, while Craig talked.

'You know, this makes the whole thing more difficult.
Whoever is doing this only needs a few sheets of doc. paper,
shielded from the light in a pocket—or a handbag—and a
desk lamp. As long as there's no other artificial light, when
you've made the exposure you switch off, put the negative
into your pocket—just a piece of white paper with no
marks on it until it's developed—and in due course go
home and fix it at your leisure.' He paused. 'That's a
thought. Somebody's got developer and fixer at home, and
some sort of fixing bath. Or, for that matter, a bidet. That
also is a thought. Thanks a lot, Jo. And now I'd better tell
you my news.'

When he had finished Ashbee was silent for quite a time.
'Is this joker Adams plain bone from the neck up?'

'I know it sounds like it, but he's not. He's got a good
brain. But he's been caught up in something where he's a
babe in arms.'

'I don't get it. Why's he acting Sir Galahad? The broad
was planted on him, it stands to reason.'

'Listen, Jo. There are three possibilities. One, Adams is
our spy and has been all along. His control decides that he
isn't doing his stuff, so he gets a girl to seduce him and takes
a photograph. Then he shows it to Adams and says do

better—or else.'

'But why push it into his hand in the street? Why not do it at the next meeting. And why ring him at the Embassy, for Jesus' sake? It don't make sense. And anyway, you said he was a hopelessly bad liar.'

'And so he is. Now, his whole manner, when he was talking to me about the Serov approach, was dead normal. He was treating it as a joke. It was only when I put it into his mind that what was happening to him now was connected with the Serov approach that he realized that it wasn't just money blackmail. I tell you, he jumped as if he'd been stung. And that, too, is the impression I got when he was talking to Mr X on the telephone. He *didn't know* who he was talking to. If Adams is our spy I'm Nicky Kruschev.'

'Then they're trying to make him one.'

'Yes, that's possibility number two. It's a simple follow-up to the Serov approach.'

Ashbee frowned. 'No *sir*. Too durned precipitate for the KGB. They're cautious operators, those bastards; they'd never risk leaving him uncertain what it's all about. They'd have got at him a different way, working on his weaknesses, getting him involved, and keeping that photograph for use when he's half on the hook. What's your third alternative?'

'It ties up with what you've just said. The reason why they know he won't tell is that the girl is someone—don't laugh—someone he *respects* and regards as above all suspicion. In fact, our spy.'

'Either Diana or Janet?'

'Yes. They've both got access to that ground floor flat in Lady Balcombe's house—Janet told me Diana still had her key—and we know the flat's empty at the moment. And that, after all, is where he was when they pushed the photograph into his hand.'

'Wait a moment. Let me get this straight. You're suggesting that one of those two girls is the spy, that she was told to get Adams to lay her and then let somebody take a picture of them in transports on the bed. That's going a bit far, isn't it, even for one of your swinging society girls?'

'She mightn't have known about the photograph. The Milanese who rents the ground floor may be a KGB stooge. The camera may have been rigged up without the girl knowing at all. If it is I'm going to find it.'

'Breaking and entering, Police Commissioner?'

'I've got to know. Then I can face Adams and break him down.'

'And which of the girls is it? I thought you said you'd crossed Janet off your list from the start. So it's the snooty-pie?'

'I suppose so. Unless Janet's been recruited since. She couldn't have been the original spy. I don't know where the hell we're getting, but at least I've got two lines. That camera and the meeting tomorrow.'

'You were right not to push Adams too far today, Peter. We've got to know who meets him. I'll do that for you.'

Craig hesitated. 'I can cope, you know.'

'I'd prefer to do it myself,' said Ashbee firmly, 'and I'll tell you why. My team know Zakharov well by now. If he makes the contact I'll know. He's still under observation, remember.'

'Right. And thanks, Jo. I'll call off the other blood-hounds or they'll be sniffing round each other. But you'll have to follow both. I'll give you a description of Adams and his mini-bus number.' He began to scribble on a leaf torn from his notebook.

'Good. We'll try to listen in to what they say, but it may be difficult, if I know my KGB friends. Depends where it is.'

'If you do that,' said Craig, standing up and stretching himself, 'and I find that hidden camera, we've got enough to put those three on the spot. It doesn't make sense, of course. Both Diana and Janet seem to regard Adams as just an annoying little man. And as for him—it beats me. There he is with five children and an adoring wife who could run rings round either of those two girls if it came to sheer magnetic charm. For God's sake, let's go out and eat some delicious food and drink a lot of wine. Come on, Jo, show me a place that isn't bugged.'

The technicians in the *Rezidentsiya* at 5 Via Gaeta had been working on the computer all morning and all afternoon. It had continued to disgorge strings of meaningless letters and the programme card was taken out, time after time, and new adjustments made. In the evening there was a conference, at which the glowering face of Rostov was very much in evidence. Then they went back to the machine and started again, and suddenly the senior technician, looking down with tired eyes at the tape, gave a shout of triumph. 'English words! It's coming through.'

It began, S.3 TO REES. ONE. YOUR TELEGRAM ONE. CRAIG SHOULD PROCEED . . . and went on to reproduce exactly the telegram Sir Watkyn had received the previous afternoon. The tape was cut and rushed down to Rostov's room.

He read it through once quickly, the thought uppermost in his mind that the method had worked. It was a new technique and the break-through was complete. Then he snatched up the tape again and read it very carefully.

He called the research section and asked what the symbol S.3 meant in a British Intelligence context. Negative. Or in the Foreign Office or Scotland Yard? Again negative. So it was something new, and that, at least, was interesting. It was a pity that the first signal in the series, the 'ONE' from Rees to S.3, should have been sent before the device was installed, but something could be guessed from this answer.

He looked again at the text. CRAIG SHOULD PROCEED WITH CASE. OUR BASIC RULE EXCLUDES USE OF WALTON. ASHBEE IS BEING BRIEFED FULLY BY WASHINGTON AND CRAIG MAY CO-ORDINATE WITH HIM DIRECT. IF FIRM EVIDENCE AGAINST SUBJECT OUR ENQUIRY IS AVAILABLE REFER BACK FOR INSTRUCTIONS. DO NOT (REPEAT NOT) CALL IN ITALIANS AT THIS STAGE. Rostov frowned. What on earth was the basic rule that excluded using Walton, the SIS man, from working with Ashbee, of CIA? And instead of Walton, Craig, the orchid-loving policeman? It didn't make sense.

And then Rostov remembered that Ashbee acted as sole liaison officer for both CIA and FBI with allied representatives. It wasn't an intelligence matter at all, but some police job. But why at this stratospheric level? Why on the Ambassador's own 'Decypher Yourself' series?

He sat up, intrigued. It must be some major scandal, something which had to be kept from the Press. A Cabinet Minister perhaps or a member of the House of Lords or a NATO general who'd been caught—what? Not spying, since it was Craig's job, not Walton's. But—narcotics, for example? S.3 might be a cover for some Anglo-American anti-narcotics agency, something super-secret, since the research section would have known, otherwise.

Suddenly Rostov burst into a roar of laughter. He would inform his own Ambassador about the message and ask him, straight-faced, if from his knowledge of Roman society he could suggest who was the target of the S.3 operation. That would make the slimy old bastard squirm.

It was half past eight and the sun was setting when Ashbee drove his big Buick out through the gate in the old walls and on to the Appia Antica, the original Appian Way, as distinct from the new road of the same name that ran parallel to it towards the Alban Hills. The intolerable cacophony of Roman traffic—the continuous hooting of infuriated drivers, the scream of tyres braked too suddenly, the roar of sports' cars driven with the one idea of showing off the owner's *virilismo*—lay behind them, and Craig breathed a sigh of contentment.

'They're the craziest drivers in the world,' he pronounced. 'It's worse than Rio, worse than the Place de la Concorde. These people *like* the noise they make.'

'Of course they do,' said Ashbee tolerantly. 'Every car is a sex symbol and it's got to be seen *and* heard. That's why they run their tyres smooth—so they'll make more squeal

going round corners. But their reflexes are fast, don't forget
that—fastest I know.'

'Where are we going?'

'Somewhere I think you'll like. Wait and see.'

After the church of Quo Vadis the road became straight-
er and more narrow, following the course of the old road
whose stones still lay beneath the tarmac. The walls closed
in on both sides and the air was full of the scent of um-
brella pines.

It was a long, low building on the right-hand side, with a
sign over the road, 'Hostaria dell'Archeologia'. Inside there
were bustling waiters and the smell of good food. The proprietor greeted Ashbee as an old friend, and Craig was
introduced. 'This friend of mine is a Scotsman, and used
only to his native dishes—'

The proprietor interrupted. 'The porridge I can provide,' he said with a twinkle in his eye, 'but the sheep's
stomach stuffed with tripe takes time to prepare.' Craig
burst out laughing. An enormous menu was put into his
hand.

'I suggest you try a little *bresaola* to start with—it's sun-
dried meat, rather salt but shaved very fine—with some
olives and celery, and then perhaps some *frutta di mare*
and afterwards either pheasant or wild boar.' He smiled at
the American. 'The pheasant is Mr Ashbee's favourite dish.
It is cooked with cinnamon, saffron, pine kernels, apricots,
prunes and mushrooms in a white wine sauce.'

'He's got his own *riserva di caccia*,' explained Ashbee
solemnly, 'and boy, are his pheasants good! And leave the
wine to him.'

Craig turned to the proprietor. 'Then that's what we'd
like. Could we eat outside?'

'But certainly.' He took them out on to a terrace paved
with old marble slabs, roofed over by the spreading arms of
a wistaria which was two feet thick at the base and covered
the whole terrace with its leaves. There was a garden
beyond, with a pool and rows of cages. Ducks and geese
were walking around, foraging under the tables. It was a

H

peaceful, pleasant place and the air, after the fume-laden heat of the city, was fresh and scented with the smell of pine needles and flowers.

Most of the tables were filled, but there was space between them and they settled down near the pond, talking about food and wine, and taking their ease while a waiter whipped off the previous tablecloth, laid another fresh from the ironing board and set out in front of them bowls of green and black olives, and celery, and dishes of *bresaola* and other kinds of hors d'oeuvre. The first wine was a thin young Marino, chilled and delicious, and they kept to that through the trout meunière. With the pheasant, served with *empressement* by the proprietor himself, came a flask of his own Chianti, made and bottled on his property in Tuscany.

As the waiter went off with the dishes Ashbee said suddenly, 'If you get the evidence you want, and Adams will play, what are you going to do next?'

Craig thought for a moment. Then he said slowly, 'There's no simple answer, Jo : it all depends. Let's say you can confirm that it's Zakharov who meets him tomorrow night. Then I'm in business. I'll have to get H.E.'s agreement—and S.3's, too, I suppose—and then tell Adams that the Embassy has been told that he's been seen in conversation with a known KGB officer. No mention of you, of course. I'll probably imply it's the Italians. If he doesn't come clean, in every detail, I'll get a warrant for his arrest and in the meantime hold him in the Embassy. Walton will have to be brought in, of course, and the Italians informed. In fact, they'll have to provide a guard while we put him on a plane to London, with me as escort. But it'd be damned awkward to arrange all that, and of course the girl has every chance of flying the coop, if she wants to. So what I'm hoping is that I can break him down, as soon as I can tell him about Zakharov. If I can make the poor fool see that he's been taken for a ride—'

'That's one way of putting it !'

'Yes, Jo. Well, if I can get him to say it's Diana I'll inter-

rogate her on Embassy premises and try and get a confession and arrest her instead. But it's darned worrying,
you know. She may deny everything; he may go on acting
Sir Galahad, as you called it, and there we are. We'll have
lost the only strong card we've got—the element of surprise. I'd give a month's pay to catch that girl red-handed.'

'I wonder whether that flat isn't a regular meeting place.
If you do pull off your breaking and entering act tomorrow, to look for the camera, couldn't you bug it?'

Craig stared at him. 'Christ, that's a thought. But I'd
have to get in an expert—no, I don't. I've got one.'

Ashbee suddenly burst into a roar of laughter. When he
could speak he muttered, mopping his eyes with his handkerchief, 'Your mysterious helper, of course.'

'Well, yes,' said Craig cautiously, 'he's good at that sort
of thing, I believe.' He looked suspiciously at the American.
'What the hell's so funny, Jo?'

'A great light has just shone. Wears dark blue mohair
suits, does he? With a red handkerchief and his initials on
it in white?'

'Blast you! *What* initials, Jo?'

'L.K.'

Craig had to laugh with him. 'You old fox! So you use
him yourself?'

'Of course. It's his surveillance team that's been working
on this Zakharov chase and I was going to ask him to lay
it on for tomorrow evening. That's what was so funny, me
telling you I didn't want to cross lines.'

'I bet he'd have done it and never said a word to me
about you.'

'That's why he's a reliable operative and earns so much
money.'

'Well, that's one job I can take off your shoulders, Jo.
I'll brief him myself, if you don't mind my explaining I'm
in touch with you.'

'Go ahead. He'll have to know some time, I can see.'

'And you think he could do that job in the flat—plant a
mike so that it couldn't be seen?'

'He could do it on his head. Luigi's the best industrial espionage expert in Rome—and remember, the Italians are pretty sophisticated in their IE operations.'

Coffee was brought, and glasses of ice-cold grappa, which was a preference of Ashbee's. They lit cigars, and Craig looked through the smoke at the big American. 'There's another thing on my mind, and I'd be glad of your advice.'

'Shoot,' said Ashbee comfortably.

'It's something that's come into my mind since we started talking about mikes. We know we've got a spy who borrows papers for copying and sends reports to the Russians, and who may have paved the way for the recruitment of Adams, right?'

'What more d'you want?'

'It's more what do the KGB want, isn't it?'

'I see what you mean. Well, they want everything secret that goes on, that's for sure. But what they get, Peter, is a different matter. It depends on the access and capability of their agent. And willingness, too. Some spies will do some things, but stick at others.'

'Exactly. But if we suppose willingness is there, all right? Either of those two girls—or both of them, if Janet is now in it too—could report a good deal. But not what's said in the Ambassador's room, for example, and not what comes and goes in "Decypher Yourself" telegrams and other papers circulated in locked red boxes, and marked "For Official Eyes Only!" In fact, the real pay dirt. I'm thinking of bugging.'

'But for God's sake, you get the offices "swept" regularly, don't you?'

'Yes, and that was the first thing S.3 did, even before I came out. They sent a "sweeper" team, pretending they were on their way somewhere else, so as not to attract attention, and they went through the rooms in Chancery with a fine comb. And found nothing.' Craig took a pull at his cigar and laid it down. 'What worries me, Jo, is that if you have someone really on the inside, who knows when the sweepers are going to do their stuff—and who can remove the mike in time—'

'Jesus! You're right. You'll have to make snap sweeps, without anybody knowing. And how are you going to do that?'

'Could Luigi do it, if I could smuggle him in?'

'Of course. It's part of his job. And he's got the latest gadgets—not those old mine-sweepers.'

'Good. That helps. Thank God the Conference doesn't meet tomorrow; they're giving us all a long week-end. And I've got a lot to do before Monday. What I want, Jo, is a break, a real break-through. Something I can get my teeth into.'

CHAPTER TWELVE

THURSDAY MORNING

It was early next morning that Craig got the break he wanted. He had agreed with Bracken to make an inspection of the boundaries of the Embassy compound at half past eight, when there would be time to make the tour before the offices opened. It was a straightforward job, part of his cover task, to check the physical security of the premises and the park surrounding them, and Bracken had offered to accompany him.

There was no entrance apart from the main gate, and after casting an eye over the locks they started off along the concrete path which ran around the edge of the park. The Embassy territory stood on land raised above the surrounding streets and beyond the path the wall dropped straight down for thirty feet or so, so that the whole park was like an impregnable island except to someone equipped with a long ladder. Down below lay busy streets, except for one corner. At this point, looking down over the parapet, Craig could see a small area of ground with a building in the middle. Its roof was quite low—not more than eight feet above the ground, and Craig was puzzled. The patch of ground was protected by high railings, with a padlocked gate.

'It's Ministry of Fine Arts property,' explained Bracken, 'and that roof is just there to cover over the remains of a Roman temple. It's got a crypt underneath, I believe, because as you see there are modern steps leading down below. I don't think anyone has been there for years. Look at the way they've let the grass grow.'

And that was precisely what Craig was doing. He had spent too many leaves in Bangasa tracking game to miss the faint marks in the long, dew-covered grass. Someone had entered the gate and walked round to the rear of the little temple, and then back again, while the dew was on the ground. But he said nothing. Perhaps the gate wasn't locked, and somebody had thought it a convenient place to relieve nature. It could be that.

When they had finished their inspection of the boundary Bracken hurried upstairs to his office. Craig walked down the drive, out of the main gate and along the road which skirted the high wall of the Embassy park. At the intersection with another road he found the railings enclosing the temple and its surrounding plot of waste ground. He paused for a moment to look through the gate, and tested the padlock. It was heavy, Italian made, and definitely locked. There was a tiny smudge of oil around the keyhole. He went farther along the second street until he found a café with a call-box, and rang Luigi's office.

A quarter of an hour later a sleek, chauffeur-driven Alfa Romeo stopped outside the café and Craig paid for his coffee and went out. The driver opened the rear door and he got in. The car moved off smoothly into the traffic.

Luigi was saying, 'A Bianchi, you said, and something like a twelve-millimetre keyhole with a central spike?' Craig nodded. 'I think I can have it open with one of these.' He pulled a ring of skeleton keys from the pocket of his immaculate blue suit. 'Now listen, Peter. We'll be dropped near and walk to the gate. When it's open we go inside, leaving the gate closed. If anyone comes up at that moment I say I'm from the Belle Arti, showing a foreigner around. As soon as we're behind the temple I gather we'll be out of sight?'

'That's it. I hope I'm not getting you out for nothing, Luigi.'

'So do I, *amico*, but from what you said it's worth trying.'

The sun was high already, and the last traces of dew had vanished. They stood in front of the gate, Craig gesticulating and pointing through the bars while Luigi tried one key after another. Then the padlock clicked open and they went inside, closing the gate after them. Craig took a casual glance back, but although people were streaming past the gate, hurrying towards the bus stop, nobody appeared to pay them the slightest attention. Archaeologists are as common in Rome as guides.

The back of the temple was about five feet high between the Corinthian columns at the corners. It was made of solid marble slabs eight inches thick, but many were missing and the top of the wall was irregular. Craig stopped Kahn from moving beyond the corner and bent down to look at the ground. Then he called him, pointing.

'Just there, to the right of the middle. Somebody stood on that stone recently—you can see the scratches. And there's a mark of a heel on the grass, there.'

Luigi laughed softly. 'I can see nothing at all, Peter, but I'll take your word for it. We'll start on those loose slabs. We can't be seen, so we can take our time. Pick up each one very carefully, noting exactly how it lies, and hand it to me here, where there's some light. Don't pick up the next until you've got the first one in position, or you may leave traces. That one at the top of the wall looks suspiciously as if it's been handled. Let's have it first.' Craig did as he was told.

'No good. Put it back. No, Peter, wait— Leave it on the ground and see if you can pick out the one below where this one was. It looks solid but I'll swear the first one had been handled.'

Craig reached one arm over the top of the broken wall and, making a sort of pincer of his hands, pulled upwards. The marble block came smoothly away from its seating; but it felt much lighter than the other block.

Then he saw that what he was holding was only the front, back and top of the block. Inside it was hollow, and where it had stood in the wall was something which Luigi pressed forward to examine, cooing with pleasure.

The little machine stood on its baseplate, which was the same size as the marble block. The machine itself was the size of two packets of twenty cigarettes, but it had every-

thing it needed to receive and record on tape the message
picked up by the tiny mono-pole antenna.

'For God's sake, Peter, don't touch it. Let me.' He lifted
the baseplate down and examined the device from all
angles. Then he chuckled. 'Very nice. *Carino*! But—that's
funny. You can't change the tape without taking the whole
thing apart. Now I wonder why. Ah, there it is. A bit
primitive, but then you've got to do it in the dark.'

'What are you talking about, Luigi?'

'I'll tell you afterwards. You want to leave it here?'

'Only when I know what's on that tape. But yes, if
possible. We don't want to scare them off yet. You can
keep a tail on this place and follow whoever comes to
service it?'

'Yes, of course. But what you really want is what's
recorded and where the transmitter is?'

'Yes. How do we do that?'

'We'll take the whole thing away and sort it out in my
laboratory.'

'You can't put it in your pocket, can you?'

The big man shuddered. 'You don't know what you're
saying. The settings are very finely adjusted. That antenna
is set exactly right for its job. Look here.' He picked up the
marble casing which Craig had lifted and pointed to a
minute hole hidden in the rough markings of the stone.
'That's what it's aimed at, and beyond that hole, I've no
doubt, some transmitting aerial in your Embassy. A lot of
very sophisticated adjustments have been made to this
machine and any jolt might damage it. So how do we get
it out of the gate without attracting unwelcome attention?'

Craig turned to the thirty-foot wall behind him. 'Up
that, I suppose, and into the Embassy grounds. But even if
I hauled it up the wall with a string I'd still have to carry
it around up there. And it might get bumped. No, Luigi,
I've got a better way. Put its cover on it and take the whole
block out of the gate and straight into your car. Can you
get your driver to stop outside?'

Kahn put his hand in his pocket and took out a small

transceiver. He pulled out the antenna and pressed a button, holding it down for ten seconds. 'He'll hear the bleep and come here at once. We'd better get it ready. If a traffic cop sees him waiting here we've had it.'

Three minutes later, still standing out of sight behind the little temple, they heard the Alfa's horn and walked to the gate, Craig holding the block with his coat slung over it. Luigi had the gate open and locked after them before Craig was in the car.

As the car drove down the Via Merulana towards the centre Luigi said, 'We've got to risk something; it'll take an hour or more to get this thing back in place and in the meantime someone may arrive to monitor the tape.'

'Have you got somebody who can look like a plain-clothes Pubblica Sicurezza agent?'

'I have indeed.' The big man chuckled. 'Good for you. I'll send one of the tailers to stand guard near the gate with a big bulge in his pocket and a white handkerchief in his breast pocket. That'll scare them off for the time being. And it's only a slight risk anyway. The obvious time to service the receiver would be at night—we know they did that—or in the afternoon. And after checking it last night they'd probably leave it alone for a day.'

'Why the white handkerchief?'

'It's one of the PS recognition signals, or used to be.' He laughed. 'Helps to stop them arresting each other.'

The car swung out of the Piazza Esedra into a quiet street of office blocks and then turned sharply through an archway under one of the tall buildings. They came out into a subterranean garage and drew up opposite the doors of a lift. Luigi spoke to the driver, who went round to the boot and produced a TWA air-bag, which he handed in through the rear window. The marble block fitted into it easily. They took the lift to the twelfth floor and entered a big mahogany door marked in gold letters 'L. Kahn e Cia.'

At the end of a corridor double doors, soundproofed on

the inside, led into a large electronics laboratory, with white-coated men busy at benches along the walls. There was a sudden hush when Luigi appeared, and his chief technician hurried up and was given instructions.

'Listen, Peter, I'm going to arrange for that watch on the gate and one or two other things. You can stay here and watch Gioacchino if you like. It's quite an experience. His main job is to record what's on the part of the tape which has been played and put it back exactly as it was. He'll also discover the receiving wavelength and make a study of the whole machine. The rest I'll explain when I return.'

Craig drew up a stool and watched, fascinated, as the Italian's long brown fingers dissected the little device. He used minute screwdrivers, spanners, callipers, pincers, probes passed into his hand by an assistant as he worked. It was like watching a surgeon and a theatre sister, the same swift anticipation of demand, the same quiet mutter of explanations and commands, the same mutual understanding. He used an oscilloscope to measure the frequency of a transistor, a stopwatch to check the speed of the tape through the magnetic heads, after carefully noting the number on the footage counter, and then took apart with especial care the coherer which operated the stop-start action. Only when he was satisfied that he understood the whole of the working of the device did he press the re-wind button. Within seconds the tape was back at its starting point, and Craig realized that very little had been recorded. Then Gioacchino brought up a large Grundig tape-recorder, inserted a blank cassette and connected it to the device through wires thrust into two minute terminals on the baseboard. He started the Grundig rotating and then, with a grin at Craig, pressed the start button on the miniature set and handed him a pair of headphones.

Craig listened, puzzled, while the short length of tape ran its course and then handed the headphones back to the Italian. '*Non me dice niente. Prove Lei.*'

Gioacchino listened, and then put down the headset and

stared at the machine in silence. He connected the Grundig to a loudspeaker and ran the tape through again. It was the same, but loud and very odd-sounding : a series of musical notes, from up and down the register, but without any coherence whatever. The Italian shook his head sorrowfully, '*Complicazioni*,' he said succinctly. '*Aspettiamo il Signor Padrone.*'

But Luigi, when he returned, was equally puzzled. He tried running the Grundig at various speeds, using a device which could be plugged into it, but the result was essentially the same. The notes might be an octave higher or lower, but they remained in their irregular groupings, meaning nothing at all.

Kahn listened to a long explanation from Gioacchino about the properties of the little machine. Then he took the Italian's chair and passed on the explanation to Craig, who had understood little of the technicalities.

'When you bug a room with something very small that can't easily be found you have to have either a recorder device or a radio relay somewhere within a few hundred yards—sometimes less, sometimes more, according to the strength of the signal you can get out of your transmitter. Now the thing we found, although quite near to your Embassy buildings, is badly blanketed by that high wall and I doubt whether it would receive speech well. But this is the point—it isn't trying to. It's geared to receive something else, those separate notes which can be magnified and analysed far more easily. What we don't know is what emits them. That's the first point.

'The second is that the machine isn't fitted with replaceable tapes or cassettes. But it has a second magnetic head, *after* the recording head. You saw the terminals?'

'Yes. Gioacchino used them to copy what was on the tape.'

'Exactly, and that's what the man who comes to monitor the device does. He brings with him a portable recorder—one he could stick into his pocket, probably—and all he has to do is to connect it, run the tape back to the place he left it at the previous time, which he can do by noting the number on the footage counter, and then he starts up both recorders and copies the tape on to the recorder he's brought with him. Are you with me?'

'Yes. But why not have replaceable tape reels?'

'I'm not quite sure. But I think there are two reasons; one, he has to operate in the dark—at least we assume he did last night—and unless he's damned careful when he fiddles with the tape he could do harm. And cassettes are not accurate enough for anything as finely adjusted as this machine. Two, whenever he wants to keep well clear of the site where the thing is hidden he can connect a relay transmitter in the same way as the recorder.'

'Let me get this straight,' said Craig slowly. 'You mean that what is on that tape may have been there for several days, for all we know. Then why didn't he scrub it after copying it on to his recorder?'

Luigi threw up his hands. 'That's what I can't understand, unless—'

'Well?'

'This machine doesn't look like a production model. It's been hand-made. I think they're preserving the tape in case they're not satisfied with the results and want to make adjustments. This, I'm pretty sure, is a prototype.'

Craig exclaimed. 'It may not have been working long at all?'

'That's very possible. Well, those are my first thoughts. But what we've got to do now is to identify these strange sounds and see what produces them.'

'One question. What's the point of the coherer?'

'It switches on the tape-recorder only when a message is coming over the air. As soon as it stops, it switches off. Saves tape, of course.'

'Could you run through the tape at the same speed that it was recorded, so that we can see how long it takes?'

Luigi glanced at Gioacchino's notes. 'He's done that. Forty-three seconds.'

'So that's all the recording it's done, unless it's going

through the tape a second time. But what the hell does it *mean*?' He looked at his watch. 'Nearly half past ten. I'm going to ditch the meeting at eleven. This is too damned important. But hadn't we better replace this thing? If it's supposed to be recording something that's going on this morning we mustn't leave too much of a gap.'

'You're prepared to risk it continuing to operate?'

'I think we must, or we'll never get at the truth. At least now, if we put it back, we can monitor it again and perhaps pick up another clue.'

'Right. And while we're away Gioacchino can do a job for us.'

The replacement of the little set went without a hitch, and within half an hour they were back in the laboratory, staring at a large piece of white paper on which a graph had been drawn. It consisted of wild zig-zags, connecting points plotted to represent the frequencies of the notes recorded.

'There it is,' said Luigi, 'just as I thought. The spacing's irregular. The notes are emitted in groups, with gaps between. Peter, how do your cypher telegrams get dispatched?'

'The ones to London go by teleprinter, and that's most of the traffic, I suppose, apart from the stuff that goes straight to the cable companies.'

'Listen, I don't want to pry into secrets, but are the groups all the same length?'

'Yes, of course. Five-figure or five-letter groups, according to the code.'

'So it's not that—I mean, we're not looking at something that represents a telegram being sent out over the wire, because the groups would be regular, and these aren't. There's a complete mixture in the number of notes in the groups.'

'And in the gaps between the groups, too.'

Luigi peered at the graph. 'You're right. And there goes my other theory.'

'What was that?'

'I wondered whether it could be reflecting the noise of a
typewriter, in some way. Then the groups would be words.
But it's no good. Any experienced typist would leave exactly
the same gap between the words, because it's just the time
it takes her to touch her space-bar. But look at the pattern
here—big gaps between some groups, then little ones, and
even the spaces between the notes in one group—look at
this one!—vary a bit. Unless you have two-finger typists!'

'Oh my God! Give me a piece of paper, quick!' He
began to make a list of numbers—3, 2, 5, 4, 4, 8, 4, 5, 6.
'That's how it began I think. How many notes are in the
first group?'

'Three. And then 2.5— You've got it, Peter! But what is
it, for heaven's sake?'

'It's a telegram the Ambassador received from London
yesterday afternoon—no, the day before, Tuesday afternoon. I put down the number of letters in each word and
included any stop which followed immediately. For example—' he hesitated; he couldn't mention S.3, presumably—'the series 4, 8, 4 stands for "your telegram one. Full
stop."'

'But I thought you said the cypher telegrams are in five-
letter groups.'

'This wasn't the cypher, Luigi; it was the de-cyphered
message which Sir Watkyn typed out, with his own two
fingers, on his own portable typewriter.'

Luigi stared at him, baffled. 'But why does he have to
type his own telegrams?'

'Thank you for that feed line, Luigi,' said Craig, ruefully.
'The answer is, for security reasons.'

'You're certain it's a portable—not an electric machine?'

'A portable. I've seen it on a small table in his office.'

'Can you borrow it, so that I can examine it?'

Craig thought it over. 'I might, but it'd mean taking
Bracken into our confidence and fetching it at night. The
only other way is for H.E. to say he needs it at the Residence for some reason, and I don't like that either—it'd

attract too much attention.' He looked at Kahn. 'And are
you sure you'd find what you want?'

'I'd find part of it, whatever makes the typewriter emit
those noises—electronically, of course. But the transmitter
may be somewhere else. The only sure way is to get me into
that office, with a lot of apparatus.'

Craig smiled suddenly. 'I'm told you've got the latest
stuff, Luigi.'

'Who told you?' asked Kahn quietly. His dark eyes
looked wary.

'Jo Ashbee. It's all right—you were perfectly correct in
not telling me you were in touch with him. Well, so am I.'

'Why? Is he on this case, too?'

'I'd better explain.' He did so; the intercepted report,
and what had followed.

'I see. So you want the same team who've been following
Zakharov to cover this meeting that Adams is going to
attend this evening. OK.'

'Good. Now back to this damned typewriter. If we
could both get into the Ambassador's office—now, for example—could we take what you want to use in our pockets
and my briefcase?'

The big man thought it out. 'Yes. Thank God, we know
the frequency. But listen, Peter. We can't check properly
unless we use the typewriter. I'll have to send someone to
immobilize the receiver while we're testing.'

'No. There's no need, I think. I've got an idea about
that.'

'And have you also an idea how we're going to get into
Sir Watkyn's office, with half an hour to spare, without
anyone suspecting anything?' He grinned. 'I'm not un-
known in this city, you know.'

'Can you change your appearance—dark glasses, for
example, as a start?'

'Better than that. I have a white wig,' explained Luigi
proudly, 'which I keep in the office for—certain occasions.
It is very distinguished.' He passed his hand, smiling, over
his bald head.

'Splendid! Then I think we can do it. The only snag is going to be His Excellency. I have an idea that he could act a part beautifully, if he wanted to. But will he?'

It was after twelve when Craig went into Janet Ransome's room.

'There's an old friend of H.E.'s sitting in the waiting-room. He's here for the Interpol Conference and he asked me yesterday if he could call on the Ambassador. He's the Chief of Police in Bogota, and they used to know each other well when H.E. was posted there. I spoke to Sir Watkyn yesterday and he said it'd be all right about now. But I'd better brief him first—I know old Suarez wants to lobby him. So if he's free I'll go in.'

She looked doubtful. 'For heaven's sake don't let the Colombian stay long. H.E.'s got a date at a quarter to one.'

'OK. Thanks.' He opened the inner door and cautiously put his head in. 'May I have a word, sir?'

Sir Watkyn looked up from his papers, startled and a little annoyed. Then he beckoned. As soon as Craig had shut the door he said, 'I assume this is something urgent, Craig?'

'It is, sir, very.'

'Sit down then, and make it as quick as you can.'

He was a good listener, and after a horrified gasp, when Craig told him of the discovery of the receiving set concealed in the temple, his face resumed its usual calm expression, with his eyes fixed on the other man's face.

'This—er—charade is the only way you can see of testing your theory, is that it?' There was the trace of a smile on his pale face.

'Yes, sir. The only sure way, if we aren't to lose time. But I'm sorry you will have to play a part in it.'

'I think I can do what you want, my dear fellow,' said His Excellency, and picked up his telephone.

'Mrs Ransome, there's a Doctor Suarez San Martin waiting to see me. Would you bring him in, please? And see that I'm not disturbed for the next half-hour, will you,

I

please? . . . Yes, yes. I won't forget the West German luncheon. Thank you, Mrs Ransome.'

When Luigi was brought in Craig looked at his appearance with satisfaction. The curling white hair, the clothes and the horn-rimmed glasses made him almost unrecognizable. 'My dear Watkyn,' he cried, putting his arm round the shrinking Ambassador, 'how delightful to see you again.'

His Excellency shook his hand warmly and led him to a chair. '*Miguel, amigo, que tal*?' he was saying as Mrs Ransome went out, 'After all these years!'

Craig opened his dispatch case and took out a small plastic box, a variometer and a dry battery, followed by a leather tool kit. Then he arrayed them on the Ambassador's desk and went quickly to the door which led directly on to the corridor, which he locked. He returned to the communicating door and took up his stand with one hand on the knob, watching Luigi.

The big man was still chatting to the Ambassador, who had suddenly seen the humour in the situation and after asking affectionately after several notional children passed smoothly into a discussion of Colombian politics, which left Luigi in trouble. But as he moved across and took the cover off the typewriter he found that Sir Watkyn realized that he knew nothing about Colombia and was phrasing his conversation so that all Luigi had to do was to say 'yes' or 'no' in the obvious places.

He turned back to the instruments which he had adjusted to the expected frequency and began to watch the dials and make minor corrections. He signalled to Craig to help him, and gave him an aerial attached to a long lead, which he took round the room as Luigi indicated. But the fingers on the dials did not move.

'We can stop our pretence, Your Excellency,' said Luigi. 'Unless another frequency is being used—and I haven't time to check completely—our speech is not being monitored. Now would you please type out this on your typewriter, quite slowly, first in small letters and then in capitals. And then again, if I signal.' The Ambassador nodded, and took the paper Luigi gave him over to the typing table.

'Peter, take this antenna and move slowly round the typing table while the machine is being used. And stop when I tell you.' He had put on a pair of headphones which he had taken from his pocket.

As the typewriter began to chatter Kahn exclaimed and held up his thumb. 'Now hold the antenna over the machine. Nearer. *Corpo di Bacco*! That's it. Finish the sentence, sir, and then stop, please.'

Craig went back to his post by the door leading into Janet Ransome's room. Sir Watkyn gave Luigi his chair at the typing table. 'Do you mean that the transmitter itself is in that machine?'

'Yes, sir, I do.' He had lowered the desk lamp and was examining the portable with a magnifying glass. Then he turned it over and shone the light into the complex arrangement of rods and bars. Swearing under his breath he picked up the typewriter and took it over to the desk. 'Please try again, sir. Just once again, slowly.' He called Craig and made him hold the antenna first over the typing table and then again over the machine on the desk, while the Ambassador was obediently typing out his sentence, first in lower case and then with the shift key depressed. 'Enough!' He took the typewriter again to the typing table and adjusted the light.

'It's in the machine somewhere—it must be. I'd thought it might be hidden in one of the legs of the table, but it's not. Let me think. Oh!' He seized the magnifying glass and began to go over the roller inch by inch. With a low cry of triumph he stood up.

'That's where it is, inside the roller, transmitter and battery, and I'll bet the frame is the antenna. Look here, sir.' He handed the Ambassador the glass. 'Look between where I've got my fingers. Now see what happens when I press hard on one side.'

Half-way along the roller Sir Watkyn saw a thin line

forming. 'You mean it screws apart?'

'Yes. That's the transmitter, all right. But how do they modulate the frequency according to which key is struck?' He turned the machine over again and screwed a jeweller's glass into his eye. Then he bent down and examined the ribbon-shift bar that ran across underneath all the key bars. He took the glass out of his eye and said quietly, 'I see how it's done, but it's still the most remarkable piece of electronics I've ever seen.'

The telephone rang. The Ambassador picked up the receiver. 'Yes, Mrs Ransome. Oh, the car's waiting?' Luigi raised his thumb. 'Thank you, Dr Suarez is just leaving.' Craig was rapidly stowing instruments away in his briefcase and pockets. Luigi picked up the rest.

'Have you had this machine cleaned or serviced recently, sir?'

'Good heavens, no. It's a new machine. I only bought it—' He broke off, suddenly realizing the significance of what he had just said. 'Thank God, Craig. Yes, I only bought it a few months ago, but what's more important, it's only been in this office a week.' He laughed suddenly. 'Until then it was used for—orchids.' He smiled at the baffled look on Luigi's face. 'For notes I was making at home for a book I am writing on the *orchis* family. But what I want to know is this. So far as you can see, Mr Kahn, the only microphone in this room is in that machine?'

'Yes, Mr Ambassador, so far as I can tell.'

'And it doesn't record speech—only what I type. But whenever I do type, the Russians know very soon afterwards just what I have written?'

'Yes, sir,' said Craig, wondering what was going on behind that smooth, distinguished face. There seemed to be the light of battle in the dark eyes, and he felt slightly uneasy.

'Good. Just so that I get it straight. Mr Kahn, I'll take another opportunity of expressing my deep gratitude for your help.' He took him by the arm and began to lead him towards the door. Then he stopped suddenly and whispered, with a portentous wink, 'We mustn't forget to play our parts. Craig, I'll see you at half-past three, at the usual place.' Then, raising his voice, 'It's been a great pleasure, Miguel. Don't forget to give my respects to Lucha and your charming daughter.' As he opened the door he put his arm affectionately round Luigi's broad shoulders, '*Y a todos, muy fuertes abrazos!*'

He almost put Luigi off his stroke, but he recovered and spoke the only words of Spanish he knew, '*Muchas gracias, amigo. Adios!*'

Craig spoke to Janet, who was waiting to show the big man out. 'Don't bother, I'll show Dr Suarez to his car.' He led him out and downstairs to the main entrance. The black Mercedes they had hastily hired for the occasion was at the bottom of the steps, with the chauffeur standing by the open door. There was nobody else near.

Craig said quickly, 'We owe you a lot, Luigi, but I've got to think this out. I'll ring you later. I'm leaving the seven-thirty meeting to you, as we arranged.'

'OK, Peter. *Ciao!*' The great car drove smoothly down the curving drive. Its place at the steps was taken by the Ambassador's Rolls, and the driver had barely opened the door when Sir Watkyn appeared on the steps, smiling, with a casual wave of his hand for Craig and looking like a man who hadn't got a care on his mind.

CHAPTER THIRTEEN

THURSDAY AFTERNOON

Craig had a lot of thinking to do. He took a bus back to the Piazza Venezia, walked through the Corso and the Via Tritone to his hotel and had a snack lunch. Then he lay down on his bed and tried to work out his plans. It was nearly three o'clock when the telephone rang.

'*La Signora Adams al telefono, Signor Craig.*'

'*Va bene.*' What on earth did she want, he wondered.

'Peter Craig?'

'Yes, Margaret, what can I do for you?'

'Come and have supper tonight. We've got a few odd bods coming and I thought you might have nothing on. Just a buffet supper, with a lot of plonk. Sorry it's such short notice.'

'I've got a bit tied up, Margaret. I'm so sorry; it was very nice of you to ask me.'

'Do come, Peter. Please.' There was a note of urgency in her voice. Craig sighed. He had to fit in both Luigi and Ashbee some time that day.

'May I leave it open?'

'You may. As long as you come. I—I want to see you again.' She attempted a provocative giggle, but it wasn't very successful.

'OK. What time?'

'Half past eight. As you are, of course. It's mostly University boffins and their birds.'

'Fine. I'll be there.'

When he entered the orchid house the Ambassador was walking up and down, smiling to himself, and glancing at some papers he held in his hand.

'Ah, there you are, Craig. I cut away from the German

Ambassador's early, so that I could think out this extra-ordinary business. And I had a chance of a word with Marchant, who was there, too.' He held up a hand. 'I'll explain later. Now, I know what you're going to ask me, and I can reassure you. The only secret message that type-writer has been used for is this.' He handed Craig the text of the signal they had received from S.3. 'This is the one which corresponds with the groups of notes you heard, isn't it?'

'Yes, sir. But what about the signal we sent—the one I drafted in here last Tuesday afternoon. Didn't you type it?'

'No. Why should I? You had written it out for me and I kept the paper. Here it is.'

'Thank God for that.' He hesitated. 'But don't you use the machine for anything else?'

'No. I bought it to use for my book, but then when Rogers came and told me about this wretched business, and explained that I should have to do the cypher work, I told Mrs Ransome to have it brought to my office. I never draft in longhand, and if I can't dictate I prefer to type. But of course all my letters and notes are usually dictated, either to Mrs Ransome or to my social secretary. So—and this is my point—the only thing the Russians have discovered is that you and Ashbee are working on something together—something obviously very secret, since a special series of cypher telegrams is used for it. But there's nothing in that telegram about a spy, is there? In fact, it looks much more as if it was something which has nothing to do with espion-age at all, since it is you, a police officer, and not my M16 representative, who is to liaise with Ashbee.'

'Yes,' said Craig, 'but—'

'I agree. We mustn't stop the series abruptly. That would arouse suspicion, wouldn't it?'

Craig had the feeling that he was being manoeuvred into position, but he nodded, waiting.

'So, Craig, point one: we must provide an innocuous explanation for what you and Ashbee are supposed to be doing. I mean innocuous in the sense of not hindering the task on which you are so skilfully engaged.'

Flattery, said Craig under his breath, will get you nowhere. 'But what explanation, sir, can possibly fit the facts?'

The Ambassador leaned forward impressively. 'You'll remember that Ashbee acts as liaison officer for both the main American intelligence services—FBI as well as the CIA?'

'Yes, sir.'

'Well, I began to think what very secret matter could be of interest to both you and Ashbee. And I think I've found the answer.' There was a glint in his eye which Craig mistrusted.

'I've been thinking on similar lines, sir,' he said hastily, and with little truth. 'I thought I'd see Ashbee this evening, since of course he is very much involved, and we'd work out a plan together.'

'So you haven't contacted him yet?' There was a trace of relief in Sir Watkyn's voice.

'I could hardly do that without consulting you first. You might have told me that you wanted to stop using the typewriter altogether.'

'Quite right. But I thought—' he coughed—'I thought I would—er—have a go, so to speak.' He went on rapidly, before Craig could interrupt, 'You see, it has to be something which would concern the FBI and also Scotland Yard, as for example a high-ranking diplomat, formerly in London and now here *en poste*, who is suspected of—shall we say drug-running, or smuggling antiques, something like that?'

'It's a bit involved, sir, surely? And why the FBI?'

'Oh, there might be American citizens involved,' said the Ambassador impatiently.

Craig thought it over. 'Well, I suppose that might fit. If this chap had a record with Special Branch in London and began to attract attention to himself here, in some American context, I suppose I might be asked to contact Ashbee and give him the background, the man's methods and so on.

But it's very unlikely.'

'Why?' asked Sir Watkyn sharply.

'Because the whole thing would have been handed over to the FBI people in London. They have a close contact with Special Branch.'

'Oh,' said the Ambassador, a little dashed. Then he rallied. 'But might there be special circumstances, especially if the person concerned were very high in rank, and both the Office and the State Department were interested in getting his activities stopped?'

Craig gave in. 'I agree. But isn't this a purely hypothetical question? I mean, you'd have to have someone in mind who really fitted the bill.'

'I have.'

Craig held his breath.

'The Soviet Ambassador,' said His Excellency calmly.

Craig jumped. 'Are you suggesting, sir, that we should invent a series of telegrams—notional telegrams, merely typed out on your machine—with the deliberate object of smearing—?'

'It would be difficult,' interrupted the Ambassador, 'to make my Soviet colleague appear worse than he is. He is known to the Western Ambassadors as "the Polecat", a name coined by Marchant, who unlike me has had acquaintance with the animal in its native state. He is right in thinking the name very à propos, because not only is Vishinsky of Polish origin but he has all the most unpleasant habits of the cat tribe. But believe me, Craig, the man is a thorn in our flesh. I am quite serious about this. He is a dedicated trouble-maker, and has done his best, to my certain knowledge, to cause an estrangement between my French colleague and me by telling him downright lies— but clever lies—about things I am supposed to have said. Luckily, de Sévigny lost his temper one night and told me, and I was able to straighten the matter out. Then again, the Lebanese and the Egyptian have both begun to avoid me, whereas we were—in all the circumstances—on very reasonable terms until three months ago.'

'Was that when Vishinsky was posted here?'

'No, rather earlier.' The Ambassador paused for effect. 'From London.'

Craig felt himself on a slippery slope. 'But sir,' he protested, 'have you any evidence that he has done anything illegal? After all, telling lies is surely not uncommon among diplomats, when they have a strategic end in view.'

'It's not my kind of diplomacy,' said Sir Watkyn coldly. 'But in fact, yes. When he was in London Vishinsky was very popular among the intellectuals of the revolutionary left, young dons from LSE and so on. He is unmarried and —er—partial to the company of young men.'

'Good God, that too? But it still isn't a crime, sir.'

'It is when you supply them with heroin, and that's what he was suspected of doing. Protocol Department had quite a job hushing it up.'

'But it sounds so extraordinary for a career Soviet diplomat.'

'It is. They usually behave with exemplary correctness in public. But then, he isn't a career diplomat. I meant to look him up in the file, but I've had no time today, since this idea came to me. But I remember that he was a general of some kind before he was posted to London.'

'He must have a hell of a pull with the Kremlin.'

'He has extraordinary liberty of movement, I can tell you that. He goes out at night to nightclubs without any member of his staff with him, so far as one can tell, and there are scandalous stories about the week-end parties he gives at his villa at Castel Fusano. But the point is, Craig, that the man is a menace.' He paused. 'We would all like to be rid of him. So—since the KGB have been kind enough to provide me with my own hot line to the Kremlin, I don't see why I shouldn't use it to get Vishinsky transferred.'

'But we're not alone in this, sir,' Craig protested.

'Don't worry about that, my boy. I've got the Americans solidly behind me.'

'But you *can't* have told Ambassador Marchant already?'

'No, there was no need.' He smiled gently. 'I told you I got him into a corner at the German Ambassador's. I simply said if I could think of a way of getting the Polecat sent home, and perhaps not a very proper way, would he back me up?'

'What did he say?'

'He said he'd double it in spades, whatever that means.'

'And you take *that* as a guarantee that whatever plan you suggest, Mr Marchant will support you?'

'I'm sure of it.' He paused, and added, with meaning, 'And what's more, Craig, he'll insist that Ashbee does the same.'

'And what about me, sir?'

'Nothing at all, my dear fellow. It's not your concern. You're here to catch our spy, and this is a separate issue on which you have no brief.' He let that sink in. 'Except that —it's just occurred to me—if we succeed in getting the KGB very interested in what you and Ashbee are supposed to be doing they might stir up their agent to find out what it is, and perhaps overreach himself.'

'I see,' said Craig slowly. And he did see. The Ambassador was establishing for himself an alibi in advance. If anyone, later, should criticize his private vendetta against Vishinsky he would say it was just a plan to make the Embassy spy show his hand—and so help Craig to catch him. The crafty old fox!

Sir Watkyn was watching his face closely, as he went into his smooth follow-up. 'Let me put it this way, Craig. We want to get the KGB worried, so that they'll force our spy to stick his neck out, as they say. (What a dreadfully sordid business espionage is!) Now I think we can do that and at the same time make things awkward for Vishinsky. And how? What *action* do we have to take? Why, we simply type a few lines on that machine. No need to encode anything, or even *write* anything. I don't even have to put a piece of paper in the machine, so far as I know. Now what is reprehensible in that? Who can object if I strum away on that machine to my heart's content? I'm not *doing* anything.' It was highly suspect pleading, thought Craig, but those mellifluous, persuasive tones could argue the hind leg off a donkey.

'You seem amused, Craig.'

'Not really, sir. I just had for a moment the idea that I was a donkey, and that one of my hind legs was feeling loose.'

His Excellency looked at him in surprise, his lips compressed. Then he suddenly burst into a roar of laughter and leant back in his chair, shaking and using a spotless white handkerchief to mop his eyes. 'I'm glad you're with me in this, Craig.'

'I didn't say— And anyway, sir, what exactly do you suggest we do?'

'Oh, that's all right, my dear fellow; I've already done it.'

'You've what?' cried Craig, feeling the sweat break out on his forehead.

'I typed out a little message to get them interested. Would you like to see it?'

'I would indeed.'

The Ambassador held out the last of the three papers he held in his hand. On it was typed, REES TO S.3. TWO. ACTION TAKEN AS IN YOUR TELEGRAM ONE. ASHBEE INFORMS CRAIG THAT V. HAS ALREADY SHOWN SIGNS OF CONTINUING ACTIVITIES ON LONDON PATTERN. REPORT FOLLOWS BY BAG.

The Ambassador smiled modestly. 'There you are, my boy. That can't do any harm, surely. It will be good for them to worry about it.' He got up from his chair and wandered over to admire a strange plant which had just bloomed. He seemed to be addressing the flower, for Craig only just caught the words. 'I will teach them,' His Excellency was saying, 'to monkey with my typewriter.'

Half an hour later Craig and Ashbee met by appointment in the safe flat in Via Ludovisi. The American listened attentively while Craig explained what had happened. Then he shook his big head, laughing helplessly.

'It looks to me, Peter, as if you can no more control your boss-man than I can mine. Holy Smoke! I hope he hasn't merely succeeded in letting the KGB know that their precious mike is under control.'

'That's what I was so scared of, but I must say he phrased that message neatly, the old fox. Of course, if the KGB have their Ambassador under constant watch, as I suppose they must have, they'll know it's a plant. That's the first thing we've got to find out, Jo, and I'm not sure how, except—and this is why I contacted you right away— they'll become very interested in us from now on.'

'You can say that again, buster. This is the last time we can go any place without having some inquisitive bastard on our tail. But that, at least, is one way of finding out whether they're taking this thing seriously. We both ought to be able to spot if we're being given the treatment.'

'All this on the assumption that Rostov, when he gets that blasted message, which he will any time now, swallows the hook and starts to ask what his boss is up to.'

'He will. If you memorized that text correctly he'll jump to the right conclusion at once. You see, it's quite true what your old man said; Vishinsky was playing some very odd games in London; and it's also true that he goes round by himself here and has gotten some very curious friends, particularly among the younger Arab diplomats. Your respected chief knows his onions. Vishinsky is a special case, and we're still trying to find out why. We *think* he's a GRU general who made his name as an illegal—just like Rostov, incidentally, but for the rival firm. And he has some sort of pull at the top, because when all the GRU top brass were looking over their shoulders after the Penkovsky purge he was sitting pretty. They gave him first the Trade Commission in Ottawa, then London and now Rome.'

'But surely it isn't usual to have an intelligence man as Ambassador in an important post?'

Ashbee stared. 'But it *is* usual. Quite a lot of the best

posts are held by either KGB or GRU men. And I can tell you something else. It isn't only with the Westerns that he's unpopular; his own staff obviously loathe his guts. It's quite evident from the way they scatter when he comes to a reception. I don't suppose your Ambassador knows all this, but there's a touch of genius in that phony message. He's dropped a hornets' nest into the middle of the Soviet Embassy. And Rostov, of all people, is going to react fast.'

'How? By watching us, as you said. But what else? Telling the spy to pull his finger out and find out what's cooking?'

'Precisely, I should think. That report that you're supposed to be sending by the pouch. He'll be told to lay his hands on that for sure.'

'Yes, that's a point. Anything else?'

'If I were Rostov I'd change that little recorder for a relay.'

'It's fitted for that. You can just plug the transmitter in. But why didn't they do it in the first place?'

'Because it's expensive—not in money, that doesn't bother them, but in time and what's more in frequencies. And the personnel who listen. It's quite an operation to keep a frequency serviced full time.' He re-filled Craig's glass. 'I must say, Peter, it was a swell bit of sleuthing to spot that receiver. And Luigi with the mike—Jesus! I'd like to know how that thing operates. He hasn't told you yet?'

'No. But he seemed to understand how it worked. And he was very much impressed.'

'I should say he was. It's new to me, and some time, Peter, I want to know the method.'

'I'll tell Luigi to explain it to you.'

'Jesus wept, boy! You can't do that. It's a Service secret. Old Gobbo would have your guts for garters.'

'I'm not in his bloody Service.'

'Well, well! I do believe you're not.'

'Oh, come off it, Jo! Let's get back to our spy. How do we force him out of cover? If Rostov reacts as you said the spy'll be told to stop that report getting into the bag, or read it first. And the bag is closed tomorrow evening and kept in the Chancery strongroom until Saturday morning, when the QM picks it up on his way to the airport.'

'What's that—QM?'

'The Queen's Messenger. But how do we know Rostov will guess right? The message only mentioned "V". We could of course dot the "i's" by sending another phony message.'

'Compound Sir Watkyn's felony and go one better?'

'I suppose so. I want action.'

'Oh boy, you're going to get it soon enough. But I'll go along with you. Listen. Let them know you're sending a tape-recording, say of a conversation between Ambassador Vishinsky and somebody else.'

'Supplied by you.'

'Heh, what's that?'

'You're the chap who's supposed to be supplying information about the erring Vishinsky. But why a recording? Why not a report?'

'First, it's direct, concrete evidence. His master's voice, all ready to be sent to Moscow. Rostov will be climbing the walls to get his hands on it. Second, you can undo an envelope and copy a report, but you can't do much with a tape-cassette, unless you take your little recorder along with you.'

'Christ! You're a genius, Jo. Wait a moment.' He began to write on a sheet from his notebook. 'What about this?'

Ashbee looked at the signal. 'REES TO S.3. THREE. FURTHER TO MY TELEGRAM TWO. TAPE-CASSETTE OF CONVERSATION BETWEEN VISHINSKY AND CONTACT WILL BE SUPPLIED TO CRAIG BY ASHBEE TOMORROW MORNING AND SENT BY BAG. 'Yes,' he said, 'that'd do it. You'd send this off now?'

'To the KGB, yes. Not to London. God forbid.'

'Haven't you told them yet?'

'No. I'd sketched out a telegram, reporting everything

that had been happening, but when I gave it to H.E. he
shook his head with well-feigned regret and said he simply
hadn't got time to en-cypher it until tomorrow.'

'But he'll type this out on his little typewriter—he'll find
time for that?'

'Try and stop him!'

'How are you going to nab the spy when he gets at that
notional tape?'

'I'll think of something. But I think we'll have to play
this thing out, Jo. Can you receive me at your Embassy
and hand me something that will look like it?'

'Yes, of course.' He looked across at Craig. 'You don't
look your usual sunny self, Peter.'

'It's this ruddy espionage business. It keeps dragging you
in deeper. And it's all shadow-boxing. You never see the
other chap.'

Ashbee leaned back comfortably in his chair and dis-
coursed on the subject. 'I've been doing this job, man and
boy, for nigh on thirty years and I hope I haven't lost my
sense of values. They're the worse for wear, like some of
my other attributes, but still operating. Listen, boy. In
these counter-intelligence capers, you *never* know the whole
truth, which to you dicks is the breath of life. You get
glimpses, and so does the other side. You both draw conclusions—just what we're trying to make Rostov do now
—and half the time they're wrong. *You may both be
wrong*, but you both go on building your card houses and
when they fall down you start again. Same cards, different
houses. Or put it this way. It's like two men in the dark.
You know the other feller is there and you've got to get
him, and you move around with your arms outstretched
and try one place after another and find sweet nothing.
You're just saying "Where the heck *is* that bastard? Does
he exist?" when your fingers touch. And then suddenly
everything is real and what you have to do is knee him in
the crotch as a starter.'

'It sounds fine,' said Craig morosely, 'except that Rostov
and Zakharov have diplomatic status, so all you can say is

"Hullo, old boy. Fancy meeting you here." The whole thing becomes a farce when you can't haul him in front of a magistrate. But if we were on our own I wouldn't give a hoot, all the same. It's having the Ambassador in on the scene that scares me. He's suddenly started to treat the whole thing as a sort of game, and at any moment he'll have another bright idea and ball up everything. But anyway, that's my problem, and of course you're right and it's a swell idea you've given me. I know we've got to theorize and probe or we get nowhere. But wouldn't I just like to get my hands on one little KGB officer, or better, one British spy.'

'You will, feller, if you play it this way. You'll get action all right.'

'OK, Jo. If I come round to your Embassy at about ten tomorrow morning and send my name up—there's no need for me to go to your office—can you send someone to the reception desk with a packet that looks as if it might contain a tape-cassette?'

'One of my girls will come down with a small flat package marked Top Secret clutched in her tiny hand and make you sign a receipt for it. That'll make the man tailing you all excited, and from then on you'd better watch out.' He grinned. 'You said you'd like to try these cheroots of mine. Packet of ten will fill the package nicely.'

'Thanks. I'll have a real tape, of course, to put in the envelope I hand in for sending off by bag, just in case anybody opens it. But I can't fake a conversation in Russian between Vishinsky and his notional contact, so I've got to make bloody sure it never leaves the Embassy.'

'Good luck then, and for God's sake be careful once you've got that packet of cigars. I take it you're going to get this second message typed out on Sir Watkyn's machine right away?'

'Yes. I'll go to the Embassy as soon as I leave here.'

'Then sometime tonight they'll have it, and they'll be itching to part you from that packet, one way or another— and if I know Rostov he'll be so keen he might get rough.

K

Wait a moment. Durned if I let you go it alone. I'll tell you what we'll do; if they start anything they'll get a little surprise.'

When he got to the Embassy he went up to the Chancery floor and along the passage, past Janet's door, and listened outside the door which led directly into the Ambassador's room. There was no sound of dictation and he opened the door cautiously and stepped inside. Sir Watkyn was reading a dispatch prepared for the outgoing bag. He saw Craig and beckoned.

'I've been talking to Ashbee, sir. He agrees that as we have—er—burnt our boats we had better go one step further and try to force the other side to show their hand.' He held out the message he had written out in the safe flat.

'That's good,' said the Ambassador approvingly. 'That leaves it nicely vague but spells out the subject of the enquiry. You want to hurry them up?'

'Yes, sir.'

'Well, as I don't have to do the encoding I suggest you add two sentences. IN MY VIEW THIS EVIDENCE JUSTIFIES APPROACH TO THE ITALIANS. PLEASE COMMENT URGENTLY. How's that?'

Craig looked at him with respect. 'That's a stroke of genius, sir.'

'You have made plans in this connection?'

'Yes. Ashbee's being very helpful.'

'I think I'd better not ask more. So all you want me to do is type this out?'

'Yes, sir. The sooner the better. But then I'm afraid you'll have to send two real signals to S.3.'

The Ambassador's face fell. 'That's rather a bore. I've got a lot still to do. And why two?'

'To correspond to the two notional signals you'll have sent—this one and the earlier message you typed out early this afternoon. It's just in case the spy—whoever it is— might know when you send a telegram in your special series.'

'Oh dear! How involved it all is. Are these the messages?'

'Yes, sir. As you see I've merely reported the finding of the receiver and the transmitter, and that with your agreement we have sent two phoney messages—corresponding to the two halves of this signal—so that the Russians do not realize that we have discovered their penetration.'

'Let me have a look. Yes—yes, that's very clear and short. And I see—' he glanced at Craig's face—'that you haven't mentioned what our notional series is about.'

'I can do so if you wish, sir, but I felt that was for you to do if you felt it necessary.'

'No,' said the Ambassador hastily, 'you're quite right.' He paused, and went on with a touch of severity in his voice. 'I don't want you to think, Craig, that I'm trying to conceal my little plan from the Office. I have every intention of reporting to them in detail, but it is impossible to summarize in a telegram—especially one I have to encypher myself—the case my colleagues and I have against this obnoxious man. Moreover,' he added with a sudden, impish grin, 'I wouldn't want poor Rogers to have a heart attack. If the plan works everybody will be so relieved that the little matter of a slanderous attack on the good name of my Soviet colleague will be forgotten.'

'And it's hardly slanderous, is it, when it isn't—strictly speaking—uttered?' Craig could not resist giving him that idea to play with. The Ambassador snapped it up.

'Exactly. How well you put it, Craig. A slander must be uttered. If it isn't uttered it isn't slander. I confess that I have been having second thoughts about my rather—well —impulsive action this afternoon. It's all rather new to me, this business which the Russians call *disinformatsiya*. It— er—tends to go to one's head, I find. But now that I see that you and Ashbee are solidly behind me I agree that we go on with it—always, of course, with the main object of forcing the enemy to show his hand. Otherwise I would never agree with this message which I will now send out on my hot line to the KGB.' He got up and walked eagerly towards the typing table. 'And naturally, my dear fellow,' he concluded, giving the machine a friendly pat, 'when the spy is caught we can always send a last message—nothing rude, mind you, but simply putting the whole thing right.' He paused. 'But only, of course, when they've recalled Vishinsky. We want to down both birds with our stone.'

'It's a bit early to think of that, sir. We first have to catch our spy. And now I'm afraid I have some rather disquieting news for you about Adams.'

CHAPTER FOURTEEN

THURSDAY EVENING

It was nearly six o'clock when he got back to his room. He rang an RCMP colleague who sat next to him at the Interpol meetings.

'Hullo, Peter,' said the Canadian. 'What have you been up to? I made excuses for you this morning, saying I'd heard you were sick—which was the message you sent me, you bastard—but when I rang the Eden they told me you'd been out all day. What's cooking?'

'Listen, Wally, I had no time to explain, but I'm taking off tomorrow as well. Be a pal and pinch-hit for me, will you? I'll explain next time I can get you alone. Just take any notes that I ought to know about and let me see your notebook for the rest of the stuff. Will you do that?'

'Willco. But goddammit, only if you let me have a look at her next week, when the first fine rapture has worn off. For land's sake, she must be a peach if the nights aren't enough for you.'

'This is duty, Wal.'

'That's what I always say. OK, Peter, I'm on.'

The more Craig thought it over, the more vital it seemed to know whether Neil Adams had been in Janet Ransome's house when the photograph had been taken. Things had begun to happen since that moment—not ten hours before —when he had seen the marks in the dewy grass by the little temple, and he had a strong feeling that they were going to happen in accelerated tempo as time went on.

And there was one thing he ought to know, and didn't. He looked at his watch again; three-quarters of an hour before the office closed. There was still time to have a sniff round. He took up his papers and walked down the passage towards Janet's room. He could hear her typing steadily and turned round. Diana's door was open and through it he could see her feeding the destructor; he dropped his papers on her desk, calling out above the noise of the shredder, 'Put those away for me, will you, sweetie?' and ran out before she could reply. So both of them were in the office and unlikely to get away before seven o'clock. As he passed the reception desk in the hall he asked one of the guards to telephone for a taxi to pick him up at the gate.

Number thirty-seven, Via Mangili, was an old house, standing back from the road and surrounded by trees and a formal garden of gravel paths and tall shrubs. The short drive divided, part leading to the stucco portico that covered the front door and a branch turning off to go along the side of the house towards the rear garden. There appeared to be nobody about and the windows were all shuttered—on the ground floor presumably because the flat was empty, and above, where Janet and her mother had their own flat, against the rays of the westering sun. The entrance door was closed, but it was worth trying, and he walked along the drive to the portico and turned the handle. The door opened.

The hall inside was square, with a broad tiled staircase leading upwards. Presumably the upstairs flat had its own front door, corresponding to the walnut door with a brass knocker and bell which Craig saw in the hall below. He also saw, to his regret, a Chubb keyhole beside a little brass frame which contained a visiting card: 'Michele Antonucci'. He rang the bell.

If anybody had answered he had intended to act dumb and ask for Lady Balcombe, but there was no sound from inside the flat. So far, so good, but he knew that he hadn't a hope of getting past the Chubb lock. Even if he'd had a piece of stiff mica, the burglar's friend, it was no use against a mortice deadlock. He walked out of the entrance, stood listening under the portico for a moment to make sure that nobody was stirring, and went along the branch drive to the back of the house.

The first floor had a terrace which jutted out from the house over a fair-sized double garage and a small annexe which had probably been built on to the ground floor flat when the conversion took place. The annexe was shorter than the garage and had a rear entrance door under the overhang of the terrace, and a shuttered window. Craig went slowly past the closed garage door and tried the handle of the door in the annexe, but it was locked. Then he had a look at the shutters.

They were made of softwood, visible in places where the paint had blistered off, and swung on hinges sunk in the wall. He thought for a moment that he could lift one of the shutters clean off, but then he saw that they were secured together on the inside by an iron rod with curved spurs which, when the rod was rotated, squeezed through iron rings at top and bottom of the shutters. It is the traditional method of securing *persiani*, and short of sawing through the woodwork or using a long jemmy there's not much you can do about it. And Craig had no wish to leave traces. He went back to the door.

It had a simple Yale-type lock, but when he pushed gently at the lower edge of the door he met at once with resistance. It was bolted. He sighed, half in relief. At least he had tried, and could get away before anybody saw him. And then he heard, faintly through the closed door, the sounds of somebody moving about inside. He put his ear tight against the door panel.

Whoever it was must have just arrived, and he wasn't bothering to keep quiet. He seemed to be dumping things on the floor of a passage near the back door. Then he went away and there was a sound of water running into a can. More steps on the stone flags of the passage, but this time they were approaching closer to the door and Craig retreated fast round the corner of the annexe. As he went he heard the bolts being slid back, one after the other, and then the sound of the door opening, and a man's steps on the gravel. Craig breathed again. The steps were going away from him towards the garage door, and a moment later he heard it being opened.

It was just as well that Craig's Scottish caution asserted itself and he remained flattened against the side wall of the annexe, because the man came back from the garage, and began to pick up the things he had dumped inside the rear door. When he could again be heard walking towards the garage Craig took a quick look round his corner.

He looked like an Italian, wearing overalls and carrying on his head a mortar board on which he had balanced four bricks and a small bag of cement. He had opened the nearer garage door wide and disappeared behind it. Craig still waited. The man returned once more to the annexe and came back with his bag of tools. There was a pause, and then came the unmistakable ring of a cold chisel. Craig turned the corner and walked quietly, on the sides of his shoes, through the rear door and into the house.

It was at once clear that the annexe had been built to include a bathroom and kitchen among the amenities of the ground-floor flat, and the shuttered window gave light to the bathroom. A passage led past both rooms and widened out when it entered the main building, where it ran through towards the front of the house until it was closed by the walnut door which he had seen from the other side. On the left were two doors, the first open and giving on to a bedroom. The sound of hammering was louder now, but still muffled, and he risked stepping into the bedroom. Opposite him was a large iron bedstead, covered with a dust sheet on which lay a picture with a frame of what looked like mirror-glass. Craig looked quickly at the wall to his left—the rear wall of the house which also formed the back of the garage. There was a big unfaded patch on the wallpaper where the picture had hung. And as he watched, there was a splutter of breaking plaster and on the edge of the patch a long crack appeared. And then he saw it, a neat round hole, quite near the crack and just where the glass frame would have covered it. By this time Craig was retreating behind the door. He had no intention of finding himself staring into the eyes of the workman who had been attacking the wall from the garage side.

He took a last look round at what he could see from behind the door and there, sure enough, neatly laid out on a table was a piece of matching wallpaper, a pair of scissors and a pot of paste.

He went into the front room, which was pleasantly furnished, in good taste, as a living-room. He went about his search with professional skill, going for the obvious hiding places first. But the drawers in the desk were empty and all measured the same. The thick leather cushions of the sofa held no secrets and there was nothing behind the pictures in this room. He went back to the door and listened, but the sounds still came from beyond the bedroom. On the other side of the passage was a formal dining-room and it was here, strapped to the underside of the sideboard with sticky tape, that he found what he had hoped for—a large black envelope. He lay on the floor, eased it open and extracted a sheet of plain white paper. He crept back to the passage, listened and then went softly along to the walnut door. It wasn't worth risking any further delay. The typewriter was hidden somewhere, no doubt, but under the floor or in a secret compartment in one of the walls. He folded the paper as he went and put it away.

He opened the walnut door and found himself again in the square hall with the entrance in front of him. He looked at his watch, and smiled. Within twenty minutes Janet would probably come in that way—or Diana. Or both. But he wouldn't give them the pleasure of entertaining him. Not just yet. Luigi's flat was within easy walking distance.

Craig was saying, 'I think what they had done was to make a square hole through into the bedroom from the garage— fill it on the bedroom side with a piece of plaster board with a hole in it through which the camera could have been sighted on the bed. The chap I saw today must have been removing the camera and patching up.'

'Wide-angle lens,' said Luigi, 'with robot gear so that all

they needed was a means of triggering it off. But anybody
might have seen the inside of the garage, so they bricked it
up on that side—one skin of bricks only—and, yes, a nail.
A nail apparently stuck in the wall, but when you pushed it
it triggered off the robot as many times as you needed.'

'But the lighting in the bedroom? The girl must have
known.'

'Not essentially, if the meetings—on the bed, that is—
took place in the afternoon. With the *persiani* half open
there'd be enough light.'

'What about the mirror-frame? Doesn't it stop a lot of
light?'

'Not with these new high-speed films. But going back to
my point. Even if the girl knew she was being photographed, it doesn't necessarily follow that she is your spy.'

'That's what I'm still hoping. You mean, the so-called
Milanese businessman might have had a fancy for taking
clandestine photographs of people using his room while he
was away? But how would he know?'

'No. I mean that the Russians could have got Adams
hooked on some quite different floozy, and just happened
to use that flat because the Milanese is in their pay.'

'It's no good, Luigi, although I'd like to think so. Look
at this.' He took the piece of white paper from his pocket,
wet his finger and tested both sides. 'On this side it's sticky.
I'll bet anything it's photographic paper.'

'Let me smell it.' Luigi licked the paper thoroughly and
then smelt it. He looked up. 'Yes, that's what it is. What's
the significance of this?'

'The spy in the Embassy uses that sort of document paper
for copying secret reports. So the spy's using that flat. So
the spy is one of those two girls.'

'That's what you thought already.'

'Yes. But this at least is a little bit of fact, not conjecture,
and it's what I want to put the screw on Adams.'

'If Adams does what he's expected to do in—' he looked
at his watch—'half an hour, you'll have all the evidence
you need to do that.'

'I suppose so. But the more I get the better. If I go for him and can't get him to reveal the girl's name, *and* all that's happened between them, he'll tip her off and she'll run for it. And I want her under arrest inside Embassy territory and with enough evidence to get her served with an extradition order. It's still damned tricky, Luigi.'

'You feel certain it's Miss Warren.'

'I can't get over the fact that Janet Ransome looks more like it. No one could have substituted the roller in the Ambassador's machine more easily.'

'*Porca miseria*, it wasn't just the roller. I told you it was something very special, didn't I? Well, this is what they did. Wait a moment while I get a portable.' He came back a moment later carrying an Adler portable typewriter. He turned it upside down and sat down with it on his lap. 'This is the same make as the Ambassador's. Now, you see that bar which runs across underneath the key-rods? Every time you depress a key you do several things at once. If all you did was to operate the striker you wouldn't make any mark on the paper, because the ribbon wouldn't be in the way of the type. So one thing the key rod does is to push down on that bar—like so—and the bar makes the ribbon pop up so that the striker hits through it at the paper. Whichever key you strike—even if it's only a full-stop— you make contact with that bar and push it down. That's how it's done.'

Craig stared at him. 'But how? The action on the bar's the same, whichever key you hit.'

'On the bar, yes. But not on what's inside the bar. I could only just see the contacts when I was looking for them with a jeweller's glass and the light full on. Hidden on the upper side of the bar, where the key-rods press down on it, are a series of tiny spring contacts, one for each key. And inside that bar, which is only about six millimetres in diameter, there must be some device which modulates the tone of the transmission differently, according to which contact is touched. Imagine, if you like, that there's a coiled resistance inside the ribbon-shiftbar. Then if you hit, say, a "K" you make contact with the coil at one end of the resistance and there's very little impedance. Strike a "Q", at the other end of the key-board, and you get a lot. That probably isn't how it's done, but you get the idea.'

'But you've still got to get your current back to the transmitter, which you said was in the roller. You'd have seen the wires.'

Luigi smiled. 'That isn't as difficult as you might think. It's a trick I've used many times, and it's a test of fine workmanship. You could pass the current through the frame to the two ends of the roller, which are insulated from each other, of course, because the roller's made of rubber. You use a little abrasive wheel, at high speed, and you cut a channel through the paint and the iron of the frame, just like chasing a groove in a brick wall to lay a power-cable. Then you lay your insulated wire in the channel, fill up with plastic padding and re-spray. Done properly, you'd see nothing at all, and it was only because we *knew* that Sir Watkyn's machine was itself operating a transmitter that I found the answer. That typewriter could be cleaned half a dozen times by a competent mechanic and he'd neither see anything amiss with it nor do any harm to the transmitter. He could take the roller out and never notice the minute contacts in the bearing at each end. And of course, that's how they'd change the battery—once every six months would be enough. A girl could do it without any difficulty, once she was shown how.'

'She could change the roller, I grant you, but what about all this other work on the machine, before they got it into operation. How long would that take?'

'The KGB have probably prepared a number of machines in this way, and this Adler portable is very common. They substituted it for the real one, I expect—changed the identification markings, even the colour, if necessary—all that could be done in a lunchtime.'

'That brings me back to where we started—the person who could most easily make the switch is Mrs Ransome, not Diana. And Janet's the one person we thought we could

eliminate for certain. Listen, Luigi, there's one way I might
be able to find out which of the two girls it was, without
depending on the unpredictable Adams. Are you in contact with Il Gobbo direct?'

The big man looked at him warily. 'Why d'you want to
know?'

'Because I want to get a message through to him without
the Ambassador knowing. He'd have a fit if he saw what I
want to know.' He saw Luigi hesitating and went on, 'It
may be something I'm not supposed to know, but it's vital
for me to get this information, and after all it's in Gobbo's
interest, too. You wouldn't be his special agent here unless
you had some emergency way of getting in touch with
him. Well, have you?'

'Yes. He'll probably give me hell, but it's his fault for not
telling you himself. How long is the message?'

'Twenty words. *En clair*, of course. You'd have to encode
it.'

'No, there's no need.'

'What d'you mean? I don't want the Russkies to get it.'

'They won't. Your message will be on the air for about
three seconds only.' He got to his feet. 'You'll have to
excuse me for a moment while I send a cable. Then, in
three hours, I'll be in contact direct. There's a quicker way
still, but this is safer.' He went out of the room, and Craig
began to write out his telegram.

When Kahn came back he took the sheet of paper,
glancing at it idly. Then he looked at Craig with a broad
grin on his face. 'Scraping the bottom of the possibilities
barrel, aren't you, Peter?'

'Yes. That's just what it is. How d'you send it off? The
Krogers' method?'

'What was that?'

'That's how they sent their regular signals to Moscow.
Recorded them in code on tape, got radio contact and then
ran it through at top speed.'

'Yes, that's how we do it. But very fast. Unless the other
side is expecting something on my wavelength they can't

possibly intercept it. But I can encode it if you wish. I've
got a one-time pad.'

'I think it might be better, if you don't mind. It gives the
whole game away, and I'm not ready for them yet.'

'OK. It's after half-past seven, Peter. We'd better see
what's happening.' He walked across to a big transceiver
and switched it on. There was no sound from the loudspeaker.

'Did you get anything interesting from the surveillance
team at lunchtime?' asked Craig.

'No. Both reports negative. Adams and Warren just went
home for lunch and returned to the Embassy at the usual
time. Incidentally, the other watchers—the men I put in
the Via Statilia to keep an eye on the gate to the temple—
they've reported nothing either. I expect the KGB will
monitor the receiver after dark.'

'Let me know, will you?' Craig grinned. 'My personal
security is involved.' He explained the events of the afternoon.

Luigi roared with laughter. 'I thought Sir Watkyn was
beginning to show talent for the game,' he said, wiping his
eyes, 'but I never guessed he'd think up a dirty trick like
that.'

'It was the invasion of his privacy that did it, and now
there's no stopping him. I'm scared to think what he'll do
next. But at least we've followed up his initiative, as I told
you, and we hope for some action tomorrow.'

'I don't like it, Peter. They're professionals.'

Craig exploded. 'What the hell d'you think I am? I
know I'm spending all my time running round to you and
Jo Ashbee, asking for help. But when it comes to a straight
security matter I can look after myself.' Kahn said nothing.
'I'm sorry,' said Craig, 'I'm acting like a prima donna. But
I want action, not all this sparring in the air.'

'From a man who's just pulled off an inside job in Via
Mangili,' said Luigi mildly, 'that's a strange remark.' The
loudspeaker bleeped and he picked up a microphone.
'*Pronto*!'

The voice from the loudspeaker spoke fast, in Italian. 'Contact established as expected. I repeat, as expected. Number Two will telephone details in five minutes. Any instructions, *padrone*?'

'No. Maintain supervision and report direct when contact is broken.'

'So it was Zakharov?' asked Craig.

'Yes.' He looked at his watch. 'They seem to be having a long conversation. Anything else, Peter, while we're waiting?'

'Could you lend me a small tape-recorder—a Grundig if you've got one, and a couple of cassettes?'

'Of course. When d'you want them, now?'

'Please.' As Luigi went towards the door the telephone rang and he picked up the receiver and listened intently. He hung up and came back to sit beside Craig.

'I'll get the recorder later. This is very odd, Peter. Adams and Zakharov met under one of the arches of the Colosseum, the Russian arriving five minutes late, which is quite usual. He wanted to make sure that Adams was there—alone, and unobserved. My men had to keep well in the background, sitting in a car, but one of them has night binoculars and although it was dark under the arch he could see the expression on Adams's face clearly. He says the man was wild with rage and made some attempt to get his hands on Zakharov, who just pushed him back against the wall and began to talk to him. Then they walked to a bench and sat down. We could not use our long-range eavesdropper because too many people were passing by, but we can reconstruct to some extent what happened. The KGB man succeeded in pacifying Adams without much difficulty.'

'He's got no guts,' said Craig disgustedly.

'Remember that Zakharov is a professional. He saw Adams on the point of ruining everything, so what would he do? I think he told Adams that he himself had had nothing to do with the taking of the photograph. Somebody else had done it—perhaps someone who made a habit of doing this sort of thing, spying on lovers and taking photographs—and Zakharov had persuaded him to hand over the photographs he had made and the negative.'

'How d'you work all that out?'

'Because the point came when Zakharov pulled out of his pocket some papers, let Adams have a good look at them, and then tore them up and handed him the pieces. It wasn't possible to see if there was a negative, but there probably was. It's as easy to keep a copy of a negative as of a print.'

'But Adams couldn't have believed all that cock, surely?'

'It's almost unbelievable what people will swallow when they're in a tough spot and can't see any way out. Anyhow, they went on talking, with Zakharov apparently putting a point of view—he was gesticulating and talking rapidly, they could see that—and it all became quite friendly. When they parted ten minutes ago—they shook hands.'

'God Almighty!' He was still staring at Luigi in sheer unbelief when Maria came into the room with a tray of drinks.

'I told Michele not to disturb you,' she explained, 'but you look as if you need something to drink now. Especially Peter. Whatever have you been saying to him, Luigi? I won't have him upset. He's my friend.' She put down the tray and mixed Craig a whisky, and went over to him with it, cooing amiably. Craig put his arm round her plump shoulders. 'Thank God, for you two at least. Your husband's a great man, Maria.'

'He's just fat, but I love him all the same. What's he been saying to you?'

'Just telling me that one of our people here is either the biggest fool it's been my misfortune to meet—or a traitor.'

'I rather doubt,' said Luigi wryly, 'whether Zakharov told Adams he was a Russian. But I'm sure he arranged to meet him again and found some reason why it should be in secret.'

'But there you are—any man who'll buy that sort of talk is a plain bloody fool.' He looked at his watch and finished his drink. 'Bless you, Maria. I needed that. I'm just going round to that man's house as his guest,' he added grimly.

Maria smiled at him. 'It's not your world, is it, Peter?'

'No, *carina*, it isn't. I don't want any part of it.'

Craig went back to the Eden to shave and change his shirt, and by the time he arrived at the party it was going well. Margaret came swishing up to him in her long dress and linked her arm through his. Her pretty face was flushed, and her eyes sparkling with excitement. 'I'm *so* glad you could come after all. Fred! Where's Fred? He's got the *negrones*. Oh, there he is.' Fred came up slowly, carrying a tray of the dark-coloured cocktails with great care and concentration, his dressing-gown cord trailing behind him. 'There! Now come and meet everybody. They're all here except the Partridges, and they're always late. Diana you know, of course, and this is Professor Lucchesi of the Faculty of Industrial Chemistry, Signora Lucchesi, Doctor Benfatti, reader in physics—is that right, Marco?—and Signorina Bianchi. Yes, well, that'll do to start with. This is Mr Peter Craig, a police officer.' She seemed cheerful enough today, thought Craig.

'*La polizia! Che orrore!*' cried Signora Lucchesi, a little woman in tight-fitting black satin. She pretended to hide behind her husband's back.

'*Che bambina!*' said the Professor, fondly. 'Are you here for the Interpol Conference, Mr Craig?'

'Yes. It's not often that we can meet in a place where we can enjoy ourselves so much after the conferences. You Romans are so hospitable.'

'We are not very fond of the police here,' said Signorina Bianchi sombrely.

'You must have something on your conscience, Signorina.'

That got him a laugh, and the next moment the long-haired young Benfatti began to talk to him earnestly about the importance, for the future of nuclear research, of Britain's entry into the Common Market. It was some time before Craig could get away.

L

Diana waved to him. Like most of the women she was
wearing a long skirt, but hers was slit at the sides to give an
entrancing sight of her slender legs. With her fair hair falling over her bare shoulders she looked delectable, and the
men were crowding near like bees round a pot of honey.
She made Craig join them.

'This is Peter Craig, visiting us from Scotland Yard, to
see that we're behaving. He hasn't made any arrests yet.' It
was impossible to tell what was going on behind that lovely,
animated face. She seemed completely assured, accepting
the admiration of the men as of right. 'Oh, there's the
Partridges. Joan dear, I don't think you've met Peter Craig
yet. Hullo, Douglas.' The blue eyes of the Major of Royal
Marines bulged slightly as he looked at her. He said
nothing.

A voice came from behind Craig's back. 'You're looking
beautiful, Diana.' A high-pitched voice with flat Yorkshire
vowels.

'Thank you, Neil. It's a lovely party.' She looked at him
for a moment with that wide, assured smile, and turned
away to talk to Joan Partridge.

Craig felt a sudden sick ache in his stomach. It was in-
decent to imagine those two locked together in a dirty
photograph. And what possible reason could the girl have
to be a spy? He turned after Adams and caught him as he
made his rounds with a bottle of Italian champagne.

'It's nice of you to ask me here, Neil. I thought we
weren't on speaking terms.'

'It was Maggie's idea, chum, but you're welcome. Put
that sweet sticky stuff down and I'll give you some of this.'
Their eyes met as Adams filled the glass. 'I'm afraid I was
bloody rude, Peter. I know you were only doing your job.'

'You look happier now, anyway,' said Craig lightly. 'I
didn't mean to pry, ' he added, lying, 'but I got the feeling
you were in a spot. Let's forget it.'

Adams gave him his sudden, flashing, infectious smile.
'I'm always getting into spots. But I get out of them. Now,
if you want to help, go and prise Douglas loose from Diana.

He'll eat the girl if he gets any hungrier, and I don't think Joan would like that.' He frowned. 'She's looking as sour as hell already. I'll go and chat her up.'

Diana didn't seemed bored with the gallant major. Her face was close to his and she was talking to him in a low voice. His back was as straight as a ramrod and he was sweating. Craig barged in on them regardless, and took Partridge off, unwilling, to talk about the Carabinieri Academy which the Interpol delegates were due to visit the following week. The man answered politely, but when Diana passed them on her way to join some friends his eyes followed her lithe body, fascinated, through the crowded room.

'Come on, you two. Grab some birds and give them food. Peter, you can have the Bianchi.' It was Maggie.

'She doesn't like policemen; she'd probably choke.'

'Then Douglas, would you please? And Peter, can you get me some of my own curry and a glass of plonk?' She looked around. 'I'll join you in a moment. Get a couple of places on the terrace before everybody else does.'

He went to the long table on which food had been laid out and took two plates of curry, added chutney, rice and poppadums, and took them out of the hot room into the cooler atmosphere of the terrace. It was lit rather attractively by candles in green glass shades and over the parapet the breeze blew fresh from the trees of the Borghese Gardens down below. He found an empty cane sofa and planked down the two plates to establish a claim, and then went back for wine. Adams was behind the improvised bar, his face flushed, pouring wine and keeping up a flow of banter in idiomatic Italian. He looked positively happy. Poor stupid sod, thought Craig, he really thinks he's in the clear.

Rostov was enjoying himself. He had set Zakharov a problem and told him to work it out and report back as quickly as possible. His cigar was drawing well and he was reading a spy story, which gave him great amusement. It was long after closing hours and his busy telephone was quiet. There was a timid knock at the door and he dropped the novel into a drawer, and picked up a report before he called.

Zakharov was white-faced. 'I am unable to understand this message, Comrade.' He hesitated and then went on, 'I cannot understand why the British Ambassador should type such nonsense on his machine. But you said there was a serious significance which you perceived in the message and pointed out that foxes are usually red. I confess failure.'

'Read me the message, Sasha.'

'It says—' his voice faltered—'it says, "The quick brown fox jumps over the lazy dog." Then it's repeated in capitals. And then all over again, several times.'

'And you actually tell me that you see no significance in the choice of those words?'

'No, Comrade.'

'Look at them carefully, Alexei Ivanovich, and you will see that every single letter in the English alphabet occurs in the sentence at least once. Hence "brown", not "red".'

'Someone was testing the typewriter, then. That's why it was repeated in the upper case. I thought it might be that, although I did not check the incidence of the letters. But what is the serious significance in that, Sergei Pavlich? It could be that an Embassy mechanic was checking to see if the type needed cleaning. Or he had cleaned them and checked afterwards. You don't think he could have discovered—?'

'No, I don't. The join in the roller would pass any routine examination.'

'But then, what is the serious significance, Comrade?' The young man's face was red with suppressed rage.

'None that I know of,' said Rostov genially. 'It was a little test for you, Sasha. You are an English-speaking officer and this is something you should have known, even if you didn't take the elementary step of checking the incidence of the letters. That is all.' He drew on his cigar and exhaled, looking at the other's face through the smoke, challenging him to protest.

There was a knock at the door and a man came in hurriedly. He was very pale. It was the duty officer serving the computer in the technical section. He held out a paper, without speaking.

Rostov read it through, his grey eyes half-closed and his face expressionless. 'This is the third message, the one you were beginning to decode when the computer failed?'

'Yes, Comrade. We only succeeded in getting it to work a few minutes ago, and I at once fed in the tape.'

'Has anyone else seen this?'

'No, Comrade. I was able to destroy the copy before anyone else saw it.'

'You did right, Pavel. You will not speak to anybody at all about the contents of this signal. Otherwise you will be responsible to me for any—leakage. Do you understand?' The technician nodded, speechless. 'All right. You may go.' The man hurried out of the room.

'He said the *third* message,' said Zakharov sullenly. 'I only know of one received today.'

'After the typewriter was tested with the amusing sentence about the brown fox it was used for two signals some time today. The first was decoded before the computer broke down and the Senior Technical Officer decided that the message should be seen by my eyes only, since in the absence of the Legal Resident on leave I am in charge of this *Rezidentsiya*. You see, my dear Sasha, he thought— and quite rightly, as it turns out—that the subject of the special enquiry entrusted to Ashbee and Craig was no less than General Vishinsky.'

'The Ambassador?' whispered Zakharov, aghast.

'Or the military neighbours' *Rezident*.* In fact, both. And on both counts he is a proper subject for our Service's vigilance.'

'But Comrade—'

'You had better see the third message, which Pavel Slavic

---

* KGB officers refer to their GRU colleagues as 'military neighbours'. (They spy on each other, just the same.)

has just brought me. It makes it quite clear who is their target. What we have to discover is why.'

Zakharov read the message. 'It could be a plant,' he muttered.

'It could be,' agreed Rostov, 'but it all fits in too well. I know you are thinking that both messages were sent out *after* the inspection of the typewriter this morning. But don't forget that the first signal in the series, the one from S.3 in London, stated that Ashbee and Craig were to collaborate in investigating something so secret that the SIS representative Walton was deliberately excluded from the discussions. And it fits, too, that Craig comes out here from London, where General Vladimir Alekseyevich Vishinsky, our esteemed chief, was GRU *Rezident* until only three months ago. And we have all heard rumours of what he has been doing here to satisfy his peculiar tastes. But yet I agree, Sasha, it may still be a plant, although I cannot see any reason for it. This doesn't alter our attitude—yours and mine—which is to keep this matter to ourselves. In fact I would not have informed you at all, except that you will have much work to do in this connection.' His tone was friendly, now, and the younger man reacted.

'The tape! The recording of the conversation between the —the General and a contact, the tape they are going to send to London by bag.'

'Yes, Sasha, that is your job. Ashbee will pass it to Craig tomorrow morning, and I rather expect he will do so personally, hand to hand, in a matter of such importance. I hope *you* are in no doubt about that importance, Comrade?'

'Of course not. We must at all cost prevent the British from using that recording to cause trouble.'

'Even if we could destroy that tape we couldn't stop them causing trouble, so long as the General is still in Rome. Obviously, Ashbee will keep a copy of the tape. No, our main task is to obtain the tape, or copy it, so that we can inform the Chairman of our Service in time to have

Vishinsky recalled before the British and the Americans act. They have to put the case to the Italians, since it is for the Italian Government to request that a foreign diplomat be recalled, and the Italians won't like doing it unless they have abundant proof. So we have some days to play with. The vital thing for us is to read that tape and report to the Chairman. It may not be very concrete evidence, but I can tell you in confidence that the Chairman will not be unhappy to have grounds for asking the Committee to remove General Vishinsky.'

'I understand,' said Zakharov eagerly, 'and will make plans for all contingencies.'

'And what are the contingencies?'

'It may be possible to get the tape cassette away from Craig before he arrives at the Embassy.'

'I hope not. You may use force if necessary. But if you fail in that respect, what then?'

'I will try to get 328 to remove it and bring it to me for copying at lunchtime. But again, this may not be feasible.'

'And if you fail again?'

'I will instruct the agent to kill the tape.'

'But if you do that, you fool, how can we tell what it contains?'

Zakharov was silent.

'Wait!' said Rostov suddenly. 'Let me think.' It was some minutes before he spoke again, and his voice was now calm and deliberate.

'You are to separate Craig from that tape-cassette. That is your first task, and you will give me a detailed report on your plans tomorrow morning at eight o'clock. You can have any technical help, cars, "rough hands", anything within reason. It will probably take you all night.'

'Yes, Comrade.'

'Everybody concerned must be rehearsed in his task and able to tell me exactly what he is to do at that time, eight o'clock. If your plan fails—and I sincerely hope, for your sake, Sasha, that it will not fail—you will have also briefed

328 so that the second plan, to borrow the cassette during the lunch hour, can be implemented. She must also have instructions and equipment so that if all fails she can kill the tape before the diplomatic pouch leaves.'

'But then, Comrade, you said—'

'Exactly. That is a last resort, to give us a few days for other action. As I said, if the tape is killed we are none the wiser, but the British will know that we have a contact in their Embassy here the moment they test the cassette. So we shall have to work fast. There is only one thing to do, and that is to capture Craig or Ashbee for interrogation.'

Zakharov looked at his chief with his jaw dropped. 'But it's against all the rules. There would be reprisals as soon as we released him and he was able to tell what we had done.' He stammered confusedly, 'Think what even the British would do, and as for the CIA—'

'Whichever of them we decided to interrogate, there would be no release afterwards—except from the sorrows of this world.'

He picked up his cigar, which had gone out, and relit it. Then he smiled at Zakharov, who was looking at him as if he had gone mad. 'You see now, Sasha, why I am insistent that you will not fail in your part of the planning, because if you do I shall have to take the drastic action I have outlined. Capture, interrogation—the Vishinsky business first, of course, but there would be a lot of other information which I could obtain afterwards—and then disposal. And I can assure you, Sasha, that if I do have to take this course nobody will even suspect that we have had anything to do with it. And why? Because the blame will fall squarely on other shoulders.'

Craig was dancing with Diana. He had been sitting comfortably on the terrace after supper, drinking grappa and talking to the Professor when somebody put a samba on the turntable of the music desk and there she was in front of him, swaying to the rhythm and calling to him to dance.

'You've just come from Brazil, you must know how to do this.'

In fact, he did. He stood up and let his body take up the deep African beat, his hips moving, his broad shoulders square—facing the girl, his arms and hands making those leisurely, graceful signals that the Cariocas use. She laughed out loud and led him on, showing off in a glittering display of gestures and glances and movements of the head and the long swathe of fair hair that flicked caressingly across her bare shoulder as she turned. The slim, moulded body swaying and trembling in the dance, and the provoking, mock-passionate look on her lovely, wanton face made her utterly desirable and Craig was amused to find his blood responding. Although their bodies were never in contact their movements were as explicit as if they were in each other's arms, and it was the girl who was making the play and the man content to respond, to admire her virtuosity, to smile back at her langorous looks, to accept all she was so patently offering in the spirit in which it was offered. She wanted a game, and he gave it.

But what was her game, he wondered. He kept his eyes on Diana, but he could sense that people were watching. Or just one man? Was all this fascinating display intended to lure one man into her net, someone—and it wasn't Peter Craig—whom she wanted as a lover or a husband or a casual date? Or just another spy for the KGB?

The music stopped and she put her arms round his neck and gave him a smooth cheek to kiss. 'You're marvellous, Peter. We must do this again. But now get me a drink, darling, please.' The other men closed in.

Craig poured out a whisky and soda and brought it back to Diana, who thanked him with a smile but made no attempt to draw him into the group around her. This suited him, and he went back to the bar.

'Give me one, too, will you, love?' It was Margaret, and she looked as if she needed it.

'Come and talk to me for a moment,' Craig said, his

hands busy with the drinks. She took her glass and linked her arm through his. 'You throw a lovely party, Maggie; everybody looks happy.'

'Except me, is what you mean. Well, since the Bird of Prey has taken her talons out of you, for the moment, you'll have to make do with me.' She led him out on to the terrace and they sat in a swing seat by a bank of potted azaleas. The scent of the flowers was heady.

'That's a wee bit bitchy, isn't it?'

'Any bird who fascinates Neil is poison, in my book.'

'It's Douglas Partridge she's fascinating at the moment.'

'Only because she knows it makes Neil roaring mad.' She turned her flushed, pretty face towards Craig. 'And of course, Douglas has got moral scruples, which makes him *so* much more interesting—the rotten, stuck-up floozy!'

'Oh, pack it in, Maggie, you know it's only a game to her.'

'Is it? That's what I thought—all this push-and-pull technique—I thought it was just for the fun of making Joan and me swallow our bile. But I'm not so sure. Can I confide in you, Peter?'

'Of course. But you don't know me very well, do you?'

'They used to say that when you wanted to know something, ask a policeman. You *look* so dependable—like Harold Wilson acting gritty and meaningful—and there's the great advantage that you're just a visiting fireman, here today and gone tomorrow.'

'You put it so tactfully.'

'I'm not a tactful person. I told you before, I don't like this diplomatic life—especially Rome. It does things to people.'

Just what Luigi had said. 'You mean, like Neil?'

'Yes, of course. He's the only one that counts. You knew, then?'

'I don't know a thing. I just thought he looked very strained, the last few days.'

'How can you see that? You didn't know him before.'

'It's what I've been trained to do, I suppose—spot when people are in trouble.'

'It *is* trouble. He's got some girl.' Her voice trembled.

He put his arm round her shoulders and said lightly, 'You're darned right, he has got some girl. He's got you, hasn't he, and that ought to be more than enough for any man.'

'Don't! You'll make me cry, and I've got to go on keeping mum, as we always said.'

'What on earth are you talking about?'

'Before we got married. We agreed then that if either wanted to have somebody else on the side the other would just shut up and make no fuss. We thought that if we both knew that, we'd always come back to each other.'

'Oh fine! And how many times have you had another man in your bed? Since you were married?'

'What a nosy thing to ask!'

'You're hedging. How many?'

'Not really. Nor Neil either, until now.'

'And you think it's Diana?'

'*I don't know.* That's the awful thing. I thought it was, but I'm not sure.'

That makes two of us, thought Craig, but he said aloud, 'Blow the understanding! Hit him over the head or seduce him or threaten to go back to mother, but *do something*. Find out what it is and then stop it. Once you know, don't tell me you couldn't outsmart the other girl, whoever she is. Damn it, use your loaf—you've got almost all the cards, you feed him, you sleep with him, you've given him children he adores and you're a sexy little crumpet, if I know a good thing when I see one. Use your talents.'

She stretched out her arms like a plump little kitten, and looked at him sideways. Her eyes glowed. 'And bust the pact into little pieces?'

'Into powder. Then mix it with castor oil and make him swallow it.'

'Your horse-sense has a nice earthy, basic smell, like manure. I like it. Would you like to kiss me?'

He kissed her soft lips. Her eyes were excited as her arms tightened round his neck. 'Peter, you're a pal. Will you do something for me?'

'I knew it wasn't just affection. What is it?'

'Help me to get all these bores the hell out of here, so that I can stalk my man.'

CHAPTER FIFTEEN

FRIDAY MORNING

With a fine feeling for one-upmanship the State Department chose for their Embassy in Rome no less a place than the Villa Margherita, the former palace of the Queen-Mother. The main building and its two equally impressive dependencies stand in the corners of a triangle of ground bordered by the Via Veneto, Via Boncompagni and Via Friuli.

'We're not actually going to ask for trouble,' Ashbee had said, 'so I'll arrange for you to be shown out the back way into Via Boncompagni. But if they're wise to that, and have stopped all the holes, we'll take care of them.'

'But I don't want to show that I know I'm being watched'.

'They'll believe that you're carrying a sort of diplomatic atom bomb, so they'll expect you to take elementary precautions, and the Via Boncompagni is a much better street for finding a cab.' He thought for a moment. 'But I agree we've got to be careful not to rouse their suspicions, so if there is action it's got to appear natural.'

Craig crossed the Veneto and went through the gates into the arched entrance of the main building. There was a small door on the right, marked 'Reception', and inside he found himself in a hall, with waiting-rooms beyond. People were talking to the security guards and receptionists, and behind him he heard the steps of two men who had followed him in. He did not look round, but when his turn came asked for Ashbee to be informed that he had arrived.

'He's expecting you to call, sir. Would you wait inside, please?'

One of the men behind him left his companion to speak at the desk and sauntered after Craig into the room beyond, which was full of people waiting.

After two minutes a girl came into the room with a small package in her hand and called his name. 'That is what you wanted, I think,' she said, giving him the package, 'and didn't you want to see someone in the Information Service building?' She had a cheerful, plain face but a spectacular figure, and looked as if life was fun.

'Yes, I did. The entrance is round the corner in Via Boncompagni, isn't it?'

'Yes, but I'll take you through the compound, if you'll come this way.'

He followed her out into the *porte cochère*. Instead of turning left towards the entrance she took him through another door at the rear which brought them out opposite a long stone ramp which led up towards the centre of the compound.

'That's shaken them,' said the girl calmly. 'One Italian, about five foot six, with big teeth, fawn suit, yellow shoes, mauve striped shirt, small Adolf Hitler moustache. We go up the ramp. The other could be East European, high cheekbones, nearly six feet, light blue suit, white shirt and blue tie, black shoes, squashed nose, grey eyes, fair hair, no hat. Rather dishy, I thought.'

'If you want another job, try Scotland Yard.'

'Thank you, sir. But I love my work.' She turned round to grin at him. 'And as a matter of fact it wasn't just lightning observation. We had you all three on closed circuit TV from the moment you came through the gates.'

'I couldn't turn round. Did you see what they did?'

'No. I was told not to look either, but I'll tell you in a minute. Let's find a quiet spot.'

At the top of the incline they came out into a very large formal garden, with a stone fountain around which Embassy drivers were washing their cars. They were walking towards a big building which stood in the farther corner of the compound. She stopped under an ilex tree as if to powder her nose, but what she took from her bag was a small transceiver.

'OK so far. Over.'

Craig heard a low crackle of speech. She signed off and dropped the set into her handbag. 'Our two friends went out of the gates, fast, and one of them blew his nose twice. There'll probably be a reception committee for you at the gate but they won't try anything there because of the guards.' She looked at her watch. 'Three minutes to go. What shall we talk about?'

'Italian men, perhaps?'

'Big Brother is always watching us innocent young girls, Mr Craig.' She sighed. 'Selected young United States officers on leave; it's almost like working in the Agency.'

'I don't believe you.'

'You're quite right.' She glanced at her wrist again. 'We'd better start walking. You don't want to go into the USIS building, do you?'

'I think for the record we'll just go inside as if to ask for somebody, and then come out again. Fellow isn't there. OK?'

'Lead on, General.'

When they emerged from the building she left him with a wave of her hand and he walked down the short curving drive to the gate which led out into Via Boncompagni. The second hand of his watch was just coming up to ten-fifteen, dead, as he passed through the gates. He felt the familiar thrill of action impending. The package was in his breast pocket, inside, with the flap buttoned down.

He stood for a moment on the pavement, between the Carabinieri guards who had machine carbines slung over their shoulders. Then the taxi came towards him and he flagged it. They had only driven twenty yards when a man stepped out into the road in front of the cab, showing a card he held in his hand and calling on the driver to stop. He wore police uniform. The driver slowed to a halt, spoke to the man in uniform and said to Craig, over his shoulder, '*Scusi, Signore, roba di polizia. Deve uscire.*'

The other man opened the door. He was in plain clothes. 'Mr Craig?'

'Yes. What's this about? I've got an appointment at the Embassy.'

'I'm sorry, sir,' said the man in careful English, 'but Superintendent Palermo would like you to come to the Direzione at once. It is a very urgent matter. He won't keep you long. He sent his car.' He pointed back to a big black Mercedes parked farther along the street, with 'Pubblica Sicurezza' clearly displayed on the rear window. It was a neat plan, thought Craig.

'That's funny,' said the driver suddenly, in Italian. 'It isn't a police number. It's not in the series. Look out, Signore, they're bandits!'

'*Zitto*!' shouted the first man, turning furiously on the driver.

But he would not be silent. '*Aiuto*!' he yelled, pushing the uniformed man in the chest. '*Sono banditi*!' The plain-clothes man yanked the rear door full open and reached in for Craig's arm, but Craig threw himself back in the seat and drove his foot into the man's chest. He staggered back across the pavement and hit the wall with a crash that nearly knocked him out. The driver raced his engine and let in the clutch and the man in uniform, who was dragging a cosh from his pocket, was menaced by the open door. Instinctively he dropped flat on the pavement and the door passed over his head. He was up in a flash, and as the taxi drew away, making a wide sweep past the Mercedes, which was backing fast towards the scene of action, Craig saw him bundle his colleague into the black car. The whole of the action had taken place in seconds, and the gate-guards were still running up when the Mercedes roared off. The taxi was already far ahead, turning right into the hectic stream of traffic in the Via Veneto.

This is it, thought Craig; this is the end of groping about in the dark. Our fingertips have touched, and from now on we slug it out. He felt relieved. 'That was a neat bit of Anglo-American co-operation, friend,' he said. 'When Jo said you'd be waiting for me I didn't think I was letting you in for a scrap.'

'It was a pleasure, Mr Craig. Like I always say, get your timing right and you make the base.' He turned off into a side-street. 'I'm stopping behind that taxi. He'll take you to the Embassy. His name's Giorgio and he's Eyetalian, but he's a good boy.'

'Thanks a lot. Incidentally, *was* the Merc's registration number wrong?'

'No *sir*. They wouldn't slip up on a piece of detail like that. It was in the series, sure thing.'

He had the cassette in his hand when he went into Diana Warren's room. She was typing furiously and looked up with an impatient jerk of her blonde head. Then she saw who it was.

'Hullo, Peter. I saw you falling for Maggie's opulent charms. You must have been sloshed.' She was smiling, but there was a bitter twist to her full lips. 'Heads together on that corny love-seat. Very surprising. I didn't think she was your cup of tea at all.'

'It shows how wrong you can be, doesn't it? Listen, Diana. I want an envelope for this.'

'Are you sending it by bag? Put it on the table. Who's the addressee?'

'Just give me the envelope; I'll address it.'

'As you like, but you'll have to tell me what it's about, so that I can get a number.'

'It's a report for Head of Security Department.'

'OK. Hang on a minute.' She picked up her receiver and dialled, then spoke to the Registrar. 'F.5902. You write that in the top right-hand corner.'

'Thanks.' He took the envelope to the table where the out-going mail was lying and addressed it, adding the number and the words 'Top Secret'. Then he put in the cassette, licked the gum and stuck it down. As he did so his thumb-nail made a light groove on the smooth surface of the brown manila. A candle was burning on the table, with a stick of red sealing-wax and an official seal lying beside it. He made a neat job of it, using little of the hot wax and

M

pressing it firmly into the fibre over both flaps and in the middle of the envelope. (Nobody is going to 'lift' those seals, he said to himself with satisfaction.) Then he dropped it on the pile of mail and went to the door. She called him back.

'Sorry, Peter, I forgot. Neil came blundering in, looking like the wrath of God. He's found something you left around last night, I think.'

He went to his room and rang, first the Ambassador and then Adams.

'Are you alone, Peter?'

'Yes. D'you want to talk?'

'I'll be right over.'

When Neil came in he wouldn't sit down, but stood by the window with his back to Craig. 'You know what you were talking to me about the other day—the Russians and all that? Spies.' He spat the word out. 'Well, I think they have made an approach to me, after all.'

'Go on.'

'It's very unpleasant. They haven't come to the point yet, but they will. I didn't think so when I was talking to him because he seemed so decent and—well, friendly. But when I'd had a night's sleep and began to think it over I knew it wasn't friendship—he was just pulling the rope in slowly.'

'Would you mind telling me what the hell you're talking about? And can't you sit down?' The man sat, and Craig continued more gently, 'Now tell me what horrible thing you've been doing? Because that's it, I suppose. Blackmail.'

'It wasn't horrible, that's what I've got to explain. Otherwise you'll think it's all so ordinary and banal, just another man playing around with a woman. It wasn't like that at all.' He stopped, looking at the floor.

'Then what was it like?' Craig prompted.

'I made a pass at a girl—half in fun, as one does, you know—nothing serious in it at all. And well, I know it sounds ridiculous, being *me*—for God's sake I'm no Olivier

—but it seemed she was in love with me. She just sort of melted—I wouldn't have believed it possible, she's so unapproachable as a rule, with me as well. I'd have thought she'd have told me to take a running jump—but she didn't. There she was one moment, all snooty as usual, and the next she was—well, she sort of came alive and all she wanted was for me to hold her and stroke her. It was something I can't get out of my mind.'

You poor, stupid sod, said Craig, but not aloud.

'The trouble is,' continued Adams, 'that I scarcely know you.'

'That's why it's easier for you, chum. You don't give a hoot what I think of you.'

'That's true.' There was an attempt at a smile. 'But you know about this sort of thing and I thought you might help.'

'You've got it the wrong way round, Neil. You've got to help *me*. If some Russian is blackmailing you it's your duty —damn it, you attended the security lectures—to report exactly what's happened and give any further help that may be required of you.'

'There you are, sounding off like a policeman.'

'What d'you expect, I *am* a policeman. You tell me the whole thing, please.'

'We've met a few times in a flat we thought was empty, but she's got the key. I suppose the tenant must be a voyeur or something. Anyway, somebody took a photograph. Have I got to spell it out?'

'You and the girl, in a clinch. Is that it? That's all I want to know.'

'Yes. Yes, that was it. It's obscene, of course, but—well, it wasn't like that. It was shown to me in the street by a man who ran away, and I tore it up. Then someone rang me and I met him—a young chap, probably Slav from the look of his face—and he said he'd persuaded the tenant of the flat, who apparently makes a habit of this sort of thing, telling girls they can use his flat while he's away, and then he's got this camera rigged up which starts shooting automatically as soon as it hears voices—it's technically feasible, you know.' He looked up at Craig.

'A voice-operated trigger with a robot camera.'

'Yes. Well, the man I met said he had a hold over this chap and had made him hand over the negative and the prints. He showed them to me and tore them up and gave me the pieces. I put them down the loo,' he added gloomily.

'Very generous of him. And what precisely did he want in return?'

'He said he was a Jugoslav research student in agronomy and he was anxious to get some books from England. He'd tried the British Council and they hadn't been very helpful; he said he wanted somebody to take an interest in his work and advise him what books were available. And so on. At the time I—well, I believed him.'

'And afterwards?'

'Oh, it was all in those security lectures you were talking about. The Russians always start by asking you to hand over something quite harmless.'

At least, thought Craig, he'd begun to show signs of rational thinking. 'That's it,' he said encouragingly, 'and then they ask for something that's on the restricted list, but not really secret. And then they make you accept money, or even theatre tickets for a visiting Russian ballet, or drink. And you're on the hook.'

Adams shivered. 'I suppose it must be like that. He seemed all right, and as I said, I believed him and we agreed to meet again.'

Craig smiled. 'But not where and when—he was going to ring you.'

'How did you know?'

'Oh, for God's sake, it's all in those bloody, boring lectures. They operate by rules; things have to be done just so. They never give you time to bug the place where you're meeting. I'm no intelligence officer, you know, but I know my standard reading.'

'But it's all such old hat—Klaus Fuchs and the Moscow cypher clerk and the Lonsdale case.'

'Exactly. It just shows you, doesn't it? The method works. Here you are, luckily with the common sense to tell somebody in time, but you mightn't have, isn't that so?'

'Yes. If it hadn't been— Anyway, I darn near didn't tell you. You see, it's the girl—I *can't* drag her into it. I'm not going to tell you who it is, you realize that? I'll only collaborate with you on those terms.'

'Listen to me, Adams. If it's a girl in the Embassy you've *got* to tell me. Either that or you go straight back to London and we let Special Branch sort you out.' As he spoke he realized that he had given the other a loophole, and cursed under his breath.

'Damn it, you're threatening me, blast you! But it's no use, Peter.' He turned away towards the window. 'It isn't anybody on the staff, I assure you. It's somebody quite different. I've told her something awful's happened—I told her about the photograph—and said we mustn't meet again for the time being. I'm not out of the wood, I know that.'

'You mean, because he's kept all the copies he needs?'

'Yes. He could have. I still don't know whether I'm being over-suspicious.'

'Oh for God's sake, Neil, what's happening to you is the classic pressure.' He paused. 'And it's very likely the girl's involved.'

Adams flared up instantly. 'You can't say that about her. It was *my* doing from the start. She couldn't have planned it.' He went on more slowly, 'Not the way it happened.'

'How did it happen, then?'

'It was in this flat, where she'd been decorating. She knew I was interested in do-it-yourself stuff and she took me there one afternoon, after lunch, to show me what she'd done. And then—I know it sounds pretty corny—I made this pass—I put my arm round her shoulders, I think—and as I told you, she sort of melted. And then she told me what she thought of me, that I was real and genuine, right through, not veneered over with manners and conventions and all that jazz—I tell you, I was so touched, it was so extraordinary that she of all people could fall for a little

runt like me that I suppose I encouraged her. As you see,'
he ended defiantly, 'it was all my fault.'

God give me strength, prayed Peter Craig. If I tell him
I know it's either Diana or Janet he'll ring the girl as soon
as he leaves here. And then she'll just fade away, and I
want that girl under interrogation. She may have planted
half a dozen other mikes for all we know. I want evidence
to arrest her on Embassy ground, so that she can't sling her
hook, and unless this gullible idiot gives evidence against
her I can't make it stick.

'Listen to me, Neil,' he said carefully. 'I realize how
strongly you feel for this woman, but I don't think you've
worked it out properly. You haven't weighed the evidence
in your mind. And there's nothing wrong with your brain,
it's trained to be logical; so use it. Don't let it get clouded
with emotional issues. Will you promise that you won't
communicate with the girl until Monday?'

'That's easy,' said Adams bitterly, 'I've told her that
already.'

'That's good. Then you won't speak to her about this
business until you've had another talk with me on Monday?'

'All right.'

'If the man you met rings, don't agree to meet him
during the week-end. I'll tell you why. I want to know in
advance where you're going to meet again and I think I
can help you. If he's blackmailing you I can put pressure
on him.'

'You mean, record what he says?' said Adams with a
flicker of interest.

'If you do as I say, yes, I think we could. The Italians
would help—and keep quiet about it,' he added hurriedly.
He tried to make this sound more truthful than it was.

'OK.' He sounded almost cheerful.

'And one last thing, Neil. You've got to tell Maggie
some time. Go back and tell her now.'

'I have.'

Good for Maggie, thought Craig. She'd done her seduction act to good effect. 'I'm very glad to hear that.'

'Yes, I decided to last night. I felt I owed it to her. Just as I owe her practically everything else,' he added simply. 'Of course she wanted to know who it was, but I wouldn't tell her.'

Blast the man's sense of honour! But she'd get it out of him over the week-end, trust Maggie. 'She's got a right to know, Neil.'

'No, she hasn't—any more than you have. If I make a bloody fool of myself I'll own up, but not drag the girl in. She's got to be in the clear.'

'You still think you're Pygmalion, don't you?' cried Craig, losing patience.

Adams stood up. He looked oddly dignified as he turned and stared Craig in the face. 'She made me think,' he said in a low voice, 'that I was God.'

CHAPTER SIXTEEN

FRIDAY AFTERNOON

It was after three when Zakharov heard her key in the lock. He waited impatiently as she crossed the hall and knocked four times on the closed door of the living-room. He unlocked the door and let her in.

'Have you got it?' he asked eagerly.

She shook her head. 'I had the envelope in my bag, all ready to bring here, and then just before lunch H.E. rang and said he wanted it back, as he hadn't heard the tape. What is this bloody tape, anyway, Sasha? It's registered out as a security report. What's so darned important about it?'

'I'll tell you later. Where is it now?'

'In H.E.'s safe, I suppose. Craig had left a tape-recorder in his room after he saw him this morning, and he was going to play it over.'

Zakharov groaned. 'You must get it back before the bag closes,' he said urgently.

'But what then? If it isn't in the bag there'll be all hell to pay in London. It'll be spotted as soon as Bag Room check the list.' She frowned. 'You're making me stick my neck out.'

'I only want you to get hold of it for a few minutes, alone. Surely you can do that?'

'I don't know. But if I can, what do I do with it?'

The Russian took from his pocket a small, heavy metal box and put it down on the table. 'Now listen carefully.'

Reg Newman, Head of Registry, was busy checking the way-bills of the out-going bag when Craig came in, and he looked up impatiently.

'I'm awfully sorry, Reg, but H.E. wants that report back. F.5902.'

'Strewth! Can't he make up his mind? He whipped it back at lunchtime and it was only ten minutes ago that somebody brought it in.'

'Who was that? Diana?'

'Yes. She said Janet had told her the Old Man hadn't had time to hear the thing after all.'

'Well, that's just it. He doesn't want it to go out until he's heard it.'

'But it's sealed up already.'

'I'm sorry, Reg, but can't you open the bag it's in and let him have it?'

'Oh all right, but I can't hold the bag open for him indefinitely.'

'He says scrub the number and he'll hold it over. There's no great hurry about it.'

'OK.' Newman picked up a knife and went over to one of the canvas sacks which stood, already sealed and tied up with their labels, against the wall. 'This is the one, I think. Yes. F.5902. It'll be near the top.'

'Thanks a lot. I'll find it.'

'No you won't, mate. My responsibility, once they're off this table. Here you are.' He cancelled the registration from the list.

'Thanks.' Craig looked down at the envelope in his hand, puzzled. He had felt pretty sure that it wouldn't be found, and then he could have stopped everybody leaving the Embassy while the search went on. But the envelope had been returned to Registry, re-entered in the lists and actually put into the sack and sealed up. He dropped it into his pocket and went back to the Ambassador's room.

While Sir Watkyn looked on impatiently, Craig examined the envelope carefully. The mark he had made with his thumbnail was still there and the seals had apparently not been disturbed.

'I don't think it's been interfered with, sir,' he said slowly.

'They didn't have much time, did they?'

'We couldn't give them much time. If they'd had it over lunch they'd have had those seals off and recorded the tape —and discovered it was a plant. So I thought they'd have tried to nick it—to remove the envelope just before it went into the bag. But there was no difficulty in recovering it either this morning or just now. You gave it to Mrs Ransome—when? About a quarter of an hour ago?'

'Yes, as you said. Perhaps a bit longer.'

'It wasn't she who took it to Registry, it was Miss Warren.'

'That may be office etiquette. It was Miss Warren who registered the envelope in the first place.'

'Well, sir. I'm afraid my plan has failed completely. But I'd better check the recording.' He went across to the small Grundig tape-recorder that stood on the Ambassador's desk, broke the seals on the envelope and inserted the cassette. Then he pressed the 'Start' button.

The tape began to run through in complete silence. Both men looked at each other in surprise. 'You told me you'd recorded something?'

'Yes, sir. A full report—just in case things went wrong. But it's not there.' He turned the cassette over and tried again, but there was still no sound from the tiny loud-speaker.

'They've changed the cassette.'

'No. How could they have known for certain what make it was? And I left a secret mark on the envelope which is still there. No, sir, it's been stripped.' He looked again at the seals on the envelope. 'And without opening the envelope, by the look of it.'

'But how, for heaven's sake?'

'There's a special device with a powerful magnet in it, which sends out an alternating magnetic force. All you have to do is to put it on the cassette and switch it on. I suppose they have them battery-powered, but it'd be heavy.'

'You mean to say that within the last half-hour somebody has operated a device like that *here*, inside Chancery?'

'Yes, sir. It must have been done here, but it could have been done this morning, if all they wanted to do was to strip the tape.'

'But why, Craig? You know, and I know, and so does Ashbee, what was supposed to go into that tape. Or that's what the Russians must think. What'll they think will happen when a blank tape arrives in London, after we have heralded it in a special telegram?'

'They're doing this for one reason only, so far as I can see, and that is to gain time. What's beginning to worry me is, why?'

'I think I can answer that,' said His Excellency, almost —but not quite—rubbing his hands. 'If they've swallowed the bait and believe that a scandal is brewing—a scandal of the magnitude we have—er—suggested, they'll find an excuse to recall Vishinsky. The Italians would never agree to declare him *persona non grata* if someone gave them a hint that he was about to be withdrawn; they'd just breathe a great sigh of relief. Don't forget the size of the Communist Party in this country.'

'I suppose that's it, but—oh my God!'

'What's the matter, Craig?'

'I've slipped up. I told Newman you wanted the cassette back so that you could hear the recording. If the spy learns that she'll know by now that we've discovered about the stripping of the tape. What a fool I was! I'm—'

The Ambassador had his hand on the telephone already. 'I'll take responsibility for this, Craig. We arranged that that was what you were going to say.' He dialled a number. 'Newman? The Ambassador here. I was sorry to cause you so much trouble over that tape recording.' He paused. 'No, it's all right, I don't want to open the bag yet again. But listen, Newman; did you inform anyone—*anyone at all*— that I had asked for the tape back? Nobody. You're quite sure? I'll explain later, but in the meantime please let it appear that the cassette went out in the bag in the normal way. And, Newman, regard this conversation as not having taken place. Yes. That's exactly what I mean. Good night.'

He put down the receiver and looked at Craig. 'He is as safe as you could wish. Apparently everybody else has gone home. I think it's quite certain that Miss Warren—if she is still the person you believe is the spy—doesn't know I have the cassette.'

Craig breathed a sigh of relief. 'Thank you, sir. Very much. But what'll you tell Newman on Monday?'

'That it was Bracken I had in mind.'

'John Bracken?'

'Yes. I asked if he'd told anyone at all about my having asked for the tape. I will tell him that I didn't want Head of Chancery to think I hadn't done my homework and listened to your recorded report. There's another outgoing bag on Tuesday, so there would scarcely be any delay.' He frowned. 'Oh dear!' he muttered with a rueful shake of his head, 'More lies. I almost wish I'd never thought of that scheme.'

'Almost, sir,' said Craig, grinning, 'but not quite, perhaps?'

'Yes,' said His Excellency, with a fleeting smile, 'not quite.' Then he frowned. 'So where do we stand now, Craig?'

'We are fighting, so to speak, on two fronts. Your *disinformatsiya* plot is working. There is no doubt that they are taking it seriously.'

'Because they stripped the tape?'

'That, and also because they tried very hard to get it off me before I could bring it into the Embassy.' He described the incident with the taxi.

The Ambassador was horror-struck. 'But my dear fellow, this is all my fault. I'm not going to go any farther with my selfish plan. We will at once compose a suitable message for me to type on that machine, making it quite clear that we are—er—pulling the KGB's leg.'

'The moment you do that they'll think we've got the spy under control, or at least know who it is. And we don't. My

elaborate plan to make the girl stick her neck out has failed
miserably.' He looked in despair at the determined expression on Sir Watkyn's face. 'The spy still doesn't know
we even suspect her. Give me till Monday, sir, at least.'

'But how will you be better off then?'

'I'm hoping Adams will come to his senses and collaborate with me voluntarily. And by then, with any luck, his
wife will have found out from him who it is.'

'Ah yes, you told me about his refusal to give the
woman's name. It shows a sense of honour, Craig, which I
must say I find rather touching in a young man as brash
and uncouth as Adams. But if he won't talk on Monday?'

'Then we'll have to have him in here and you put it to
him formally. And then the spy will know something's up
—and fly the coop.'

'I see. And you think that if Mrs Adams finds out who
the girl is she'll tell you?'

'Yes. But I'll ring her and make sure. She won't believe
for a moment that the woman is innocent, and the best
way of breaking Adams's infatuation for her is to show her
up for what she is.'

'And when you know for certain, what will you do?'

'Well, we've got to keep her ignorant of our suspicions
until we can arrest her here, on Embassy territory. And
then I'm afraid she'll have to be kept on the premises under
guard. That's where we'll have to tell John Bracken everything, I suppose, and get a warrant sworn out in London
and sent to us by the first plane. And with that we can
apply to the Italians for deportation.'

'But the first step—arresting her here in Chancery. Can
you do that without a warrant?'

'Yes, sir. But only in order to hold her on suspicion for a
short period. We'll have to act very fast after that.'

'I see. Well, Craig, you've done your best. I'll stay on a
bit and catch up with my boxes. Tell Mrs Ransome as you
go out that I'll lock them up in my safe when I've finished,
so she can go now. The poor girl's had a long day.'

CHAPTER SEVENTEEN

FRIDAY EVENING

As soon as Craig got back to his hotel he rang the Adams's flat. Maggie answered.

'Peter Craig here. Just to thank you for a wonderful party last night. Is Neil with you?'

'He's putting the twins to bed.'

'Good. Listen, Maggie dear. Thanks to you he told me everything—except the one thing I want to know. Find out for me, will you?'

'I don't care who it is. He won't see her any more. He promised.'

'This is what I want to say, for you only, d'you understand? She's not an innocent party, as Neil thinks. She's in it up to her neck.'

'Are you sure? I thought she was just a bloody home-breaker.'

'No, she's a spy. I *know* this.' He heard her gasp. 'So for Neil's sake you've got to find out who she is, and when you do *tell me*. Then we can be sure to keep him in the clear. But on no account tell Neil what I've just said. He's such a —well, I won't say what he is, but he might warn her off.'

'He's *not* a fool, Peter, and—anyway, he's my man and he's adorable.'

'Fine. But do as I say, won't you? Promise?'

'Promise. I'll have to try tears, I suppose.'

'If it'll work.'

'You haven't heard me cry. It takes me a bit of time to work up to it, but it's real boo-hoo stuff. Earth-moving.'

'As long as you can move your favourite bit of earth I don't mind how you do it, but he's got to come clean on Monday morning or he'll have to be sorted out by H.E. As soon as you know, if you can't get him to tell me direct,

wait till you can get to a telephone without being overheard and ring me here, at the Eden. If I'm not in leave a
message.'

'OK. He's coming.' He heard the click as she put down
the receiver.

He took a shower and put on fresh clothes and then rang
Ashbee's flat. A girl's voice answered.

'Gee, Mr Craig, I'm sorry but they're both out and won't
be back till late. This is Betty.' And about fourteen, by the
sound of her.

'OK, Betty, thanks. I'll ring him tomorrow.'

'No, there's a message for you. Pop said if you rang I
was to say we're all going to the beach tomorrow for a
picnic. And you're coming too.'

'Am I?'

'Gee, that's me again! Mom says we'll be happy if you'll
come. We'll pick you up at your hotel at ten o'clock. OK?'

'That'll be fine, Betty. I'd love to come.'

'Swell. Bring your swimsuit.'

Craig had invited Luigi and Maria to dine with him at
Alfredo's in Trastevere, and they were sitting at a table
against the artificial hedge which separated the dining area
from the rest of the ancient square. The Romanesque tower
and the pediment of the church were floodlit, and the
brilliant mosaic figures of the Wise and Foolish Virgins
stood out against their background of glowing gold. The
Roman artichokes and the *ossi buchi* had been excellent,
and there was still half a bottle of young, slightly *pétillant*
wine from the Alban Hills to drink while they waited for
coffee. At a table near-by a man was singing Roman
stornelli to a guitar accompaniment, and people had
stopped chattering to listen. It was a peaceful place, too
pleasant, thought Craig, for talk of espionage.

Luigi was saying, 'There's no joy for you in the surveillance reports for lunchtime. Ransome went home as usual,
Adams did the same and Warren didn't appear to leave the

Embassy at all.'

'She had a pile of stuff for the bag at the end of the morning, and she probably had lunch there. There's a staff canteen.'

Luigi was relieved. 'So that was it! I was afraid my boys had failed to spot her in the personnel bus. It's difficult to see from outside.'

'It'd be quite normal to lunch in the canteen on a Bag day. There's always a last-minute rush. And she could hardly have got over the wall. No, I think what she did was report by telephone, in some sort of code, that she couldn't borrow the cassette over lunch. Then they told her to strip it. Which she did, all too efficiently.'

'I don't like the way they're showing their hand, Peter. First that attempt to snatch you this morning, and then scrubbing the tape so that you know for certain they've got someone in the Embassy.'

'They weren't trying to snatch me. They'd have turned me over—wallet, notebook, identification papers—and the tape—and let me go. We made it easy for them by shouting "bandits".'

'It was a big risk, all the same, right in the middle of Rome, and one of them in uniform. So they were crazy to lay their hands on that cassette. And they'll still be. You don't imagine they swallowed that "bandit" bluff, do you? I know quite a bit about Rostov and how his mind works. The moment he heard what you'd done to his men he would check the number of the taxi, if they got it, and find it was phony. And besides, the whole thing was too neat. Roman taxi drivers are tough, but not that tough. Rostov will have concluded that you expected trouble and took precautions—you and Jo Ashbee. And he'll want to know why. Are you armed?'

'Good God, no. I never carry a gun.'

'But why not, Peter?' cried Maria. 'They may try to kidnap you, and do it properly this time.'

'*Macché*! Not kidnapping,' said Luigi, soothing the agitated Maria with a wave of his big hand. 'I agree with

Peter, they wouldn't try that. It'd reveal too much, for one thing, and for another they're scared of reprisals. They have a sort of, quote, gentleman's agreement, unquote, with both MI6 and CIA—and with the French SDECE, too, I think —about not touching other services' intelligence officers, and I suppose it would cover Peter. But they might get rough, all the same. You'd better have a gun. I've got a small Colt with a shoulder holster at home, I'll lend you that.'

'All right, then. Thanks, Luigi. But they won't try anything this week-end. They can't imagine I'll be carrying anything very secret around with me. I shall be with the Ashbees at the beach tomorrow and probably take them out afterwards, and on Sunday the Brackens have asked me to have lunch at a villa they've got up in the Castelli. I'm not going to be wandering around alone, as you see. But I'll be glad to pick up the gun on Monday.'

'You will take it this evening, to please me.' Maria's eyes were flashing and there was little Craig could do.

'All right,' he said meekly. 'As the Signora orders.'

CHAPTER EIGHTEEN

SATURDAY AFTERNOON

The sea was still rather cold for bathing, and after a long swim Craig was glad to lie on the hot sand and talk to Fay Ashbee. She was a handsome dark woman, tall and elegant in Bermuda slacks and a sun top. Jo and Betty—all brown legs and arms in her diminutive bikini—were playing deck tennis. They had found a part of the beach which was almost empty, and Craig felt ashamed of the hard bulge in the rolled-up jacket under his head.

'Your husband covers the ground pretty fast, doesn't he?'

'It's time he started to let her beat him,' she said placidly. 'That man of mine can't forget he was an All-American tackle before the war. I tell you, when he joined the OSS I was right glad. It was so much safer.'

'I'll say it was. We play a more gentlemanly game.'

'Then how did your nose get broken?'

He smiled, fingering his twisted nose nostalgically. 'I used to box a bit.'

'Is that a British under-statement?'

He grinned. 'I got my half-blue at Cambridge, but as you see I wasn't as good as all that. There he goes, slowing up a bit, as you said.'

She sighed. 'That's just what he won't do in his work. He can afford to take it easy now. But not my Jo—work first, wife and children afterwards.'

'Is Betty the youngest?'

'For land's sake, yes. What do you take me for? The others are all at college. Go on, Peter, call them in before Jo gets a stroke.'

As he strolled towards them Betty threw her quoit high in the air. 'I've beaten Pop. Did you see, Mr Craig? He's just darn lazy. I've beaten him, Mom.' She rushed past Craig, flushed with excitement.

'All right, Toots. Now come and give us all a nice cold dry Martini. There's some Coke for you somewhere.'

Later, they moved back to where the Buick was parked under the shade of the pines and brought out the picnic hamper. It was a good lunch and afterwards they lay smoking cigars and talking while Betty made coffee. Fay went gracefully to sleep.

Ashbee gave his cup back to the girl and stood up.

'D'you want another game, Pop?'

'No, sweetheart, I do not. Mr Craig and I will take a little walk for the sake of our digestion while you pack everything up. And don't wake your mother,' he added in a lowered tone.

'OK, OK. So I'll be the slave, as usual.'

In this part of the *pineta* there seemed to be little roads everywhere, some metalled, some sand, running down to the beach from the coastal highway or sideways through the trees. The two men took one of the sandy paths which ran parallel to the beach. The afternoon was hot, and they both wore only shirt and trousers.

'The trouble is,' said Craig, 'that if Luigi's right Rostov will know we're on our guard, and he may tell the spy to keep her head down.'

'Why? There's no connection, necessarily, between the two things. There might be any number of reasons why we would be scared that somebody might try to lay their hands on that tape—not connected with your spy at all. After all, how am I supposed to have got hold of the tape in the first place? He doesn't know, and I don't know—because the tape doesn't exist—but there might have been a leak there, for all he can tell.'

'That's true. If only Adams will come clean. I hope Maggie gives him hell until he does.'

'What *is* eating that little man? What makes him so durned sure that the girl isn't involved?'

'I told you. He was conned—and by an expert. He's

convinced that he made all the running, so it can't be her
fault.'

'But he's grown-up, isn't he? He's heard of Samson and
Delilah, hasn't he? Not to speak of Mata Hari. He can't be
as dumb as all that.'

'If she was a girl of his own—well, class, I suppose—he
wouldn't have been taken in. But he said something to me,
the day I first met him, about Diana—and the same would
apply to Janet. He said he was fascinated by people like
that, born with a silver spoon in their mouths. He said you
couldn't get near the girl, and he wanted to know what
made her tick.'

'He seems to have found the answer,' said Ashbee drily.
'He's discovered he's the handsome prince who wakes her
with a tender kiss. It makes me want to throw up. Why
didn't you just hold him incommunicado and press him
until the juice ran out?'

They had reached the next cross-road and turned right,
towards the beach. Craig said, 'It's all a question of *proof*,
Jo. You must see that. If he names the girl, it still doesn't
mean definitely she's the spy. Not enough for a warrant.
But it'll give me enough grounds for holding her until
we've gone to that flat, exposed the evidence and con-
fronted the girl with it. Then, with any luck, she'll break.
But I'd have given a lot to catch her red-handed yesterday, stuffing that damned cassette into her handbag.'

'Red-handed,' said Ashbee thoughtfully. 'Yes, and that
reminds me. You spoke the other day about a tell-tale
powder.' He reached for his hip pocket. 'Do you still want
it?'

'Well, thanks. I might be able to cook up another trap—
one that works, for a change.'

Ashbee put into his hand a small bottle. It contained a
colourless powder and was sealed with wax. 'This is the
best stuff I know. No colour, as you see, but get it on your
hands or any clothes where there's the least trace of sweat
in the fibres and it turns bright blue. It takes quite a time,
so that you don't notice anything at once, and then it's too

late to do anything about it. It's hell to wash off.'

'Thanks a lot. I'll think of something.' He dropped it into his trouser pocket.

Just ahead of them was another of the cross-paths, which would lead them back to the road on which the car was parked. Two men were standing at the turning, irresolute, as if uncertain which way to go. They were wearing sports shirts and light-weight slacks, with bathing-trunks in their hands. One of them waited until Ashbee came up and spoke to him.

'*Scusi, signore,*' he said, '*dov'è il quiosque?*'

'We didn't see one of those kiosks for drinks near here, did we?' said Ashbee, turning to Craig. But Craig was looking down at the muzzle of an automatic, with a silencer attached, which pointed at the middle of his stomach. The swimsuit lay on the sand.

The man who had spoken, the taller of the two, said softly, 'Put your hands on your heads, *quick.*' He was speaking Italian, with a marked southern accent. 'Now walk, side by side, down that path. No tricks, or you'll get a bullet in your liver.'

They went along the path, parallel with the beach, until they came to another of the metalled roads which led to the beach. A grey Fiat 1300 was waiting. As they approached it the tall man went forward behind Ashbee and at the same time Craig felt a hand behind him, pulling him back by the neck of his shirt. The gun was poking painfully into the small of his back. He stopped.

The driver, a short, stocky man with oily black hair and a drooping moustache, had got out and opened the back door. 'Get in, Ashbee,' said the tall man quietly.

For a moment Craig was scared that Ashbee would start something; which would have been useless, for these men were professionals. Ashbee hesitated for a second and then got into the back seat. The tall man followed immediately, the driver slammed the door and got back behind the wheel. He drove off fast towards the coast road.

'You, man. What's your name?' said the voice behind Craig, softly. They were still standing in the loose sand of the path.

'Craig. What the hell—?'

'*Silenzio*! And don't turn round.' His hand was still gripping Craig's collar. 'American?'

'No, British. And I have diplomatic status.' It wasn't strictly true. He had no accreditation in Italy.

'You will not be harmed if you do as you're told.' The voice had the same thick southern accent—could be a Sicilian. 'We will take you for a little ride and then let you go. But no tricks.' The hissed '*sènza scherzi*' held a cold menace.

Two minutes later Ashbee's big Buick came up, with another man driving. He had a nylon stocking pulled over his face. The other gunman moved to open the rear door, but his eyes never left Craig, who stepped forward as if willing to enter the car. It was just a chance, but he took it. As his left foot came down on the door frame he pushed back violently and fell on the man behind him, twisting round to get at the gun. But it had fallen out of reach. They grappled for a moment and the man's hat fell off and Craig had a glimpse of a shining bald pate above the fringe of black hair.

Then he felt himself being lifted bodily and flung to one side. The driver was a gorilla of a man, with muscles bulging under his striped T-shirt. He stood above Craig with a gun in his hand. '*Calma-ti, calma-ti*!' he said genially, like a mother reproving a child in a temper.

The other man was not so friendly. He found his hat, crammed it on his head and then went over to kick Craig viciously in the ribs. This done, he retrieved his automatic. His eyes were glinting dangerously, as if daring Craig to try something else. But he knew better, and when he could get his breath back, he got up slowly and crawled into the car. The pain in his side was like fire.

The bald man followed, to sit in his corner, leaving a wide stretch of leather seat between him and the English-

man. The car began backing down the narrow road, fast
and straight, until it came to the highway. Then it turned
towards Castel Fusano.

As they passed the turning where they had picnicked
Craig saw Betty rushing towards the main road, screaming,
and behind her, Fay, staring horrified at the fast-moving
Buick. She called her daughter back, sharply. Then they
were lost to view.

They drove fast through a small village and then on into
a wider part of the *pineta*. Craig had an idea of what was
going to happen. The little bottle of powder was in his
right-hand trouser pocket. He took out his handkerchief,
under the watchful eyes of the man in the other seat, and
began to mop his forehead. Then he lowered the handkerchief, with the bottle inside it, on to his lap.

After several miles the bald man leaned forward and
spoke to the driver. 'The next turning,' he said, 'away from
the sea. Go down it three hundred metres and stop.' He
turned quickly to look at Craig, but by this time the plastic
stopper was out and the contents of the little bottle tipped
out on to the seat between Craig's legs.

They took the side road and after a little while stopped.
The bald man got out, his automatic pointing backwards
at Craig. 'Get out. Come on! Move! *Non far compli-
menti*!' Craig obeyed, sliding sideways across the length of
the seat and climbing out, to stand blinking in the fierce
sunlight. It was a place of tussocks, dunes and canebrakes,
and the side road was half covered with drifting sand.

'Over there, behind that hill.'

As he obeyed, he heard the bald man following him
close behind, and had time to pray that his behind had
spread the powder well over the back seat and if only— At
this point in his cogitations he was neatly and effectively
sapped. He crumpled up and lay on the sand behind the
little dune that hid his body from the road.

He had dreams—quite pleasant dreams, although he
couldn't remember them afterwards—and when he opened

his eyes he saw two faces above him, staring down at him
solemnly. Then the pain came, agonizingly, and he lay
back with a groan and closed his eyes. He heard their
voices, dimly through the pain.

'*E morto*,' whispered the girl.

'*Macché morto. E ubriaco.*'

'I'm not drunk, you fool,' muttered Craig. 'It's my head.
La testa. Fa male.' He felt hands lifting his head gently and
feeling the lump behind his ear. The girl squeaked.

'*Senti Nino. E stato colpito. Senti qua.*'

The man's hand found the spot, more roughly, and Craig
groaned. It was hurting like hell. He opened his eyes again.
They were a wild-looking pair of youngsters, the girl wearing a flowered dress like a gypsy and the boy—he couldn't
be more than seventeen—jeans and a fringed leather jacket.
He wore his hair over his shoulders and a wispy Che
Guevara moustache. But they looked very concerned about
him, standing now hand in hand, wondering what to do.

'Were you hit?' asked the boy, in English.

'I was hit. Can you help me to stand up?'

The boy pulled Craig's arm over his shoulder and hauled
him to his feet. He stood swaying, while his mind picked up
what it could remember. 'Oh my God! I must get back to
Rome. Have you a car—*una macchina*? *Devo chiamare
la polizia.*'

He saw them both stiffen and the boy said firmly, '*Niente
polizia.*' He turned to the girl and whispered. Then he
continued, 'We'll take you to telephone.' He pointed to a
Vespa leaning against a tree. At the same time Craig
noticed a faint whiff of marihuana. So that was it. They
wouldn't want any contact with the police.

The boy said, 'You sit behind me. Maria can run.' The
girl nodded. They helped him to sit on the pillion and the
girl held him there while the boy mounted. Then she had
an idea. '*Aspetta!*' They waited while she took a rope
from the saddle bag underneath Craig's leg and tied it
round the two men's waists so that he couldn't fall off.

Then she took the end of the rope in her hand and called
'*Andiamo*!'

They started off slowly, with Maria running behind,
half towed by the rope, and bumped towards the main
road. Craig's head took exception to this treatment and he
had to bury his face in Nino's long hair to prevent himself
shouting with pain. But on the tarmac road it was easier.
Every so often they stopped and the couple changed places,
taking turns to drive and run, with Craig tied to each in
turn. Oddly enough, they both smelled tolerably clean.
After a mile, they were all exhausted and sat in a row on
the grass verge, too tired to speak.

Craig never knew who his benefactors were. A big car
came up, with a middle-aged man driving and a woman by
his side. He hooted frantically when Nino seized Maria by
the hand and ran out in front of him. But he had to stop,
and there was a furious altercation in Italian before Craig
was bundled into the back seat, the door slammed and the
car drove off. Craig looked through the back window and
waved. They stood there, hand in hand, waving wearily
until they were lost to sight. If they were typical, thought
Craig, of the *capelloni*, the wild youth of Italy, he'd swop
them for half Carnaby Street.

In the front seat he saw two rigid backs, expressing disgust. 'Hotel Eden, *per piacere*,' he said—and then realized
that although the address sounded more respectable the
driver might not like his car being treated like a taxi. He
apologized, and then went on in English, 'I'm very sorry to
bother you, but I must get quickly to my hotel or to the
British Embassy.' No reply. '*L'Ambasciata Britannica*,' he
explained hopefully, and this at last had an effect. The
woman in front turned round.

'You are in the Embassy?' she asked in English.

'Yes, I was attacked. I must report to the police.'

He had made that mistake again. The man's shoulders
hunched in a tremendous gesture of distaste. 'I will take
you to the hotel. Not the police, they would keep us all day,
you understand?'

'Thank you. That'll be fine.'

The driver grunted, but speeded up and half an hour later they stopped outside the portals of the Eden. Craig got out stiffly and thanked him. Then he felt vaguely for his wallet and realized that everything, including his visiting cards, was in the jacket that he had left at the picnic site. But there was something in his hip pocket, something there had not been before. Somebody had slipped in a dirty envelope and he pulled it out and stared at it. He was still reading the address, written in block capitals with a ball pen, when the driver gave a final shrug and drove off. '*S.E. L'Ambasciatore degli Stati Uniti*', that's what it said. It was a note for the American Ambassador.

It was fortunate for Craig that the Eden commissionaire, who by now was a good friend of his, was a man of great presence of mind, because he himself was in no mood to care for his personal appearance. Giorgio snapped his fingers, and when a page came running up gave him whispered instructions. Then he moved out of the doorway so that he was standing behind Craig.

'Signor Craig.'

'Oh hullo, Giorgio,' said Craig absent-mindedly. He thrust the envelope into his pocket, and was turning to go into the hotel when Giorgio stopped him.

'Wait here for a moment, please.'

'Sorry, I'm in a hurry. What's the matter?'

'The seat of your pants, sir.' When he saw the delighted grin on Craig's face he continued reprovingly, 'You cannot go through the foyer like that, sir.'

'What's wrong with my trousers?'

'The seat is blue, sir. Bright blue.'

Craig thought quickly. Then he said, 'So that's what they did; I suppose they thought it was funny.'

'Who, sir?'

'The *capelloni*. I was in the *pineta* and a gang of them came up and knocked me out—look at this bruise. I was out cold, and when I came to they'd gone.'

'*Porca miseria*! The young brutes!'

'What do I look like, a blue-arsed baboon?'

'Well, yes, sir. That was probably the idea. They have no respect, these *capelloni*.' The page came up, carrying a dust-coat. 'Put this on, Mr Craig. It'll look odd, but not—like it was.'

'Thank you, Giorgio. They pinched my coat, too, so I can't—'

'*Non c'è di che, Signor Craig*.'

As soon as he got to his room he took out the envelope. It was not securely stuck down and he eased it open with the blunt end of the pen provided by the hotel. The message was in Italian, typed on poor-quality paper. It was addressed, as on the envelope, to His Excellency the Ambassador of the United States, and ran:

'The relatives of the four Italian-Americans Lorenzo Sarti, Giulio Spadafora, Mario Bellomo and Ernesto Siracusa, wrongfully arrested in Chicago on 3rd April on suspicion of fraudulent practices in the Congressional Elections, make known to Your Excellency that Jonas Ashbee, the notorious head of the sinister Central Intelligence Agency in Italy, will be executed in ten days' time unless the above-mentioned innocent gentlemen are released and freely allowed to leave United States territory in an Italian aircraft proceeding directly to an Italian airport.

'If any attempt is made to inform the Italian police or the national or international press of this request Mr Ashbee will be liquidated without mercy or delay.'

Craig picked up the telephone and asked for the American Embassy.

'This is Craig, British Embassy. Would you put me through to someone in Mr Ashbee's department?'

'The offices are closed, sir.'

'This is urgent. There'll be somebody there on duty. Put me through, please.'

'I don't think—'

'I don't care what you think. I told you, this is very urgent. If you can't help me I'll ring Mr Marchant.'

'Hold on, sir.' There was a pause and then another voice spoke. Craig told him curtly that Ashbee had been kidnapped and that he had been given a letter for the Ambassador by the men who did it. He asked for someone from Ashbee's department to come to the Eden at once and added that the matter must be handled as Top Secret, since Ashbee's life was at stake.

The startled voice at the other end asked him to come to the Embassy, but Craig refused. 'Sorry, but I've been coshed—yes, coshed, sapped, hit on the head, d'you get that?—and I need some help. You're only a few minutes away, so step on it, lad. But don't inform the police at this stage, is that understood? I'll explain why when I see you —or whoever it is.'

'OK, Mr Craig. I'll be right round.'

He took off his trousers, looked at the sky-blue seat ruefully, and stripped down. He had had a quick shower, dressed in other clothes and was finishing a stiff whisky when there was a knock at the door.

The young man who came in was tall and crew-cut and looked tough; he had a hand in his jacket pocket and pushed Craig gently back into the room while he took a look round. Then he spoke. 'I've left a Marine guard outside, just in case. Now talk, please.'

'Have a whisky. You'll need it.'

'No, sir. Please get to the point.'

'Sit down. Are you on Jo Ashbee's staff? I've got to know because otherwise you won't know what the hell I'm talking about.' He saw the man hesitating. 'Come on. Jo's in serious danger and we've got to act fast. Do you know what I've been doing during the past week?'

'OK, then. Yes, I do. And my name's Hank Jensen.'

'Listen Mr Jensen. I was on a picnic with Jo, Fay and Betty near Castel Fusano. He was snatched. So was his car. Mrs Ashbee and Betty were left without transport. I was knocked out and when I came to had a job getting back and I've only just arrived. I don't know what's happened to Fay and Betty. Can you ring the Embassy and get a car

sent out at once?' Jensen was lifting the telephone before
he had finished speaking.

He gave rapid orders to the Marines officer on duty,
relaying Craig's description of the exact site of the picnic.
Then he came back to Craig. 'What about that letter, sir?'

'I opened it—and take that truculent expression off your
face, Hank. I'll explain why. Look at the message.' He
handed him the open letter.

'Jesus! The Mafia have got him.'

'That's what we're supposed to think. Those four names
are all Mafiosi, are they?'

'Suspected Mafiosi, yes. It was a plot to rig the Chicago
elections. They're as guilty as hell.' He looked at Craig. 'I
suppose it's the Rome Mafia that's hit on this scheme to
buy them off.'

'No. I told you. That's what we're intended to think. It's
the KGB that've got Jo.'

Jensen stared at him. 'They'd never dare.'

'They would if there was something they couldn't get by
other means—and that's just what they think Jo's got in his
head. *And*—this is the point—if they could make us all
think it isn't them at all, but the Mafia.'

'But when he's released—Ugh!' It was a grunt of sheer
horror. 'You think,' he went on slowly, 'that those bastards
would have the neck to bump Jo off when they've got out
of him what they want?'

'Yes,' said Craig flatly. 'They wouldn't have any other
option, would they?' He filled a tumbler half-full of whisky
and added a little water. Hank looked at it for a moment,
dumbly, and then took a long swallow. 'You see, they know
that, one, you can't release the Mafiosi without explaining
why, and two, that you can't do anything without the
Italian police. So their conditions aren't fulfilled and they
can take the action they threaten. It's as simple as that.'

'It's Rostov,' muttered Jensen between his teeth. 'Jesus,
I'd like to get my hands on that son of a bitch. It's his
doing.'

'We'll try and work it so that you can. But first, there's

somebody else in this city who'd like to do the same thing. The head of the Rome Mafia.'

Jensen's head came up with a jerk. 'Yes, *sir*. They won't like it a little bit.' He hesitated. 'I think I could get indirect contact—'

'But you can't convince the Mafia that their name's been smeared unless you show them the letter—and an indirect contact's no good for that. Or unless it comes out in the press.' Jensen shuddered. 'So,' continued Craig, 'I want you to leave that side of the action to me—with the letter.'

'But I've got to have it,' cried Jensen. 'Mr Marchant'll have to see it and we'll have to examine it forensically—'

'For the moment it's mine,' said Craig firmly. 'Even the KGB can't be sure I'm going to hand it over just yet. Look. You copy the text.' He handed him a piece of writing paper from his desk. 'Then go back and get started on the signal to Washington, and Hank—'

'Yes.'

'If I may suggest something to you I'd not show the letter to the Ambassador yet—in fact, not till you've had a reply from the Agency. Incidentally, you must point out to your people that we *know* it's the KGB behind this ploy, and why. But the KGB *can't know* we know that, and they'll probably expect your Embassy to swallow the hook. And for God's sake don't let anyone hear about the letter outside your Embassy. It's just the excuse the KGB are waiting for. Let's have a few hours while they aren't sure what's happened. I'm going to find Jo if it's the last thing I do, and Christ! I need time.'

'And you think I'm going to sit on my fanny? Goddammit, he's my boss. I'm not going to leave you this letter unless you swear you'll bring me in the moment you have a line.'

'OK. I promise that. Leave me some telephone numbers where I can get hold of you.'

Jensen wrote them down on a fresh piece of paper and then went on copying out the text. Then he sat and thought for a moment. 'I've got a standing watch on the main entrance of the Soviet Embassy—we can actually see inside the gate in the Via Gaeta—so I'll know if they bring him in there. But I think it's doubtful. They'll have got him in some hide-out in the country, somewhere. All the same I'll chase up Rostov and Zakharov at every address they use.'

'Do that, as long as they don't know you're doing it. You do see that, don't you? They mustn't suspect for a moment that we know they're behind the snatch.'

'Yes sir. It's tricky, though, isn't it?'

'It's the trickiest thing I've ever struck. Now I'm going to see if I can't explode a bomb in Mafia headquarters. So long, Hank.' He saw him out.

Luigi read the letter and whistled. 'Old Cozzeferrate isn't going to like this. Not one little bit.'

'The head of the Mafia?'

'Yes. The Rome lot. A very tough old man. I'll ring him at once. He prides himself on his relations, under the counter, with the police, but if this got out they'd be grilling him in Regina Coeli within the hour. I must have the letter.'

'You know him well?'

Luigi avoided Craig's amused glance. 'Let's say I'm on good terms of mutual respect. I've had to negotiate with him on occasions.'

'I'm coming with you.'

'No, Peter, he wouldn't talk in front of a stranger.'

'Look, Luigi. There's no time to waste. They may have started pumping truth drugs into Ashbee already. I *must* be with you, I can describe what happened and the men who did it.'

'All right. I'll try.'

Twenty minutes later they were sitting round a table in a highly respectable café in the Borgo San Lorenzo, on the other side of the Tiber. But Craig noticed that the tables near them were not occupied—everybody else seemed to prefer to sit farther away.

Luca Cozzeferrate was an old man of immense presence. He stood about five foot three, with an enormous barrel chest under his tightly buttoned blue serge suit. Although he was over seventy he had a full head of frizzy grey hair and a sweeping moustache curled into wide points.

Craig waited impatiently while the ceremonious greetings were exchanged and he was introduced as a dear friend of Luigi's of very long standing. The fact that he was a police officer was not mentioned. He gave his account of what had happened and turned round so that the old man could examine, with professional curiosity, the lump on the back of his head. Then he produced the letter.

Cozzeferrate's first reaction was to laugh heartily, wiping his rheumy old eyes with a spotless white handkerchief. Then he looked again at the names and went purple in the face. '*Che schifo!*' he exploded. 'But it's impossible. They'd never have dared to write this. *E uno scandalo!*' He turned to Craig and seized his arm in a grip of iron. 'Who did it?'

'The letter is a fake,' said Craig flatly. 'It was not the relatives of the men in Chicago who wrote this. It was the Russians.'

The old man looked baffled, and Luigi hastened to explain. The Russian intelligence had used this excuse to seize an American official and torture him to death. All the blame would be on the Mafia.

Old Luca gave a roar of rage. At the other tables several men got up and quietly left the café. 'Ask him—' he pointed to Craig—'to describe the men, all he can remember. But wait—my son-in-law must hear this.' He raised his hand and a young man hurried forward. He was dressed immaculately in a purplish suit with wide, padded shoulders. His face was pale, with black eyes and a hooked nose. He moved like a cat.

He was introduced as Marcantonio, known as Tonino, and sat down with his dark eyes fixed on Craig's face as he described again what had happened and added rough descriptions of the men involved.

'The driver of the Buick,' he concluded, 'was a man of

medium height but very broad, like a gorilla, with very long arms. I couldn't see his face, because he had a stocking over it, but I think he was just a strong man, not a killer. The other man—the one who coshed me—was about the same height, say one metre seventy-five, with a bald head and a fringe of black hair, wearing a dark brown sports' shirt and light beige trousers and a brown hat.'

'If he was wearing a hat, how did you know he was bald?' asked the young man softly, in Italian.

'It fell off when I tackled him. He looked like a gunman —that sort of mouth—and he had narrow brown eyes, ears pointed and sticking out, and a small scar at the right hand side of his mouth.'

'His right side—or yours?'

'His.' There were no flies on this boy, thought Craig. 'He had a Mauser H SC 7 mm., no silencer.' He paused, then grinned suddenly. 'There is one other thing. If he got into the back of the Buick when it drove off, as he probably did because the driver was on his side of the car and he'd have been in a hurry, the seat of his trousers—and the skin underneath—will by now be bright blue.' He pulled out of his pocket the pair of cotton trunks he had been wearing at the time of the snatch and threw them on the table. 'That colour.'

'*Perbacco*!' said Cozzeferrate.

Ashbee was still blindfolded when they took him into the small room under the stairs. Then they took the thing off. The windows were closely barred. The place smelled of damp and the air was stale. There was a table and chairs and a camp bed along one wall.

The tall man signed to him to sit down and then patted his pockets to see if he had anything concealed. It was all done politely, but the automatic in the man's hand called for obedience. He went out and closed the door behind him. Ashbee heard the sound of a heavy bolt being shot into place.

It was half an hour afterwards that Rostov came in. He

o

sat down with the table between him and the American, holding his Walther PKK in his lap. For a time they looked at each other silently. Then Rostov spoke.

'We needn't beat about the bush, Mr Ashbee.' His English was surprisingly good. 'We've both met on occasions at cocktail parties and receptions. More frequently, perhaps, we have been aware of each other's existence at second hand—professionally. Let me say at once that I have a respect for your intelligence, in both senses of the word.'

'What is the meaning of this charade, Rostov?'

'I apologize for the dramatics. But really, it seemed the only way of having a quiet talk with you.'

'Why not a quiet cup of coffee at Doney's?'

'Oh yes, coffee. Let's have it now. I asked them to have it ready.' He went to the wall and pressed a bell-push. 'There you are, you see. If there's anything you want, ring for it.' When the door opened he called out something in Russian. They heard the sound of the bolt as the door was closed.

'Now let me see, yes, you asked why we could not have met socially. It's simple. I don't want anyone at all to know that we *have* met. If you are sensible you will leave here and forget all about this meeting.'

'Don't be a fool. You're not going to be able to get away with this. Twenty-four hours after I leave this place you'll be *persona non grata* to the Italian Government, I can assure you of that. Have you got Craig here as well?'

'I think I'll leave you in ignorance for the time being about Mr Craig, if that is the man you were with.' There was again the sound of the heavy bolt and the tall man came in with a tray bearing a coffee-pot, two cups and saucers, sugar and a small bottle of transparent liquid.

'Do you like a *caffè corretto*?' This is good Kirsch and the coffee is our best Caucasian.'

'Thank you.' He waited until Rostov had poured the coffee and added Kirsch. 'Not that cup, Rostov, the other one.'

'How mistrustful you are!' said Rostov, laughing. He

had taken the Walther from his lap and had it on the table in front of him, near to his hand. 'Here you are.'

'Come to the point, Rostov.'

'All right. I will tell you what I want to know, and you will see that it won't hurt you in the least to tell me. Whereas otherwise—well, we'll leave that for the moment. Explain why you are taking such a close interest in my Ambassador.'

'How do you know I am?'

'Oh, there have been signs,' said Rostov airily, 'such things as close surveillance of his movements, enquiries into his contacts and so on. All very cleverly done. But why? That is what you are going to tell me, Ashbee. Why?'

'It wouldn't be unnatural for me to take an interest in a new Ambassador of the USSR. He's only been here three months. But all the same, what you're saying is quite untrue. I'm not investigating him.'

'You're lying.'

'You wouldn't say that outside this place of yours.'

'But I do say it here, because you are at present in my power. I can do what I like with you. Nobody knows you're here. Nor will they know. That's why you have nothing to lose by telling me what I want to know. Then you can go home, with a story that you were kidnapped in mistake for someone else.'

'Kidnapped?'

'Why, yes. In fact, I think I'll tell you a little more. Craig was set free with a note from the kidnappers, asking for the release of the four Mafiosi held in Chicago—in exchange for your life.'

'Mafiosi?' Ashbee stared at him for a second. Then he said slowly, 'So the Mafia here will be blamed?'

'That's the idea—and I'm rather proud of it. You see, the note made it clear that if anyone told the Press or the Italian police you would be liquidated at once. And that's what we could do with you, Ashbee, and no one would be a penny the wiser. But I want you to give your help freely.'

'Freely! Go on, tell me what happens if I don't tell you

what you want to know—and I can't anyway, because you've got it all wrong.'

'Well, then I'm afraid we shall have to use quite ruthless but sophisticated methods of interrogation, and as you know very well, that is one thing in which my service is extremely competent. We shall get it all out of you, don't be in any doubt about that. But afterwards, we may well decide, as I said, to let you go, provided you don't talk about what's happened here.'

'And if I do?'

'You want it spelt out, do you? I shall have taken the precaution of drugging you, stripping you of your clothes and taking photographs of you in bed with an attractive girl. One of our secretaries is really very good-looking, and she hasn't the slightest objection to being photographed in the nude. She's done it before. So if you do open your mouth copies will be sent not just to the Rome press and your Agency, but to your family in the United States and, if ever you were to be posted abroad again—which I would think unlikely—more copies would be sent to each post for distribution as most effective.' He smiled at Ashbee's troubled face, then said sharply, 'So make up your mind, man. Talk!'

Ashbee stretched out a trembling hand for his coffee and raised it towards his lips. Then he leaned forward across the table. 'You wouldn't do that, Rostov. I've only got two years to go before I retire. There'd be reprisals against your men. You *can't* ignore all the rules of the game—' He was speaking in a low tone, appealingly.

Rostov laughed and peered into the big man's face. 'But I will, Ashbee—' The scalding contents of the coffee-cup, with the added fiery sting of the alcohol, took him full in the eyes. He screamed with pain, but the gun was under his hand and he found the trigger and pulled. He aimed blindly at what a moment before had been Jonas Ashbee. The bullet sped through empty air until it hit the stone wall with a vicious crack.

The American had slid sideways from his chair and

found Rostov's outstretched foot under the table. He braced himself against the table leg and hauled. As the Russian came flopping on to the floor Ashbee twisted the foot and turned him over on to his face. He heard the thud of running feet, but for a moment he was protected by the heavy table above him. He snatched the automatic from Rostov's hand and hit him with the butt on the back of the head with all his strength. And he was a very strong man.

Then the table was lifted in the air and thrown aside, and the blows rained down on him. In the half-second before he lost consciousness he had the feeling of a job well done. It would be some time before anyone could get much sense out of Rostov—or out of him either, and that was the object of the exercise.

CHAPTER NINETEEN

SATURDAY EVENING

It was infuriating, sitting in the comfort of Luigi's flat and unable to do anything but ring people up, hoping for news. Craig tried Ashbee's flat again, and this time heard Fay's voice. It was lifeless, but quite firm. In a crisis she didn't waste time on tears.

'Hullo, Peter. I've got your jacket. It had a gun in it. There are two rounds missing now.'

'Good God! What happened?'

'I flagged a car. Two passed and wouldn't stop, the bastards, so I stood in the middle of the road and fired in the air. Tell me where you are and I'll send the coat. It's got your wallet in it and everything.'

'I'm at Luigi's. I must stay here, Fay, because—'

'Yes, I know you're doing your best. Hank's been here. He says you're trying to do it yourself. Hadn't you better leave it to the pros, Peter? I don't want to be rude, but as far as I can see you got Jo into this mess.' There was no bitterness in her voice. She was just stating a point of view.

'That's why I've got to get him out of it. As soon as I have a line I'll ring Hank and—'

'And what's happening to Jo in the meantime?'

There was nothing Craig could say. He muttered some words of sympathy and hung up.

Luigi came in, and Craig burst out, 'It's like looking for a needle in a haystack. How can your Mafia pals comb through the whole of the Rome underworld in time for us to do *anything*? We'd better tell the KGB we know they've got him and let the police in.'

Luigi sat down. 'It's too risky, Peter. They could still liquidate Ashbee and deny everything. You've got no proof, nothing you could show. We must wait a bit longer. Cozzeferrate has a lot of contacts.'

'Contacts!' said Craig scornfully.

'And,' added Luigi, 'he has three hundred and forty little walkie-talkies. I know; I supplied them.' He looked at Craig's astonished face. 'I wasn't going to tell you, because it's one of the deals I don't usually talk about. But it's as well, in my job, to keep on good terms with the Mafia. At present there are at least three hundred men in touch with their HQ, and I'd expect them to be well spread throughout Rome. There's a really good chance of identifying one or more of the men involved in the snatch.'

'But that doesn't mean we can lay hands on them. They've got to ditch that Buick, to start with.'

The bell rang, and a moment later the Mafiosi chief's son-in-law came into the room, with a cheerful grin on his face. He began to talk to Luigi fast, partly in Sicilian dialect, and Craig couldn't understand a word. Luigi turned to him.

'They've got one of them. A man called Gianni, the bald one with the scar.'

'Where—?'

'Somewhere in Trastevere. He hasn't talked yet, but it's him all right. He'd changed his pants, but they stripped him and his bottom was bright blue, even,' he added with a cold smile, 'before they started in on him.'

'Get Tonino to take me there,' said Craig urgently. 'I'll make him talk. He'll know it's all up when he sees me.'

Luigi talked to Tonino, who nodded, and then began to make a condition, explaining something at length. Craig listened impatiently to the strange, clipped Italian. Luigi said, 'He'll only agree if you're blindfolded.'

Craig said nothing but took out his handkerchief and offered it to the Italian, who smiled and waved it away. 'Not yet,' he said courteously, and led the way to the door.

Luigi's Alfa Romeo followed the big Fiat down to the Via Flaminia and into the Piazza del Popolo, then right until they found the Tiber and could join the smooth rush of traffic along the Lungotevere. They passed under the

Castel Sant'Angelo and finally reached the edge of the ancient district of Trastevere—all narrow streets and winding alleys, the heart of the Roman underworld. They came out into the big square in which Craig and the Kahns had dined the previous night, but went on, skirting Santa Maria, into a maze of small stone-paved alleys. The Fiat drew up.

Luigi stopped his car and reached into his pocket. 'You'd better have this,' he said, handing him a Walther automatic, 'but keep it hidden. You'll join them in the Fiat now, and they'll cover your eyes. Good luck! I'll be at home if you want me.'

It was some minutes later that Craig heard the creak of the big wooden doors and sensed, although he could not see, that the Fiat had entered a garage. The doors were closed, and Tonino, with apologies, removed the bandage they had tied round his head. He helped Craig out and led him to a small stone doorway at the rear of the garage. They went down steps and, after an elaborate business of passwords called through a heavy oak door, were let in.

It was a cellar, by the look of the damp walls and the trickle of water running across the floor, but it was furnished adequately with leather chairs, cupboards and a long table. There were no windows, and the air smelled stale. Tonino took a paraffin lamp from the man who had opened the door and led Craig to the opposite wall. It appeared to be blank, the old stone blocks fitting closely, but the Sicilian gleefully drew his attention to a crack between two blocks. He bent down and whistled through it, and as if by magic a whole section of the wall swung outwards to reveal a room beyond. The short dark man who had pushed open the door had a rubber cosh in his hand.

Beyond him, on a bed against the wall of the small cell in which they found themselves, a man was lying. His wrists and legs were bound and there was a bandage round his eyes. There were marks of violence on his jaw and body. He was quite naked. He groaned deeply as he heard the footsteps.

Tonino had drawn a rubber truncheon from his pocket and was swinging it in his hand. Craig said, 'Listen, Tonino. I think I can make him talk. But he must see my face. Stand on the other side of the door, all of you, so that he can't recognize you afterwards. Then I'll take the scarf off. OK?'

The Mafioso agreed, rather reluctantly, and the man set the lamp on the table by the bed. They went out, leaving the door half open.

Craig went up to the bed and untied the blindfold. Then he held the lamp so that the man could see his face. Gianni stared at him without expression and turned away. Craig slapped his face. 'Look at me,' he ordered. 'You know me, don't you?'

'Yes,' said the man, sullenly.

'And you know what was in that letter you put in my pocket?'

'No,' said Gianni boldly. But he was beginning to look frightened.

'It was signed by the Mafia. But it was your masters who wrote it—the Russians.'

Gianni turned his face away, then saw that Craig was raising his hand again and faced him. 'I didn't know,' he muttered.

'It doesn't matter, Gianni. It won't help you. Those men behind the door are members of the Brotherhood. *They believe* you know about that trick the Russians played with their good name, and they want to make an example of you, so that no one again will do the same. Of course, they will kill you in the end, but it will not be an easy death and it will not only be you. They will take their revenge on all your family, your wife and children, and your father and mother, and every one of your relatives. That is what they have taught the members of the Brotherhood to expect if they betray their oath.'

'But I am not a member,' the man shouted. 'I've never had anything to do with them. I haven't betrayed them.'

'You have done something they think is worse. As an out-

sider you have dared to use their name as a cover for your
own crimes. That is why they want their revenge.'

'*Animali!*' he cried, twisting and jerking at his bonds.

'Yes, you can say that,' said Craig inexorably. He hated
this melodramatic rhetoric, but it might work when violence failed. 'But what will your wife and your children
say, when the executioners come in the night?' He turned
towards the door. 'What words will your mother scream
out, before they cut her throat? Curses on *you*, Gianni, not
on the Mafia. And you will hear her curses in hell.'

'Stop!' The man was struggling to get up. 'If I take you
where they've taken the American, will they swear to let
me go and not harm my family?'

'I don't know,' said Craig. 'I will ask them.'

He tied the scarf again round the terror-stricken eyes
and went to the door. On the other side Tonino and the
other two men were all smiles. Tonino explained to them,
'*Il sistema psicologico. Molto effettivo.*' He turned to Craig.
'It sounded good, Signore. I will go in now and make an
oath, perhaps?'

'Yes. Have you got a Crucifix?'

'But of course.' He pulled it out of his shirt—a charming
cross of gold and enamel—and kissed it reverently. 'Now
leave it to me.'

He went into the room with Craig, who remained silent
while Tonino spoke in a solemn voice. 'I swear on the
Cross of Christ and by the Virgin Mary that if you will
help us now and in the future your family will not be hurt.
You will pay a fine, but we shall not harm you either. All
this I swear in the name of the Brotherhood.' Then he
lowered the Crucifix on to Gianni's naked chest and
brought his tied hands to feel it. 'Do you agree?'

'Yes.' The man stood up, swaying, and they untied his
feet and led him into the other room. The driver produced
a bottle of red wine and some glasses, and poured it out.
They removed the rope from Gianni's wrists but left the
scarf on his eyes. Then he was given a glass and after he
had swallowed the wine helped into his clothes. He was

told to sit down.

'How many men are with the American?' asked Craig. 'And where is he?'

'We were all at the monastery this morning. It is a house owned by a rich Roman, near Lake Nemi, in the Castelli. I didn't know there were Russians there. The man who hired me and Giacomino, who drove the Buick after the snatch, was Il Capitano. I've worked for him before.'

'And who else?'

'He hired two other men, whose names I don't know. They drove in the snatch car. I was to put the envelope in your pocket after—putting you to sleep. But I didn't know what was in it. The tall man—I think they called him Marco—had lifted the big Fiat during the night from a car-park, he told us, and he was going to take the American back to the monastery. That's all I know.'

'What about the Buick?'

'I don't know. Giacomino was to ditch it. He dropped me in the city.'

Craig took Tonino aside. 'I want to put through a telephone call. You can tie my eyes if you wish.'

'There's no need. Come with me.' He took him out of the door and up the steps into the garage and then across to another door, which he unlocked. It led into a passage, with rooms on both sides. There was a wall telephone. 'I'll stay outside.'

'No. Please stay with me. I may want to consult you.' He rang the first number Jensen had given him. The young American answered.

'Listen, Hank, we've got the address.'

'It's too late, Mr Craig.' His voice sounded utterly depressed. 'I've just had a report. Rostov's car arrived at the Embassy half an hour ago. As I told you, they can see inside the gates, and they saw Zakharov get out, and then he and the driver carried somebody into the building. There were bandages round his head. Well, he reported that and then ten minutes ago rang me again. He said Zakharov had come out driving his own car. No sign of

Rostov. In fact, he hasn't been seen all day. Another of our men tried to follow Zakharov, but got shaken in the old town.' He paused. 'I may be jumping to conclusions, Craig, but I think that's it. They've got him inside. I'll have to go and see Mr Marchant; those are my orders.'

Craig was silent, but he was thinking furiously. 'Jumping to conclusions'. It was Ashbee who had said that: 'You both draw conclusions, and half the time they're wrong.' It could be, he thought.

'What's Zakharov's car?'

'Lancia Fulvia. Roma 684 CD.' A pause. 'Why d'you want to know? You're not going there—wherever it is?'

'Just in case I see him somewhere.'

'Now look, Mr Craig, if you're going there I'll follow as soon as I've seen the boss.' His voice was loud enough for Tonino to hear, and he signalled furiously, shaking his head.

'You keep out of this, Hank. It's likely to be a wildgoose chase, but there's nothing else I can do. I'll ring you as soon as I can.' He rang off, silencing a loud protesting noise from Jensen's end. Then turned an enquiring eye on Tonino.

'If you go, Signor Craig, we go with you. It's still our business and I don't want Americans swarming all over the place. I'll just tell Luigi and let him report what's happened to the old man.'

'You don't want to ring him direct?' said Craig, grinning.

'No, he might say not to go.' He picked up the telephone.

When he had finished speaking they went back through the garage and down the steps. Once again, passwords exchanged through the closed door, and then it was opened. Gianni was sitting at the table, talking, while the gaoler re-tied his wrists.

'He has explained where the monastery is, and I can find it. It's off the Via dei Laghi, past the turning to Monte Cavo, an old stone house with very thick walls, built against the hill-side, and there's about a quarter of a

hectare of land round it, mostly olive trees, with a bare
space near the house. They parked at the end of a rough
road that leads only to the house, and went through a gate
in a wall and up a winding path to the front entrance.'

'*Va bene*,' said Tonino. 'Marco, take him back inside
and tie his feet. Then come back here.' When the man
returned Craig was formally introduced, and the two
Sicilians bowed and offered their hands.

Marco was a little dark man with a sallow face marred
by a long knife wound down his cheek. Lucio was big for a
Southerner, good-looking, with flashing black eyes, and
sculptured whiskers. They sat down.

Tonino spoke. 'There are three men there, at least—the
two who went off with the American and the boss they call
the Capitano. And perhaps Giacomino, too, the driver of
the Buick.'

'And any Russians who may be on the job. There is one
in particular I want to meet—the one who planned the
whole thing.'

'It is he I would like to meet, too,' said Tonino with a
slight smile. 'What do you want to do, Mr Craig?'

'I heard just now on the telephone that the American
seems to have been taken to the Russian Embassy.' He saw
the puzzled look on Tonino's face. 'Yes, I know it looks as
if there's no point in going out to this house that Gianni
spoke about. But there's just a chance that one of the
Russian intelligence officers is still there. If I could get hold
of him I could ransom him for Ashbee before—things go
too far. But it means acting very fast.'

'We are ready.'

'You've done enough already. I don't want to run your
neck into a noose.'

'It is our business as well as yours. The men who wrote
that letter must be punished. Marco must stay here, to guard
the prisoner, but Lucio and I will come with you. We are
armed.'

'What with?' asked Craig cautiously. He feared they
might only have the knives which are the traditional weap-

on of the Mafia.

'I have this,' he pulled out from under his arm a 9 mm. Luger, 'and Lucio has a machine-pistol in the car—a Schmeisser.'

'Good God!' said Craig cheerfully, 'that's more like it. All I've got is what Luigi gave me just now.' He reached into his side-pocket and pulled out a .32 Walther. 'But with twenty-eight rounds in your Schmeisser you could do a lot of persuading.' He got up. He had burnt his boats already by not telling Hank where the monastery lay. He wanted action, *now*, and couldn't wait for Hank or Cozze-ferrate or the police; if anything could be done to help Jo it had to be at once. It was a pretty forlorn hope, but better than waiting around.

To save time, as he entered the Fiat he bound his own eyes while Tonino made apologies. Then the big car was driv-ing fast through the narrow streets back to the Lungo-tevere. Once there the bandage was taken off and he could see where they were going.

They crossed the river and worked their way along the crowded streets until they could pass through the walls and get on to the New Appian Way, and here the car began to pick up speed. Twenty minutes later Lucio turned off to the left and came out on to the Via dei Laghi, the spectacular road that runs along the edges of the volcanic craters which contain the lakes of Albano and Nemi. The moon was rising, and they could dimly see the woods sloping steeply upwards towards Monte Cavo. Then the car slowed to a halt. Lucio reached under the driving seat and pulled out a folded-up Schmeisser, which he proceeded to set up and load, talking as he did so.

'You see that kilometre stone ahead? That's where Gianni said the little approach road to the monastery leads off, only you can't see it for the trees. It's about half a kilo-metre long and not far from the end there's a place he saw where we could park the car. I'll turn so it faces back this way, right?'

'OK. Get moving, then.'

The Fiat turned left-handed into the narrow dirt road and some way down it they saw what Gianni had meant. A cart track led off through the trees. Lucio backed into it and stopped the engine. Then they went forward, silently, along the road.

It came to an end in an open space. Beyond this was a high stone wall which crossed their line of vision at right angles and disappeared into the trees on both sides. There was a gate in it, open, and through it they could see the ground rising steeply towards a building in the background. But their eyes were more occupied with a car which they could just see in the gloom, parked under the trees on one side of the open space. The three men froze in their tracks, then slid sideways under the trees.

Craig whispered, 'I'll go first,' and began to work his way round through the trees. He had been afraid that the town-bred Sicilians would make too much noise, but he could scarcely hear them as they cautiously followed him until they were standing near the car, with its bulk hiding them from anyone who might come through the gate. It was the Lancia, all right, and empty, but there was plenty of heat still coming from the engine. Craig took out the ignition key and slipped it into his pocket. Then he signed to Tonino and Lucio to cross the open space at one side and take up a position by the gate.

He walked forward without trying to deaden the slight noise of his footsteps, but nobody challenged him and he passed through the gateway.

The monks, who had come to live there in the thirteenth century, had chosen the site well. It backed on to a precipitous spur of Monte Cavo, which sheltered it from winter gales, and so they had been able to grow olives, and some of the ancient trees, gnarled, twisting, with their concrete fillings and props, looked as if they had been there from the beginning. Someone had given a coat of white to the lower trunks, and they glimmered in the moonlight.

From the gate a path, with occasional stone steps, wound

its way upwards through the eerie maze of white trunks.
The three men spread out—Craig on the path and the
others on each side, climbing through the coarse grass—and
went forward slowly, pausing every few seconds to listen.
But apart from the silvery rustle of the leaves and the creak
of ancient boughs there was no sound at all. Then the trees
came to an end, and across a ragged patch of gravel they
could see the squat, massive shape of the abbey in front of
them. It was quite small.

The entrance consisted of a deep stone archway; the door
itself was hidden in the shadows. The building stood four-
square with deeply inset windows, all barred, and above the
low roof a sturdy little bell-tower appeared. There was a
glint of light between the drawn curtains of a room to the
right of the entrance, but no other sign of life whatever.

Suddenly, as they stood watching, each man hidden behind the thick bole of an olive tree, there was the sound of
a door opening in the shadow beneath the archway, and a
flashing glimpse of light within. Then the door closed and
was locked—they heard the sound of the heavy key turning
—and a figure came out into the dim moonlight. It was the
man who had driven the Buick; there was no mistaking
those broad shoulders and long arms. He had a shotgun
under his arm and stood looking out for a moment. Then
he took a torch from his pocket and began to walk slowly
round the side of the building, flashing his torch at the
trees. They watched until the light disappeared behind the
rear of the house and then acted very fast.

At a whispered command from Craig he and Tonino
ran silently across the open space and crouched inside the
archway, hidden by the stone columns that stood out on
each side. Lucio remained where he was, well hidden behind a massive trunk.

They heard the guard coming round the other side of the
house, and waited, tensely. Lucio played his part well. As
the guard reached the archway there was the sharp crackle
of a twig from his tree.

The man was instantly alert, but his left hand was trying

to hold the light of the torch on the tree and support the shotgun at the same time, and it was during his momentary fumbling that Tonino's gun-butt caught him on the back of the head. Craig grabbed him as he fell and lowered him to the ground. Then he whirled round, but there was neither light nor sound from the dark building behind him.

They carried the guard into the trees and bound his arms behind him with his own belt. Tonino felt in his pockets and found the great key of the front door. Then they gagged him, took his shotgun and left him.

The lock groaned as Craig turned the key, and he pushed it open and stood back. But there was no sign of life, and only the dim light of a dusty lantern hung high up under the vaulted ceiling. On the right was a closed door leading presumably into the room from which they had seen light escaping between the curtains. There was also another door on the left, and straight ahead, beyond the curving stone staircase, a door was ajar and they could see light beyond. Craig moved towards it on the tips of his toes, while Lucio took up his stand beside the door on the right and Tonino remained in the centre of the hall, his automatic in his hand.

Craig swung the door open quietly and stepped inside. A man was bending over a bed placed against the opposite wall. He was fair-haired and young. He spun round.

Craig spoke softly in English. 'Don't try to shout, Zakharov, or I'll kill you.' There was no mistaking the menace in his voice or the gesture with the Walther in his hand, and the man froze, his eyes glancing sideways at the gun he had left on the table beside the bed.

Then Craig saw that it was Ashbee lying there, and his heart gave a great leap. There was a rough bandage round his head, to stop bleeding, but nothing had been done about the welter of cuts and bruises on his face.

'Is he dead?' said Craig coldly.

'Find out,' said the Russian, and changed the weight on his legs, ready to spring for the gun. Craig moved forward and picked it up—it was a twenty-shot Stechkin, 9 mm.,

P

only nine inches long but capable of being fired fully automatic; not a weapon to leave in an enemy's possession for
long. He thrust it into his pocket. Afterwards he admitted
to himself, ruefully, that he went near the Russian hoping
to provoke him into starting something. He certainly succeeded.

Zakharov chopped with the edge of his hand, like lightning, at his gun-arm, and the automatic dropped from
fingers that could not hold it. But as the Russian stooped to
pick it up—and he moved very fast—Craig's left fist caught
him on the side of his jaw. It was a perfect counter, deliv-
ered with a lot of pent-up hate behind it, and Zakharov's
sudden movement doubled the effect. He went over backwards and lay on his back near the bed.

Craig rubbed his right arm and picked up the Walther
with his left. Then he went to look at his friend. Ashbee's
eyes were closed, but he was speaking in a low, monotonous
babble of sound, the words indistinguishable. Craig thought
he must be delirious, until he saw the hypodermic syringe
which had fallen from the Russian's hand.

Craig always liked to think of himself as a reasonable,
rather unemotional man, although he knew there were
times when the label didn't fit. And this was one of them.
He had a policeman's loathing of drugs, but they were a
fact of life in his world and you dealt with addicts and even
pushers equitably and humanely. But to him the ultimate
horror, far worse than physical torture, was to inject serum
or drugs into a helpless man to make him talk; it was a
crime against a man's persona. For a moment he had in
mind to put down Zakharov like a mad dog and he lifted
the automatic with his finger on the trigger. Then the rage
passed; the problem was to immobilize the Russian absolutely and there was neither time nor rope to do it conven-
tionally. He cut the rope that bound Ashbee's legs together,
but there was only enough for Zakharov's wrists. He heard
a sound at the door and spun round, but it was Tonino,
who had heard the noise of Zakharov's fall. He waved him

back; his presence in the hall was essential.

Suddenly he smiled grimly and looked around for a strong bar, but there was nothing in the room but the bed and a table and chair. He tipped over the table and with a vicious kick broke off one of the legs. It was a piece of deal about two inches square in section and thirty inches long. He pulled the Russian into a sitting position, with his knees drawn up to his chin and his arms, tightly bound at the wrists, encircling them. Then he took the table leg and thrust it through the space under the man's bent knees and above his elbows. It was a tight fit and he had to kneel on Zakharov's shoulders to get the wooden bar through. Then he stood back.

The man was coming to and groaning with pain, but Craig was satisfied that he could be left alone; the pressure of the insides of his knees and elbows on the square table-leg would give him no chance of working it out. It was all done in half a minute, and he went back into the hall. Tonino was startled at the look on his face.

'The American is there,' said Craig tersely. 'I don't understand why, but he is. And he's still alive.' He hadn't bothered to lower his voice. They heard the scrape of a chair inside the closed room, then footsteps, and the door opened. The man who came out was the tall gunman who had been in charge of the kidnapping. He was evidently expecting to see Zakharov or the guard, because he was unarmed and unsuspecting. Not that it would have made much difference—Lucio had a knife prodding his ribs before he could take a further step, and Craig and Tonino pushed past him and burst into the lighted room.

It was big, and comfortably furnished, with a long dining table at one end and at the other sofas and arm-chairs arranged in a semi-circle round a fire of olive logs. Heavy velvet curtains hung against the high windows and the ceiling, like the hall, was vaulted in stone, with a Venetian chandelier hanging high in the smoke-laden air. Behind one of the arm-chairs, conveniently to hand, was a small marble table on which lay a telephone. And also a

Beretta automatic.

The short dark man who had been sitting at his ease in the chair, smoking a cigar, twisted round to see what was happening and lunged for the gun. Tonino's quick eye had seen the danger the moment he entered the room and he dived full length for the pedestal of the table and knocked it over. But Il Capitano had his hand on the gun already when Craig fired.

He aimed at the automatic, but missed, and hit a brightly burning log in the fireplace. The result was spectacular. The log exploded, and the Capitano's figure was framed in a whirlwind of flying embers. The man dropped the automatic and screamed, slapping the back of his neck and jumping up to throw off a still burning piece of wood that had landed, fortuitously, on his lap. But by that time Craig was standing over him. He slowly raised his hands above his head.

Tonino was up in a flash, retrieved the gun, and poked the barrel roughly into parts of the man's body where he might have had another weapon. Then he backed away and looked down at his purple suiting. '*Ci manca un bottone,*' he said resentfully.

'Never mind that,' cried Craig, 'the bloody carpet's burning.' Smoke was rising in a dozen places and Tonino went round, stamping out the smouldering wool. Then he found the missing button and put it away carefully in his pocket. He looked at the Capitano with an expression that made the man blink.

'So you are the pig who sets himself up against the Brotherhood,' he said softly, and took a slow step nearer.

'You have no right—' he began, but he had trodden back on a large piece of red-hot wood, and his attempt at dignity failed in his convulsive leap to safety. Tonino gave a roar of laughter.

'You are the one they call Capitano?' asked Craig, contemptuously.

'I am,' said the little man, drawing himself up.

'Where is the other Russian?'

'I do not speak with bandits.'

'Show him a knife, Tonino,' said Craig coldly.

The Sicilian went towards him with a knife projecting upwards from his right fist, which he held low in front of him. The man was tough but he recognized the gesture and turned pale. 'You are Mafiosi,' he muttered.

'Tell him why you are angry with him, Tonino.'

Tonino did so, adding in bloodcurdling detail what he proposed to do about it.

'I didn't know,' the man screamed.

'But that is what the Russians did,' explained Craig. 'If you don't know it's too bad for you. If you want mercy you had better do what we say. Where is Rostov?'

'He was hurt by the big American. Badly. His skull was broken. They took him away.' Then Craig understood. The bandaged figure carried into the Embassy had been the Russian.

'What other man was here?'

'The guard, and the man who went out of this room before you came in, and the tall Russian.'

'And the other man? The second driver, who drove the Buick?'

'He went into Albano for food.'

'Were there no other Russians?'

'No. He—Rostov—said there was no need.'

'I see.' Craig went across to the window and wrenched away the thick cord which closed the curtains. 'Get the other man in and tie them up and gag them.' He didn't know the word for 'gag' but pretended to stuff his handkerchief into his mouth. Tonino nodded, and called to Lucio to bring in his prisoner. They made a quick, professional job of it and Craig looked on with approval.

'We can't wait to bring in the other man, the one who was on guard. We've got to get the American to a doctor quickly. Lucio had better guard the door in case the other driver returns.' He went across to the fallen telephone, put it on the sofa beside him and telephoned.

'We've got your boss, Hank, and he's all right.' There

was an excited babble at the other end. 'Yes, it was Rostov whom you saw taken into the Embassy. Jo's been badly beaten up, and they must have given him some damned truth serum. But it's gone wrong. He's talking, but doesn't make sense. Tell your doctor that and bring him out here quick. I haven't had time to examine him yet. We've had a bit of a scrap. But I don't think we ought to move him till the doctor comes, so make it quick. You've got a doctor?'

'Yes, sir.'

'Good. This is where we are.' And he told him, adding the telephone number. 'Bring two men with you, armed, and be careful as you come in. One man's still missing. But we've got Zakharov.' He rang off.

Tonino picked up the receiver. 'I'll tell Luigi.' Craig nodded and went back into the hall and unbolted the oak door beyond the stairs.

He ignored Zakharov, who was rolling from side to side, a human bundle of frustration as he sought to free himself from the wooden bar that locked his body together, and went straight to the bed.

Ashbee was still mumbling interminably, but his pulse, although 'thready', was not dangerously weak.

Tonino came in, and stood staring astonished at the human ball in the middle of the floor. *'Perbacco!'* he said, with respect in his voice. 'That's neat. Is that what you do with them in England?'

'No,' said Craig, thinking of British courts of enquiry. 'Not exactly. I saw a picture of it in Brazil. It's an old slave-overseer's trick.' He wasn't proud of using it, but he looked at the result with cold satisfaction. The man's face was purple with rage and the veins on his forehead stood out in knots. Craig wanted him to feel utterly humiliated, lying in a bundle on the floor, at the mercy of anyone who cared to take a kick at him. The gentler treatment could come later.

'What drug did you use?' he asked harshly.

The young man spat. Craig lifted his foot, and then

instead of kicking him rocked him from side to side with his toe.

'I haven't time to waste. You speak English, I know, so you understand. I have to get my friend to a doctor. If he dies you will be responsible. It's immaterial to me whether you live or not, but I will do anything—anything at all—to save Ashbee. Tell me quickly what I want to know, or I take him away and leave you with the Mafiosi.'

'The Mafia!' cried Zakharov, startled.

'What did you expect when you sent off that note? Did you think they'd like it?' He turned to the door. 'You'll soon see how they like it.'

'I told him,' the young man muttered. Craig turned back.

'You told Rostov, did you? What?'

'I told him it was too dangerous.'

'And he told you not to be a fool. He said by the time the Americans had decided to call in the police, thus risking Ashbee's life, he'd be dead already. And no trace? Is that it?'

The young man's body was motionless. His grey eyes looked at Craig without expression. Craig knew he had guessed right. He bent down and shouted, 'But when you were left to get on with the interrogation you didn't hesitate, did you? Did you?' he repeated, seizing the man's hair and forcing him to look up. 'You injected him with some damned truth drug, didn't you?'

'No.' The word was forced out.

'Don't lie. You had the hypodermic in your hand.'

'No. They telephoned from the Section before I got back and told the Capitano what to do. The drug was here already. Ros—my colleague was going to use it, but the American half-killed him.' He looked up at Craig's sceptical face. 'But they used too much. What I was trying to do was stimulate his heart.'

Craig picked up the syringe and smelled it. 'Yes, it's camphor. But why did you do that? To make him talk coherently, wasn't that it?'

'That, too,' admitted Zakharov. 'But he would have died if I hadn't.'

Craig turned to look at Ashbee. His lips were still moving, but his breathing was easier and the babble of sound had stopped. He was asleep.

'This is the state you wanted him in, isn't it, Zakharov? Just about now you would have splashed water on his face to wake him up?'

No reply.

'Then you would have begun to interrogate him gently and insistently, coaxing him to tell you the things he would never have said otherwise. Then another splash of water, perhaps, if he showed signs of going to sleep again. And perhaps a little more camphor or some glucose to give him strength. And then more questions—all very friendly, until he showed the slightest sign of resistance, when you would use other methods.' He was rocking the man's body backwards and forwards with his foot as he spoke. Tonino was watching, fascinated. 'This man is my friend, Zakharov, and it would give me great pleasure to stamp on your face. Think about that. And yes, you'd better think about the Mafia, too, because they don't like you, either.'

'I will not speak,' said the young man.

'Oh yes, you will,' said Craig calmly. Then he turned to Tonino and said in a brisk, practical tone, 'You can have him later, and do what you like with him. I don't want him dead or alive. The lake is handy, after all. Now let's get Mr Ashbee moved into the other room, out of the smell of this vermin.'

'I won't speak,' shouted Zakharov.

CHAPTER TWENTY

SATURDAY NIGHT

They moved Ashbee, bed and all, into the big room and Tonino found blankets in one of the rooms upstairs to keep him covered. The door on the opposite side of the hall gave on to a large farmhouse kitchen, and beyond it was a larder, with barred windows and a good lock. Here they stowed the Capitano and the tall man, laid out on the stone floor. As they came back into the hall they heard a scuffle and saw the man who had been on guard outside sitting on a chair with his head in his hands and his hands tied together. Lucio was standing over him, grinning.

'He just walked in, staggering, and I gave him a little tap. He's all right. He's got a head like a piece of rock.' The man looked up and blinked at them sheepishly.

Craig looked at him thoughtfully. 'Don't put him with the others. Just tie his legs to the chair and keep an eye on him.' He glanced at his watch. 'Jensen won't be here for another quarter of an hour at least. I'll have another go at Zakharov.'

Tonino pulled his rubber cosh from his pocket. 'It would go quickly with this.' Craig declined the offer with thanks.

'I'm not sure. He's a trained man and has plenty of guts. I think you'd knock him out before he'd speak, but I've got an idea that's worth trying.'

The telephone in the big room rang. They looked at each other. 'I'll go,' said Craig. 'It's probably Luigi or Jensen.' He ran into the room and picked up the receiver. 'Craig here,' he said. There was a startled exclamation in Russian at the other end. Then the receiver was slammed down.

The Sicilians saw the look on his face as he came back into the hall. 'What's happened?'

'I've just done something extremely silly. I've let the Russians know I'm here. They'll be coming out to investigate, and quick.'

'But that's all right,' said Tonino confidently. 'The other Americans will be here by then.'

'They'll have enough to do to get Ashbee to safety. We can't stand here and fight off an attack. We'll have to shift the Russian out as soon as the Americans come.'

'We can do that. There are two cars.'

'My God, you're right! But listen, Tonino, I've got an idea. Give me ten minutes with him alone.'

'*Va bene.*' He unbolted the door at the rear and Craig went in.

Zakharov was lying on his side, facing the door, looking at him unblinkingly. Craig went up to him, put his foot on his thigh and pulled at the projecting end of the table leg. It seemed to be held tight.

'Bend your head forward, man, help me,' he ordered. The fair head bent and Craig could feel the pressure on the wooden bar slacken. But it was still difficult to draw out, and he guessed that the young man's legs and lower arms had swollen in his efforts to free himself. He pulled him into a sitting position so that he could kneel on his shoulders, and at last got the bar out. The Russian slowly straightened his legs, biting his lips until they bled at the pain of the blood flowing back into his hands and feet. Craig helped him into a chair and stood back. But there was no fight left in him—at least, no physical fight.

'Don't try anything,' he said. 'I'm still quite happy to put a bullet into you if you do.'

'I shall report your treatment—' began Zakharov in a shaking voice.

Craig laughed, looking down at him and shaking his head. 'You can't be such a fool as to think that. You look quite intelligent—a good deal more intelligent than the cretin who thought up this kidnapping game. Yet he's senior to you—Rostov, I mean. It's unbelievable.' The

young man looked at him without a word, but Craig knew
he had struck the right chord.

'I shall be taking you away from here to a place where
you can be shut up until you talk. I'm having difficulty
preventing the Mafiosi getting at you now.'

'Who are you?'

'Who d'you think? I'm Craig, the one your thug tried to
kill this morning.'

'He did not—'

'There, you see, you're admitting it already. That's
better. You have the sense to realize that all the cards are on
our side. Suppose I hand you over to the Americans?
What would happen? It's not just that you and Rostov
would be declared *personae non gratae*. There would be so
much pressure on the Italian Government that they'd have
to break off diplomatic relations. And *you* would be responsible.'

'Not me, I told you.'

'Yes, of course. Not you, but Rostov. But that wouldn't
help you much. You were here, and the KGB would blame
you for bungling this part of the operation. And besides,'
he added casually, 'there's also the mess you made of pene-
trating the British Embassy. They won't like that either,
will they?'

Zakharov had been too well trained to show surprise, but
his face froze and when he spoke it was with difficulty. 'I
don't know what you mean.'

'Oh yes, you do. That little game we played with you,
pretending we were investigating your Ambassador. That's
another thing that's going to make your Service look very
silly.' He laughed. 'There are going to be a lot of broad
smiles in Prague and Warsaw and Budapest when the Press
get that story.'

Zakharov had control of himself now. He was staring at
Craig silently, his face burning. Then he said slowly, 'The
last thing your Embassy can do is admit that you were
trying to compromise my Ambassador.'

He had a point there, as Craig knew, but he brushed it aside. 'Nonsense! *We* should admit nothing. But I think the NTS or some other White Russian organization wouldn't mind acting as foster-father to that little scheme.' His tone changed. 'But,' he added coldly, 'we shall have no hesitation about accusing you, Alexei Zakharov, of recruiting a spy inside our Embassy.'

Zakharov winced and looked down at his hands. 'That is untrue,' he said loudly. But Craig sensed the bitter disappointment flooding into the young man's mind. He suddenly felt that the spy operation was Zakharov's own doing; the kidnapping was Rostov's, and he would stand the blame, but the thought that his own agent had been blown was too much to be borne.

The Russian looked up suddenly. 'Who is it you mean?' he asked, and there was no mistaking the urgency in his voice.

'I don't know,' said Craig deliberately. It was quite true, of course, but this was the point he had to ram home if his plan were to succeed. 'Not for certain. That is why I want you to tell me. I want a full statement from you. I've told you the alternative—I shall leave the Mafia to find out from you in their own way. Be sensible, Zakharov. You know your stay in Rome will be short even if you are released. Your interest in this agent is at an end. Your whole career is compromised, even if you *were* acting under Rostov's orders, because the Kremlin does not like the taste of failure. If you refuse to tell me you are only causing me a few hours of extra work because we have the fingerprints that were on that de-magnetizer—' he saw the man's jaw muscles tighten—'and as soon as the staff come into the Embassy on Monday they will have to offer their prints. But do as you please. It's as simple as this: if you help me I will square the Mafia. If I say you were not responsible for that note to the American Ambassador they will believe me. If I say it was all your idea, they will be content to deal with you, who are in their hands, and not wait for Rostov to appear in public. But I assure you—oh yes, Zakharov, I assure you they will be revenged on one or other of you.'

The Russian's face was drained of colour, but he stood up and squared his shoulders. 'I will not tell you,' he said simply.

Craig went to the door and called. Tonino came in. Craig shook his head. Zakharov made no resistance when they bound his legs together, tested the knots on his wrists, and flung him on to the floor. Craig put the hypodermic into his pocket, wrapped in a piece of his handkerchief. Then he felt through Zakharov's clothes, removed his wallet and a knife and a bunch of keys. There was also a diplomatic card in red leather. He looked at that for a moment and then slipped it, too, into his pocket.

He went to the door and turned. 'It's your choice,' he said casually. But the Russian turned his face to the wall and shook his head. Craig and the Mafiosi went out and bolted the door behind them.

They heard sounds coming from the big room and a voice speaking with an American accent. Jensen was bending over Ashbee, who appeared fast asleep. His face had been cleaned up but was half covered with sticking plaster. Another man was putting things into a medical bag. He nodded to Craig. 'He's OK. I've given him a sedative. Very badly bruised—I've never seen such a mess, but his bones are as tough as oak. Nothing broken. We can move him.'

Craig gave him the hypodermic, explaining how he had found it. 'I think it's camphor, but you'd better regard it as Exhibit A.' He took Jensen's arm and led him to the farther end of the room.

'Listen, Hank, we've got to get out of here fast. The Russians are on their way. My fault, but I'll explain later.'

'I've got a couple of Marines.'

'Good, but we've got to get Jo away and into his own bed.'

'That's what the medic said.'

'Right. Now this is the point. I'm pretty sure that it was all Rostov's idea, not young Zakharov's.'

'That checks.'

'If we leave him here I won't be responsible for what the Mafiosi do to Zakharov, all the same.'

'He's got it coming to him, Mr Craig.' He saw the look on Craig's face. 'Sure, you're right. We'll take care of him. I've got a safe house; I'll take him there.' A thought struck him and he grinned with delight. 'I might get him to defect. He knows the skids'll be under him if he gets loose.'

'He won't defect, I assure you. He's just refused to tell me what I want although he knows the alternative is whatever the Mafia can think up. No, Hank.' He looked at him and said slowly, 'I want to let him go.'

'Jesus! You can't do that, Craig. We've got him—I know it was all your doing, but still—he's *ours*. We can't just let him go. We can turn him over to the Carabinieri—'

'And what then? They can't hold a diplomat. Here's his card, by the way, you'd better have it. If we ever had to produce proof we found him here in the act of pushing stuff into Jo, that's a good bit of evidence.'

'Well, thanks, but say—'

'And besides, Hank, are you sure that's what your Agency would want?'

Jensen was silent for a moment. Then he said, 'I'd better ring the office again. They'd warned us there was a long signal coming through but I couldn't wait. Hang on.' He went across to the telephone. When he returned his healthy face was creased with a tremendous frown. 'Well, you sure were right. So far as I can get it, from the way my buddy was wrapping up the message, they won't want any, repeat any, publicity at all. In fact,' he added bitterly, 'they want the whole durn thing hushed up if in any way possible. How the heck do they think we can do that?'

'That settles it. We let him go, but only the way I've worked out. Can I borrow one of your Marines?'

'Sure. But we'll get Jo off first. Hell, I'd like to stay and see what you've got in your locker, but I'm going to protect Jo until he gets home, where I've got more fellows to take over guarding him.' He glanced at Craig curiously. 'What d'you want the Marine for?'

'Oh, just to lie possum in the back of Zakharov's car with a gun in his hand.'

'Oh, sure, sure,' said Hank, grinning, 'just routine dooty. And what happens when Zakharov looks in the back when he gets in?'

'He won't have time, chum, I'll see to that. He'll be in one hell of a hurry.'

The most difficult part was persuading Tonino to play, and he had to ring his father-in-law to get permission. But the old man gave it without hesitation. He had no wish to get involved with the Russians.

Then the guard was given his choice. As Craig had thought, he proved to be a genial, simple soul, always willing to sell his impressive strength and his ability as a get-away driver for twenty thousand lire a day, but very unhappy to have fallen foul of the dreaded Mafia. He agreed to play his part with a broad grin.

Zakharov heard the bolt thrown back and braced himself. Tonino came in with a long knife in his hand. He cut loose the bonds from his wrists and feet and told him curtly to get up.

'The Englishman has gone, and we are taking you to a place where my friends and I can have a comfortable talk with you. You must not be seen with your hands tied, but I shall be with you all the time and if you speak or try to escape you will get this in your tripes.' He prodded him with the point of the knife in the region in question and Zakharov caught his breath sharply. 'All right. *Avanti*!'

They walked out into the hall. Lucio was still standing in the main doorway. Tonino called to him, 'Didn't you find the guard? What happened?'

'The animal must have worked himself free and run away. I searched the grounds.'

'The Russian's car is at the steps?'

'Yes. I left it with the engine running.'

'*Accidente*! *Ma non importa, andiamo.*'

It was only afterwards, and too late, that Zakharov realized what it was that had struck him as odd. They were not talking dialect, but an Italian he could understand.

They went down the path, Lucio in front, then Zakharov with Tonino close behind him. As they came round the final curve the Russian could see his car at the gate, with the doors open. He could hear the low growl of the Lancia engine.

'Suddenly he heard a gruff voice cry out, '*Mani in alto*!' The big silhouette of the guard appeared from behind the wall and faced them, the light of the moon glinting on the long barrel of the shotgun which was pointed at the little group. Zakharov heard Tonino swear furiously and the tinkle made by his automatic falling on the stones, and saw Lucio drop his gun and raise his hands. Then the guard shouted, '*File, Signore, scappe*! I'll release the Capitano.'

The Russian needed no urging. He was a brave man, but the chance of escape was too good to miss, and he had an urgent task to perform. He brushed past the guard and was in his car, letting in the clutch, within five seconds. The Lancia surged forward, accelerating under full throttle.

There was a roar of laughter from the three men as Craig drove up in the big Fiat. Tonino flung his arm round the guard's shoulders. '*Bravo, ragazzo*! You did that like a Brother.' He took the useless shotgun from the man's hand —there were no cartridges in it—and thrust it into the back of the car. Tonino recovered the automatics; he still had Craig's in his pocket, in case things had turned the wrong way. Then he got in beside Craig, with the other two in the back. He began talking in dialect into his transceiver. He turned to Craig. 'You're sure he'll go back to Rome?'

'He must,' said Craig confidently. 'He'll do anything to warn his agent that the heat's on. Have you got contact yet with Luigi's car? It should be on the Appia Nuova, waiting to follow the Lancia.' Then he heard a crackle of speech from the transceiver, and Tonino shouted above the roar of the engine, 'OK. They're in position.'

He got all the speed he could from the car, but by the time he was passing Castel Gandolfo Luigi's Fiat was already chasing the Lancia down on the plain, within five miles from the city walls. Zakharov was in a hurry.

Craig expected the man to stop somewhere and telephone, to make the appointment, but the trail car reported that he had entered the city walls at Porta San Giovanni and was heading down Emanuele Filiberto. He hadn't stopped. Craig followed the same route, past the station and then by way of Via XX Settembre to Piazza Fiume. Neil Adams was standing where he had been told to wait. He was obviously in a bad temper when Craig picked him up. But Craig was in no mood to be tactful.

'Get in the back. The other two are friends.'

'What the hell's this about, Peter? You were bloody rude on the phone.'

'Just shut up, Neil, there's a good chap. As I told you, this is your one chance of getting yourself off the hook. And for good.'

Tonino interrupted. 'He's going round by the Zoo. Hasn't stopped.'

'It's as I thought, he's driving straight to Via Mangili.' He heard Adams exclaim behind his back. 'Listen, Neil. The man we're following, the same chap you met, who is a Russian intelligence officer, as you suspected, is going to Janet Ransome's house. To that flat you know all too well.'

'What d'you mean?'

'Oh, can it! It was he who put the camera in the wall. I want the key.'

'I haven't got it.'

'You bloody fool. Won't you grow up? Do I have to stop the car and get it off you?'

Q

'You're a bastard, Craig.'

'Maybe, but hand it over. Give it to this man here. That's better.'

'The Lancia's stopped. Luigi's car is parked some way behind. The Russian's gone in.' Tonino listened again and laughed. 'They've just seen another man get out of the Lancia and can't understand.' He called into his microphone, '*Sta bene! Già sappiamo.*' Craig grinned. The Marine must have had an uncomfortable ride. Two minutes later he drove past Luigi's Fiat 1300 and parked behind the Lancia, opposite the house he had visited two days ago. It seemed like two years.

He spoke in a low voice to Tonino. 'You and I go in. Lucio at the back of the house. That's the only other exit unless they open the shutters, and we'd hear that. If anyone goes out at the back he should stop them, but not harm them if possible.'

'OK. And this Englishman?'

'Our other friend had better bring him into the hall and see he stays there until I call. You understand, Neil?'

'Oh, all right.'

'Good. Let Lucio go ahead.'

The house seemed to be asleep, and there was no sound except the rustling of the acacias as they walked up the short drive. There was not a glimmer of light through the shuttered windows. And the outer door was closed. Craig had no key to that and was thinking of either ringing, or breaking in at the back when he heard Neil's voice behind him. 'It's in that flower pot,' he said dully. He picked out the key and handed it over.

To Craig's surprise the door had not been bolted. Zakharov had thought he had left the team accounted for. Tonino switched on the light inside. The front door of the flat was opposite, and light appeared underneath. Craig signed to Adams to wait and inserted the key in the lock. The door opened without noise; it had been well greased. But they heard the faint sound of a buzzer from somewhere within. The living-room door was open. Tonino slipped inside and switched the light on, then he came out and shook his head. Craig went straight to the bedroom door and pushed it wide open, expecting a rush. But none came. He went in, his automatic in his hand.

'Hullo, Peter,' said Janet. 'What d'you think you're doing?'

CHAPTER TWENTY-ONE

RETURN OF IL GOBBO

She was standing by a large Cinquecento wardrobe, which Craig had not seen on his previous visit because it stood behind the door. She had a duster in her hand and was running it over the ornate mouldings. Her expression of surprise and alarm was completely natural.

'Catching spies,' said Craig. 'Two spies.' He took a quick look round. 'I think he's in there, Janet. Tell him to come out with his hands on his head.'

'You are mad, I suppose. This is our flat, you know.'

'Certainly, and it's the tenant you've got in that cupboard. Open it.' Tonino moved forward with a gun in his hand.

'All right.' She shrugged her shoulders. 'But you'll be sorry. Come out, Sasha,' she added, opening the wardrobe door. 'There's company.'

Zakharov stepped out, and stood looking at Craig impassively. Tonino ran his hands over the man's body, but he was still unarmed. Meanwhile, the girl stood looking at Craig, her chin up, calm and imperious in the face of his cold stare. It was as if nobody else was in the room.

'You're a bit late, aren't you? You were going to take me out this evening. I waited for you for half an hour, but I'm not used to being ditched so I rang Sasha.'

'Who d'you think this man is?'

'Sasha? He's my boy-friend, aren't you, darling?' She went up to him and put her arm round his shoulders.

'Another?' He called over his shoulder. 'Come in, Neil.'

She started, and instinctively held on to Zakharov more tightly as Adams came in. He stared at them for a long moment. Then he put his head in his hands.

'Neil,' she cried urgently, 'look at me.' She disengaged

herself from the Russian. 'I didn't know about the photograph, I swear to you I didn't. He's only just told me.'

He raised his head. 'No,' he muttered, 'no. You couldn't
have done that.'

'But she did,' said Craig harshly. 'You've just seen her
with her arm round the man who had the photographs. If
that doesn't convince you take down that picture. Go on,
take it down.' He pointed.

Adams shook his head, and Craig backed towards the
wall, twitched it off its hook and handed it to Adams. 'Look
at the wall where it hung. They papered over the hole. You
can see. Look at it, man.'

'The hole?'

'The hole for the camera. Now look through the frame
—yes, *through* it. D'you think all that was set up without
her knowing? D'you think she didn't know what the frame
was for?'

Adams stood turning the frame over in his hands; then
he held it up to the light, slowly, reluctantly; willing it to be
decent and opaque. He took a long, shuddering breath and
threw it down to smash on the floor. As he stumbled to the
door he turned back.

'When I told Maggie who you were,' he said slowly,
'she said—she said she could imagine you sending her a
print of that—thing, and laughing. And I hit her. But she
was right. And all your talk about other ways than one to
make money— You're almost as big a fool as I am if you
thought I'd work for that gang of cut-throats.' He pointed
to Zakharov, who had not moved. Then he went out of the
door.

Tonino said, 'He needs help. I'll ask Lucio to take him
home. The other man can take his place, OK?' Craig
nodded.

'Poor little man!' said Janet scornfully. 'He's off his
rocker. It's true he pestered me a lot and I was kind to him.
But that's all—and you'll have a job proving anything
different, Peter.'

'Drop all this, it won't wash. This man's a known KGB

officer and you're his agent.' He waited until Tonino
returned, then said, 'Pick up your bag, Janet, and let's go.'

'You can't arrest me,' she said calmly, 'this is Italian soil.
And without positive proof you can't even turn me in to
the Italians. I know the law, you see, even if you don't.'

It was true, thought Craig, that he had no *proof*—only
a mass of utterly convincing circumstantial evidence. There
was the document paper under the sideboard in the dining-
room, but this was a rented flat, no necessary connection
with her. She would be sacked, of course, if only for con-
sorting with a Soviet national without reporting it—but
there was nothing like enough to get her where he wanted
her—in the dock at the Old Bailey.

It was as if she could read his thoughts. 'If you take me
by force to the Embassy you'll find yourself in trouble. No
one would issue you a warrant after that.'

But, even if it broke him, he was not going to let her get
away now. 'Come on, Janet, we're going. Give her her
handbag, Tonino.'

The Mafioso took a quick stride to the table, but she was
quicker. She had her hand on it when his fingers closed
over her wrist. He squeezed, and she gave a cry of pain.
Then he lifted the bag in his hand and took a step backwards. 'It's *heavy*,' he said, with his gun pointing at the
girl, and tossed the bag to Craig.

He opened the clasp. Inside there was—not an automatic, as he had expected, but a small metal box, very
heavy for its size. Craig's heart lifted.

'That's the positive proof I wanted. It's what you used to
strip the tape and this is the first chance you've had of
returning it.' He was watching Zakharov, who had moved
a step forward. 'Keep still! Just try anything and I'll kill
you in self-defence.' The Russian stood still, but his eyes
were feverishly bright and Craig had a premonition of
danger.

He put his gun away and looked at the remaining contents of the bag. There was nothing concealed in the lining,
and nothing there at all but a purse, a passport, which he

took, some keys, two lipsticks and a powder-compact. He threw the bag back to Tonino, who gave it to the girl.

'I'm going to leave now,' said Zakharov. 'My car's outside, with the key in the ignition.'

'Be quiet!' shouted Craig, puzzled. Why had he said that, about the key? He was watching Janet closely as she opened the bag and took out her lipstick. Two lipsticks, thought Craig, *two* lipsticks—but he was too late. She suddenly pointed the little gold cylinder at Tonino and twisted the base. Craig saw a faint mist around Tonino's face and the man staggered back with a loud cry of pain, his hands over his eyes.

Janet sprang past him and got to the door, with Craig after her. Then he felt Zakharov's arms round his waist. He dropped the metal box to get at his gun, but the Russian fell backwards and pulled him to the ground, swinging his body so that he was on top. Craig felt the man's strong fingers on his throat, searching for the knock-out points. He got his thumbs into the Russian's eyes just in time, and as the other's hands lost their grip he flung his arms out sideways to get enough push from the floor to throw him off. His hand closed on the metal box, and thankfully he slammed it against the side of Zakharov's head.

That was enough, and he rose shakily to his feet, dropped the box into his pocket and picked up the gun. Zakharov lay motionless, and Craig snatched the coverlet from the bed and rolled it tightly round him. Then he turned to Tonino, who was at the basin, washing his eyes. The air was full of the smell of ammonia.

'Are you all right?'

'Yes. The bitch wasn't close enough to do them real harm.' He dabbed his eyes with a towel. 'I still can't see properly. What happened?'

Craig didn't answer. Two men stood in the doorway, Luigi and the man he called Il Gobbo.

Craig was in no mood to be polite. 'Where the hell did you spring from?'

'We got your telegram yesterday on Luigi's link, but it

took some time to find the answer. We had to get people to
go on searching this morning. They're damned sloppy in
their records. But then of course I took the first plane.
What's happened to her?'

'She threw ammonia into this man's face and scarpered.
I would have stopped her, but the Russian tackled me.' He
pointed to the bundle on the floor.

'Who's he?'

'Zakharov. Ashbee cracked Rostov's skull.'

'I know.' He bent over Zakharov.

Luigi explained. 'Cozzeferrate gave me the frequencies
his men were using so that I could monitor the messages.
And then my old colleague arrived. I brought him up to
date on the way.'

'Did you see any cars in front of the house as you came
up?' asked Craig urgently.

'Oh yes, we saw Zakharov's Lancia going off very fast. I
was going to follow, but Gobbo said no.'

'Oh, did he?' said Craig furiously. He turned on the
Englishman. 'Blast you! I still don't know your name, but
you put me in charge of this operation. I want that girl
where I can make an arrest.'

'My name's Duncan. Colonel. I didn't know it was Janet
Ransome,' said Gobbo mildly, 'but I should have acted just
the same. I'll explain in a moment. And I'll take charge
now, Craig.' He scarcely raised his voice, but there was no
contesting his authority. 'This man's bleeding from the ear,
but his pulse isn't bad. What did you hit him with?'

Craig pulled the metal box from his pocket. 'Not hard
enough to crack his skull.' He gave a twisted laugh. 'I just
gave it everything I'd got, but I wasn't in a position to do
much damage, unfortunately.'

'What's got into you, Craig? You know damn' well you'd
have been in a spot if you'd killed him.'

'I do indeed, but that wouldn't have stopped me. And if
you don't like that you can—'

Duncan interrupted him. 'Let's go into the other room.'
He turned his back on Craig and went up to Tonino, hold-

ing out his hand and introducing himself. Then he com-
plimented him in smooth, flowery Italian on the success
of the operation and on his personal bravery, finishing with
words of commiseration about his smarting eyes, which he
examined carefully. Tonino, who had been worried by
Craig's outburst, looked more cheerful.

'Don't bother about this *canaglia*, Signor Craig,' he said,
pointing his foot at Zakharov, 'I'll look after him.'

As they went out of the door the S.3 man took Craig's
arm. 'You've done a very good job, in circumstances in
which we had no right to involve you.'

That spiked Craig's guns to some extent, but as they sat
down in the living-room he said bitterly, 'That's cock, and
you know it. I've failed. She'll get away.'

'Yes, I think she will,' said Duncan calmly. 'They will
have had an escape route all arranged, and she'll be either
out of the country by tomorrow or in a really safe house.
She'll be in Moscow in a week. That'll teach her.'

'If I could have got her back to the Embassy she'd
be in Brixton in a week. That'd have taught her even more.'

'Would it? I wonder. Anyway, that isn't what we
wanted. I don't hanker after another spy trial, thank you.
And you ought to know what holes a good counsel could
make in your case.'

'I suppose so,' muttered Craig. 'Didn't know he was a
Russian, all an affair of the heart, didn't know the flat
owner had spied on her, the ammonia spray—just an
obvious precaution for a widow woman in Rome. Oh yes,
they could fight us, all right. And the one who would be
really hurt would be Mrs Adams.' He looked at Duncan.
'She's solid gold, that girl.'

'Maybe. But the point is, Craig, we don't want a fight.
We just wanted the spy identified and nullified, and you've
done it, and we're very grateful. But I still don't know how
you knew he'd come straight here.'

Luigi came in. 'I must get in touch with Cozzeferrate and
tell him the news. And then home to bed. You've got the
key to my flat, Gobbino. I'll send the car back for you.'

Duncan nodded. When Kahn had gone he looked at Craig questioningly.

'I told Zakharov we knew all about his spy, except who it was. Then I arranged for him to escape, in the belief that we were all taken care of. By this time he was in something of a state, and didn't stop to think it out. I expected him to telephone her first, but he must have thought we'd got her line tapped and he came straight here.'

'You were taking one hell of a risk.'

'If I'd left him to the Mafiosi they might have killed him. He's got a lot of guts.'

Duncan laughed suddenly. 'Well, it worked. And I have a lot of respect for people who have that kind of luck. But of course we've got to let Zakharov go.'

'Only when Adams has made a signed statement.'

'Don't you trust him to?'

'It's not that. I want to show it to Zakharov and then tell him that if he should ever take any action with the other prints of that photograph we'll show the statement to the Italians and demand that he is recalled. I can suggest that if he keeps his mouth shut nobody need know how we used him to lead us to the spy. I don't suppose he'll want to admit what a mess he made of it.'

'You seem to want to go to a lot of trouble to protect him—and Adams,' said Duncan, raising his eyebrows.

'They're really not bad types, either of them. But it's Adams's wife I'm thinking of, as I told you.'

'And what do you suggest doing with Zakharov in the meantime?'

'Hand him over to the Americans for tonight. Young Jensen wants to try and make him defect. He won't succeed, but he'll be grateful for the chance.'

'Worked it all out, haven't you? Nursemaid to all the nice young people.'

Craig ignored that crack. 'I'll ring Jensen. When he's taken delivery of the Russian I'll go and see Ashbee, if he's awake, and then—' he yawned— 'with your permission, Colonel Duncan, I'll get some sleep.'

'You look as if you needed it. All right, I'll go along with your plans. But there's one thing, Craig, that Luigi wouldn't explain. I still don't understand *why* they took this extraordinary step of kidnapping Ashbee. And what were those phony messages you sent to the KGB? Sir Watkyn's telegram didn't say.'

'They gave the impression that Ashbee and I were working on some aspects of the Soviet Ambassador's activities that would have made him a subject for *persona non grata*. It was H.E.'s idea.'

Duncan sat up straight in his chair. 'Great God Almighty! *Sir Watkyn* thought that up.' He looked searchingly at Craig. 'This wasn't another of your crazy schemes?'

'No, it was his all right. He got bitten by this bloody intelligence bug.'

'But why, for God's sake?'

'He pretended it was to force the Russians to show their hand, which they did, as you know. But his main thought was to get his Soviet colleague recalled in disgrace.' He saw Duncan start. 'What's the matter?'

'General Vishinsky was being seen off by his staff when I landed at Fiumicino this afternoon. Moscow plane.'

'H.E. will be pleased. And it's just as well it's happened. I told Zakharov it was all our bit of fun.'

'Jesus Christ! You did what?'

'I was trying to break him down by making him feel we knew everything. And anyway,' he added, a little primly, 'I prefer not to be involved in smearing operations.'

Duncan drew a deep breath. 'And do you think the Ambassador will be pleased when you tell him you've blown his little plan to bits?'

'I'm not sure. He might even be a bit relieved. I think he was having second thoughts.'

The S.3 man suddenly exploded in a great roar of laughter. Craig was too tired to do more than watch him sombrely. 'You've got it both ways,' said Duncan, wiping his eyes, 'you've salved your precious conscience and it won't make a blind bit of difference. They won't send him back from Moscow.'

'Why not, for God's sake?'

'You don't think the KGB are going to take *your* word,
do you, even if Zakharov talks? They'll think it's all part of
a plot. They'll have Vishinsky under a bright light before
many hours have passed, and serve him right. I knew him
in London.' He paused. 'And now I'll tell you the answer to
your telegram.'

Fay Ashbee threw her arms round Craig's neck and kissed
him. 'You're my pin-up boy. Who says the limeys have lost
their touch?'

'How's Jo?'

'He's fine.'

'You mean—?'

'He's drinking a large bourbon and talking his head off.
There's a little square man with him, a Cavagliere Cozzeferrate, with a big moustache, who told us what you'd
done, and they're having a glorious *post mortem*.' She
laughed, but there were tears in her fine eyes. 'It nearly
was a *post mortem*, Hank told me.'

Craig found the big American sitting up in bed, with a
stack of pillows behind his head. Cozzeferrate jumped to his
feet and threw an arm round Craig. 'Look at him, Signor
Craig.' He punched Ashbee in the chest. 'He's as strong as
a Sicilian.'

He didn't look too good, thought Craig, seeing the welter
of bandages. 'I'm very sorry about this, Jo. We shouldn't
have dragged you into it.'

'Nonsense, I wouldn't have missed that crack I gave
Rostov for worlds. Give this unlicensed shamus a drink,
Fay; he's got to tell us the whole story.'

'He's going to make it a short one, Jo. And then you're
both going to eat and sleep.' She overruled Craig's protest.
'Of course you'll sleep here. Now tell that story fast.'

It was eleven o'clock on Sunday morning when Craig
entered the orchid house—and quite fitting, he thought, to

have their final consultation where it had all begun six days ago, in that exotic setting.

Sir Watkyn was pottering around very neatly with a long syringe. He was wearing light slacks and an old college blazer and large horn-rimmed spectacles which had settled on the end of his nose. He looked at Craig reproachfully. 'I was trying to get in touch with you all yesterday evening, you know, but the hotel said you'd gone on a picnic and hadn't returned, not even at ten o'clock. It must have been an extended picnic.'

'That,' said Craig with mild irony, 'would be one way of describing it. But why did you want me, sir?'

'I had another of those S.3 telegrams and had to go into Chancery to decode it. It was a reply to one you had sent through Kahn, without my knowledge.' He looked at Craig over his glasses, like a prep-school master at a boy who has used a dirty word. 'I must say I was surprised, Craig.'

'It was just an idea, sir, and I didn't want to worry you.'

Sir Watkyn sighed. 'Exactly what my heads of department say when they know they should have consulted me.'

'It was a long message, sir.'

'All right,' said the Ambassador with a shudder, 'let's forget it. But what was it all about?'

'Then the signal you received didn't say?'

'No. Here it is.' He fished a piece of paper from his pocket and smoothed it out on the damp table. REFERENCE CRAIG'S UNNUMBERED TELEGRAM VIA KAHN. DUNCAN WILL ADVISE. HIS ETA ROME 1935 HOURS TODAY. ENDS.

It was hand-written; at least the old boy had had the sense not to type it. His Excellency added, 'Who is this Duncan? He must have arrived before I finished decoding. Incidentally, he's coming here in half an hour.'

'He's the S.3 man in charge of our operation, sir. Which, by the way, is now concluded.'

'So I heard. Very satisfactory, indeed. He left yesterday.' He saw the puzzled look on Craig's face. 'Vishinsky, I mean. That was well done, Craig. Marchant is delighted.

But tell me what your signal was about.'

Craig explained. 'Apart from the fact that Mrs Ransome was in England when the first document was copied all the evidence pointed equally at her and Miss Warren. Now, although Miss Warren has been under tension I came to the conclusion that it was a personal matter. I think she's been making a big play for the affections of Major Partridge—' he saw the horrified look on Sir Watkyn's face and hurried on— 'but Mrs Ransome struck me as a woman with hidden motivations, and I thought it would be worth checking if all her absence in the UK last March was accounted for. S.3 discovered that she had volunteered at the end of her official leave—you remember, sir, you said it was extended for some reason—for a week's work in Scientific Department, to replace a girl who had gone sick. She had access to the document in question.'

There was a long silence. 'Do you really suspect her, Craig?'

'There's no doubt, sir. And I'm afraid you won't see her again.'

'What, man, what? What's been happening?' Craig told him.

Sir Watkyn sat for a time looking at the floor. His handsome face was strained and white. 'I must accept part of the blame. She was a woman with a mind of her own, and it was a very good mind. Even I could see that at times she was bored to tears with the job she did for me, and I knew how she had taken to heart her failure to pass into the Service. I ought to have wondered why she stuck with us, but when you're the head of a big mission like this you do tend, you know, to expect that people are happy to work under your orders. It's built into the system.'

'She was recruited before you were posted here, you know.'

'Yes, so she was, I'm glad of that.' He paused. 'And Adams? Will he have to go?'

'That'll be for you and Security Department, I suppose. And Personnel. He's made a very full and well-drafted statement—spent half the night on it, I should think. Technically he's in the clear, because as soon as he suspected Zakharov of being an intelligence officer he told me, even if he still wouldn't say who his mistress was. I'll speak up for him, of course, as I've no doubt you'd wish me to.'

'Yes, do that, please. Well, Craig—' an awkward matter had been satisfactorily settled and now it was time to say the right things to those responsible. The charming, mellifluous voice took on a warmer tone. 'I think both you and Ashbee have shown great resourcefulness and courage in dealing with this affair, and I am deeply grateful. You must dine with us tonight, if you're free, and tell us the whole story. My wife must not miss a word. And I suppose I had better invite this Duncan, too. Good heavens, one of the servants is coming from the Residence. He must have arrived already.'

'*Colonel* Duncan, sir. A very senior intelligence officer.'

'Thank you. Of course, he would be. This sad intelligence business.' He looked at Craig from the corner of his eye. 'I must be careful what I say. After all, I suppose I may claim a little credit myself. My—er—ruse did succeed in drawing the fox out of his hole, didn't it?'

'Yes, sir. Although it nearly caused the death of a colleague.'

'Yes, yes, I see that. What a brave fellow he must be!'

Craig spelled it out deliberately. 'When Ashbee attacked Rostov he knew he hadn't a chance of escaping. There were too many people around. He decided that to get him off the Russian they'd have to beat him into insensibility.'

'But—'

'He did it to gain time. He didn't like the thought of being filled with truth drugs.'

'Good gracious!' His Excellency shivered. 'What cold, deliberate courage the man has. I've never heard anything like it. I must go and thank him personally. Will you arrange that, please, at some time when it is convenient to him? Now I must see Duncan and expose my ignorance of what young Walton is doing.' His spirits were recovering rapidly. 'But I can tell him honestly that I shall take a greater interest in Walton's work in future. You know, my dear fellow, I think I may have an aptitude, after all, for this sordid intelligence business. I may be able to give Derek some tips.'

Craig's heart bled for the MI6 representative.